On the Outside of Everything

^^^^^^

Tiffany Renée

Library of Congress Cataloging-in-publication Data

Names: Renée, Tiffany, author.

Title: On the outside of everything / Tiffany Renée.

Identifiers: ISBN 9798991101608 (paperback) | ISBN 9798991101615 (hardcover) |

Subjects: romance fiction. Novels.

The story, all names, characters, and incidents portrayed in this production are fictitious. No identification with actual persons (living or deceased), business establishments, events, or products are intended or should be inferred.

Book Cover by Katarina Naskovski

1st edition, 2024

For anyone who has ever wondered

where they belong,

and everyone who still believes in love.

1

Now

Emma

Here's the truth about everything I know. The mountains look just as pretty in the snow as they do in the sunshine. A house is not a home unless it's filled with the people you love, and love is not as simple as it should be.

∧∧∧∧∧∧

There's a big porch with a row of rocking chairs looking out over the valley. Tatumn sits beside me with a green smoothie in her hand and her legs pulled into her chest. We're both still a little sweaty from our run, and the bits of hair that are stuck to her head are made more visible by the ones floating in the wind.

Her eyes dart to the side and she looks over at me and asks, "Do you think it's actually possible to die from happiness?"

"I don't know, but I bet at least a few men have gone out *in flagranti*."

She gives me a questioning look, "Only men?"

I nod and her eyes roll, "Figures."

"Well in all fairness, they do tend to do most of the heavy lifting." She reaches over to slap my arm, "Hey, I'm no slouch, and I'm serious. Look at him."

She pulls her phone out and turns it toward me. It's a cute picture. Agatha is sitting on Ethan's shoulders. His hands are lifted in the air, and she has her palms wrapped around his fingertips. Her eyes are bright, just like her mother's, and the little smile on her face is enough to know that this is what is best for them.

That right now, love means letting go.

"He's so cute with her." she says in this helpless sort of way, "I don't have any weapons to fight back against that kind of warfare."

I look over, but her eyes shift away from mine, "Why would you want to fight back you're marrying him?"

"I know. I know I am, but… are you sure you don't want to come with us?"

There's something in her voice, a sort of longing disguised as playfulness, and yes, of course I want to go with them. "Tate, you know I can't do that."

Her eyes roll upward as she leans forward in her chair and looks over at me. "Actually, I know you could. We have lots of extra room, and I can't stomach the thought of leaving you here anyway. I mean what am I supposed to do without you? I don't know how to do anything on my own anymore."

"That's not true."

She pins me with a serious look, "It is too."

"Tate, just a moment ago you were so happy you thought you might die from it."

"I am. I am happy… but you could be happy too." She says it like a promise, and I want to turn to her and tell her that I'm already happy. That she doesn't need to worry about me, but something about the cool breeze on my cheek and the firmness of the boards beneath my feet makes it impossible to look her way.

"You could stay with us. Seattle's a big city, I'm sure there are MFA programs there too. Just think of all the dark city scenes you could write, and all the cute coffee shops you could write them in. I bet they're full of hip artsy guys who wear fedoras unironically, *to keep the rain out of their eyes*, and order things like oat milk lattes that they drink while they read Kafka for fun."

I look over at her, and despite her overt claim to incandescent happiness, I can see the apprehension in her eyes. "Nobody reads Kafka for fun."

"I bet they do in Seattle. The Pacific Northwest is known as the literary hub of America. You could meet a posh coffee shop guy, have the quintessential kiss in the rain and lots of dirty sex in inappropriate places all over the city. You'll be so sated that when he asks you to marry him, standing at the top of the space needle with his arms wrapped around your waist and his breath brushing against your ear, you won't even try to argue your way out of it. You'll just say yes, and then we'll meet for tea, and you'll tell me how much you love him, how great he is in bed, and how you can't wait to have all his babies."

I rock back in my chair, "You really have this all figured out, don't you?" Her lips purse, and she looks away from me, out over the mountains. "Well, I've got a wild imagination and a very empty bed to think about it all in."

She gives me a look tinged with sorrow, and I almost tell her, her bed won't be empty for long, but then she says, "It could work. I know it could."

She sounds so sincere that I have to remind myself that she is happy. That when Ethan asked her to marry him, she didn't hesitate at all. This past year has been a blur of venue checks and cake tastings, and Tatumn has loved every minute of it. Ethan is already there, they already have a home, and Tatumn never looks happier than when she and Agatha set the iPad up on the coffee table and face time him in the evening.

She puts one foot down and presses her chair back. "Think about Agatha. She would love it so much."

It's a good tactic, and I can hear the granule of hope in her voice as she says it. She's not wrong either, Agatha would love it. I would love it too. Not for posh coffee shop guys, or kisses in the rain, but for morning coffee with Tatumn, and an endless supply of tiny kisses on my cheek.

It would be so easy to give into her, to leave this place and never look back. I know what it's like to miss someone here. I know that even after they're gone. I'll see them everywhere I turn, and that is not something I'm looking forward to.

"Yeah, but what would Ethan think?"

She leans back in her chair, and her face wrinkles up in this way that says, *Ethan who?* As if Ethan isn't the most important person in her life. The father of her child and the only man she's ever loved.

She looks over at me with a splinter of pity in her eyes, and I feel my shoulders tense. We don't talk about him much, but she gives me the same pitiful look every time she brings him up. Her knee starts bouncing, and I have to fight the urge to stand up and walk away. She says, "You can't keep waiting on him. He's not coming back."

There's something in her voice that wasn't there before. A certainty I'm not prepared to deal with. Which doesn't make any sense at all because I know he's not coming back. It's been five years. That's enough time for the ground to settle over a grave, or a river to cut through rock. If he wanted to be here, he would be.

If I had been enough. He wouldn't have left.

It still hurts to think of him, but time has muddled the image of his face. So, instead of being tortured by his sharp jaw line and full lips. I get a mirage of a man with dark hair and grey eyes. I get whispers of his fingers running over my skin, and echoes of his voice in my mind. I get flashes of a one-sided text thread, and whiffs of his scent on the clothes he left behind. I can't remember the exact shade of his skin tone, somewhere between olive and tan, but I'll never forget the way it felt to lay in his arms.

"I'm not waiting on anyone." I say a bit defensively.

Tatumn puts her drink down on the table beside her and her eyes tighten at the corners. "I'm serious. You can come with me. You don't have to stay here… alone."

^^^^^^

There's a lounge in the basement of the Rivulet. It's the sort of place where the lights are kept dim and groups of men gather to sit in oversized club chairs as they sip whiskey. The event was supposed to be small, just a few of us having appetizers and cocktails on the night the wedding party was set to arrive.

Tatumn planned the whole thing, in this very loose sort of way, with mood boards and multiple trips out to find the perfect pair of shoes to go with her dress. I had been the one in touch with Alissa, answering all of her questions about allergies and approximate head counts.

Tatumn looks divine. She's wearing a sheer dress with a plunging neckline and crystals sewn into the fabric, but she's surrounded by a few more people than we were expecting.

The appetizer table is more empty platters than food, and I haven't seen the chef once since we arrived. Tatumn's flitting around the room, obliviously welcoming each guest with an even bigger smile than the last.

I look around, trying to locate the wait staff in this crowd of button-down shirts and elevated hemlines. Only to see the blur of a woman holding a tray full of drinks, winding herself in and out of the small spaces people naturally leave between them.

Mom and Dani are sitting at the bar. They have a nearly empty bottle of wine in front of them, and when I walk up, they say my name like it's a celebration. I lean in and give them both a quick squeeze as I attempt to get the attention of the bartender behind them.

"You really outdid yourself with this thing." Dani says as I pull away and take another look around the room. "Yeah, it's a bit bigger than I expected it to be though."

"What can I do for you, Ms. Ward?" The bartender, Alan, asks.

The way he looks at me, like the unwieldy crowd behind me doesn't exist, puts my mind at ease. I introduce myself and insist that he call me Emma, before pointing out the fact that we're wildly overcount and quickly running out of food. He gives me a tight smile and I say, "I would ask half of them to leave, but I'm a terrible coward… and they look hungry." I playfully tilt my shoulder up and Alan's lips pick up at the edge.

He looks away from me, his eyes ticking over every person here. Every beat squeezes on the ball of nerves that has settled at the base of my gut. His jaw tightens, and I can see he's assessed the situation in the same way I have. *It's a lost cause* flashes in bright neon lights across his eyes.

I catch another glimpse of Tatumn, Don and his wife have just arrived, she and Ethan are talking with them. Tatumn's head tilts back on a laugh and then she motions toward the appetizer table.

I swallow the lump in my throat and speak up. "Listen, Alan, I know this is a lot. It's too much really, but this is my best friend's wedding, and I will not survive if I screw this up. I mean that literally. She will take me out, and if she doesn't her two-hundred-and-thirty-pound linebacker of a husband will do it for her… and I know I led with a joke, but I can't actually ask them to leave." He gives me a quick glance, and a small smile.

I can tell he's amused. I just hope he's amused enough to help me.

When Tatumn asked me to be her maid of honor it was more of a formality than anything else. I didn't actually think about it because I knew it wasn't really a choice. I just said yes, even though I had no idea what it actually meant to be a maid of honor.

My search history quickly became cluttered with questions like *how to host a proper party*, and *what is a canapé?* I looked up absolutely everything I could think of. I spent my free time reading articles from *The Knot* and meeting vendors at various locations around town with Tatumn and Alissa, but somehow, I overlooked the most obvious fact. The pull of the Martin – Ellis names in Bozeman Montana.

Tatumn is the kind of person that thinks that the meaning of the word stranger is just a friend you haven't met yet, and Ethan just signed with the Seahawks. She's the town sweetheart and he's a local celebrity, and they are hosting a party with an open bar.

Alan looks back over at me, his brow wrinkled in thought. I almost open my mouth again, this time to beg, but he quickly spins away and then turns back with a glass of red wine in his hands. "Here. I'll go talk to the kitchen."

"Oh my God, thank you." I take the glass of wine and head back into the crowd to say hello to Eli. He leans down and wraps me up in a hug so tight my feet lift off the ground. Cool air hits the top of my thighs and I wiggle to try to get away from him. He misreads my apprehension for enthusiasm and squeezes tighter, so I look at him and say, "Eli, you're about to shine the moon over Bozeman."

His cheeks flush, and he puts me down and takes a step back. He apologizes and I tell him it's alright, "I'm just not trying to throw that kind of a party."

I've barely been let go when Cash steps up behind me. He leans in and puts his lips right next to my ear, wrapping his arm around my waist and pulling me tight up against him. "Damn Emma… you trying to kill a man?" His hand tightens on my side as he nuzzles into my hair, "I know this isn't the actual wedding, but I'm pretty sure you're not supposed to outshine the bride." His voice is quiet, but I can tell Eli heard him by the stiff set of his shoulders.

I turn around to look Cash in the eyes and I see exactly what I know I will. It's not that he's insincere, he means what he says, it's just that what he says doesn't mean anything. Not really. Cash looks down at my chest and bites down on his lower lip. "Seriously, I mean it. I don't think your tits have ever looked better. You're going to have me hobbling around on three legs all night."

Eli clears his throat, Cash looks up, and I give him a quick jab with my elbow.

He lets me go and looks up at Eli like he's just realized he's there. "Eli, good to see you man, it's been a while." Eli looks down at me and Cash steps to the side. "Yeah, I guess it has." Cash looks around the room, "Our girl did a good job here, huh?" Eli gives me a scathing look and my eyes roll to the top of my head. Cash says, "I'm sorry, am I missing something?"

Eli shrugs, "No, just didn't realize Emma was your girl."

Cash says, "Well…" in this cocky *it's only a matter of time* sort of way, just as I say, "I'm not." Eli nods and Cash says, "Sweetness, you're breaking my heart."

I take an exaggerated look around the room. "I'm sure any number of these nice girls would be willing to put it back together for you later." He nods, like that's a given, and leans in a little closer, "Yeah, but you know one of these days you're going to have to learn how to clean up your own mess."

Cash has this way about him, dark eyes and a light smile that make him easy to forgive. "My daddy issues don't run that deep, Cash." His head tilts in my direction, dark blue eyes burning into mine. "Daddy issues are my specialty, Sweetness."

Eli coughs into his beer and then reaches up to wipe his face on his sleeve. "Dude, that's my sister." Cash looks him up and down, "Alright fine, I'll help you too, but separately."

I look back at Cash, "You know there is actually something wrong with you right?" Eli says, "Nah, thanks man, but I think I'll stick with my therapist." Cash shrugs like he's the one missing out and Eli says, "You know what Sis, I'll catch up with you later."

Cash pulls his shoulders back and his eyes dart to mine. "Alone at last." I push him away and tell him he's incorrigible, just as a petite blonde walks in the room and he seems to lose all focus. He gives me a distracted, *maybe*, and I watch as she catches his eye. He says, "I think I'd better go. You know so I don't upset your brother anymore." I nod, and he turns to go over to her.

The band comes on and the crowd gravitates to the front of the room. I take the opportunity to check in with the wait staff. They aren't worried about the extra people. The kitchen is preparing a few more dishes to accommodate the extra guests and the bar is fully stocked. People are happy. Tatumn is happy. I can see her now. She's dancing with Ethan.

Alan hands me another glass of wine, and I lean my back on the bar and listen to my mom and Dani as they laugh about nothing. Tatumn sees me standing on the edge of the crowd and waves me over. I try to tell her no with a wave of my own hand, but we have a prearranged agreement. It was the only request she made. I can't say no, or in her words *"You can't plan it all, and then just watch it happen like you always do."*

She takes my hand in hers and twirls me around. A bit of wine sloshes over the edge of my glass and the soft liquid runs down the back of my hand. I lift the glass to my lips and make quick work of finishing it off. I don't have anywhere to put it down, but Tatumn doesn't care.

She is in her moment, and right now I get to be there with her. I let the music wash over me and the two of us dance with my empty wine glass held carelessly between us. She lets me go and I just move, until the song stops, and I realize that Tatumn is staring at me.

The way she's looking at me makes me think I've done something wrong, but then I see her look over at Dani. Whose face lights up like the sun as she jumps up from her chair and rushes toward the door… and I realize I haven't, but she has.

2

Eleven Years ago

The first time I saw Camden Pierce I was thirteen years old. He had just climbed out of his Aunt Dani's truck, and I couldn't take my eyes off of him.

Mom ran out of the house to stand at the edge of the porch and even before the truck stopped, I knew something had changed. At first all I could see were his shoes, dirty soles, and a toe poking out at the corner. A cloud of dust rose up around his feet, and Dani reached out to ruffle his hair. He hadn't looked up yet, but he did when she did that, and I could tell he didn't like it.

I'd been coming to the ranch my whole life, it was more like home than home was, but Camden had never been here before. It had always been just me, my brother Eli, and Tate. Tatumn and I were more like sisters than friends. We didn't live close to each other during the school year, but in the summer, we ran wild across these hills.

Camden had a bit of wild in him too. I could tell by the way his eyes refused to settle, quickly darting away from any contact. Mom left the porch and started walking my way. Somewhere in the fuzzy parts of my mind I was aware that she'd been watching me, and I knew it was because I'd been watching him. She hadn't said anything, we hadn't even made eye contact, but I could feel her admonishment all the same. Mostly because in the clearer parts of my mind I knew that what I was doing was strange.

I had never looked at anyone the way I was looking at him. It wasn't okay, and I wasn't normally a rebellious child, but something about the soft sounds of her sandals sliding across the dirt made me feel almost frantic for more of him.

He shoved both of his hands in his pockets and even though I couldn't see much of his face, I could tell he was chewing on his lower lip. Mom put her hand on my shoulder and the weight of it startled me.

I don't know if it was just the magic of summer, or if the ranch really held some sort of special power, but Mom was different here. Back home she was always busy, grading papers and running us around. Dad traveled a lot for work, so she spent a lot of her time alone.

Here she had Dani, and the two of them spent all their time drinking wine and doing yoga. In the evenings they sat on the porch to soak up the sun, and they laughed… a lot. Mom always laughed more when Dani was around. She told me once that she was her person. That everyone had a person and one day I would find mine.

Camden Pierce was Dani's nephew. His mom wasn't with him, no one was, and even though he was standing right beside Dani, he looked alone. Tatumn looked up with a bored expression on her face and said, "Oh, he's here." like it was an imposition. I felt a strange prickle of discomfort spread out over my skin.

"Tatumn come and say hello to your cousin." Dani said.

Tate turned to me and gave me a conspiratorial look. As if we were in this together. As if the thought of walking over to him was as repulsive to me as it was to her. It wasn't. In fact, if I'd had my way, I would have wiggled free of Mom and gone to stand between them.

Tate reluctantly dropped her water gun on the driveway and headed in his direction. I could tell Tatumn was talking, though I couldn't make out what she was saying. I was too focused on him. The way he seemed to be trying to climb inside himself. Shoulders slumped over, gaze cast down and hidden behind a dark curtain of hair. Tatumn just kept talking. She always had something to say, and though I loved her, she was somewhat oblivious to the discomfort of others.

Camden didn't speak a word. His eyes only met Tatumn's for a moment at a time. Dani kept looking at her like she wasn't doing enough, but from where I stood it looked like she was doing too much. She asked him something, but I could tell by the way he looked up at Dani that he didn't want to answer. Tatumn looked up at her mom without even trying to hide the irritation in her eyes, and he looked over at me.

His eyes were the color of the sky when it was about to rain. I've always loved rainy days, but his eyes looked like a hurricane. There was so much he wasn't saying. So much he should be saying, but I could tell he didn't have anyone to say it to.

I was so fascinated by him that I forgot to look away. He didn't though. The moment his eyes left mine I wanted them back. I felt myself lurch forward, and if it weren't for my mom's hand on my shoulder, I would have gone to say hello just to find out what his voice sounded like when he spoke. She didn't want me to though, and as I looked at him, I realized he didn't either.

It wasn't long before Tatumn grabbed my hand, and we were off again. The ranch was the only place I was allowed to run free.

We lived in a nice neighborhood in a little suburb of Chicago. It was the kind of town with cute little parks and bike paths lined with trees, but Mom never let me leave our yard back home. She trusted me, or at least she said she did, it was the rest of the world that she was skeptical of.

On the ranch though, there was no yard. There was a fence, but it was mostly for decoration because the ranch went on forever.

The only thing we had to watch out for at the ranch was wildlife. There were a lot of elk. We'd seen a couple of moose down by the river. Mom said there were bears and wolves, but I'd never seen them. Thankfully, we didn't see any that day either.

We came home from the creek with mud on our feet and grass in our hair. I watched Camden all through dinner, but he never looked up from his plate.

He never took a bite either.

He wasn't like my brother, Eli never stopped eating, and he certainly wasn't quiet. I finished my plate and then Tatumn and I took a shower in our swimsuits. We took turns singing into the water, making our voices bubble, and laughing so hard we had to crumple to the floor and curl up beneath the spray of the shower just to catch our breath.

We all slept in the game room. Dani and Mom took turns reading us stories before bed. This year it was *The Outsiders*, and I really loved the way Dani's voice deepened when she read *Dally's* lines. The bunks were carved into the wall, so even though we were all literally piled on top of each other, it felt like we all had our own little nooks to settle into.

Eli and Tatumn passed out the moment the lights went off, but I never could go to sleep that quickly, especially at the ranch, images from the day would always run through my head like a movie. The ranch was my favorite place. It was where I made all my happiest memories, and for some reason I never could live them just once.

This time I mostly thought of him. The way his eyes carefully scanned his surroundings when he thought no one was watching. Dani hovering over him all evening. His index finger rubbing a continual circle over his thumb as he sat and stared at the floor.

The room was pitch black, and the wind was howling. At first, I hadn't realized it was him making that noise. I listened for a while just to make sure, wondering the whole time what could make a boy like him cry like that. I didn't think I wanted to know, because even though I knew almost nothing about him, I knew I didn't want him to hurt like that.

It was him though. His howl was different than the winds. It came in shorter burst, and instead of soothing me to sleep, it made me feel like I might never rest again.

I reached over into the jar I kept by my bed and pulled out a chocolate kiss. It wasn't much, but it wasn't nothing either. I rolled over and pushed the covers off my legs. The boys had taken the top bunks. He was sleeping above Tatumn. I climbed up the ladder. His back was turned to me, and I could tell he didn't know I was there by the way his shoulders kept shaking.

"Camden?" I whispered.

His head jerked to the side, and he pulled the covers up to wipe the tears from his cheeks. It was obvious he didn't want me to see him like this. I looked down at the end of his bed as I climbed the last couple of rungs on the ladder and found a spot by his feet.

"What are you doing?"

I wasn't really sure how to answer him, so I just held out my hand and said, "I brought you something."

He gave me a wary look.

"It's chocolate." I explained.

He didn't move, so I popped up on my knees and held it closer.

"Take it. It'll help."

His eyes narrowed and then he reached out from under the covers and took the kiss from my hand. I still remember the way it felt when he touched me. His hand was rough, *dry and scratchy*… nothing at all like Tatumn's.

"Thanks." he said, as he pulled the covers back up and rolled away from me.

3

I don't have to turn around to know it's him. It isn't just the way Tatumn is looking at me either. It's this slight tightness in my shoulder blades and a soft wave of sensation that travels from the back of my neck to the edges of my body. I can't be sure he's looking at me, but the way Tatumn's eyes keep darting over my shoulder makes me feel like he is.

I have lived this moment before.

Not in this room. Not surrounded by all these people, but in the shadowy parts of my mind. Where things feel almost dream like. In that place it's easy to look at him.

Here it feels fraught with danger.

I hear the moment that Dani crashes into him. The low rumble of his voice carries across the crowd, and I feel my breath catch in my throat. Tatumn looks over at me, searching my face for signs of collapse. I can feel it, the need to crumble, but I won't give into it. I refuse to be reduced to rubble by the same man twice. Instead, I pull myself up a bit and look over at her like nothing's the matter.

I would give anything, including my own soul, to be able to evaporate into thin air. To avoid turning around and seeing the way he's standing there, chatting nonchalantly with everyone that comes his way.

I look back toward the bar, wishing I was the kind of person that could do one of those casual one fingered waves that would get me another drink, and realize that my mom is watching me.

I can tell by the look on her face that she doesn't want me to turn around either. It shouldn't bother me, she's right, but I look away from her anyway. My attention gets caught on the disapproving faces of the couple standing beside her and my eyes sweep the room. There are murmurs of curiosity and expressions of thinly veiled disdain everywhere.

Tatumn steps in and puts her hand on my shoulder, "I swear I didn't know." Her eyes are wide and filled with remorse. Something about her tone and the way she's looking at me, like she desperately needs me to believe her, makes her words from earlier float through my mind.

You can't keep waiting on him. He's not coming back.

I hear it as clearly as I did yesterday, only now I understand why she said it with such certainty. She invited him and judging by the look on her face he declined, or more likely he just didn't reply at all. Either way she knew this was a possibility and she chose not to tell me.

I'm still trying to decide if that makes me angry when Eli walks past and calls out his name. I try not to wince, but my eyes close anyway. When they open again, every head in the room is turned his way. Dani's voice is bright, so is Eli's, but the rest of them are looking at him in derisive silence.

When I thought about seeing him again, my thoughts were always for myself. I knew it wouldn't be easy. For me. I never thought about how difficult it would be for him. Small towns like this have long memories, and Camden Pierce is absolutely unforgettable. I don't know what my plan is, but I know I can't stand here anymore. I turn around and shake free of Tatumn's grip.

He is as cool as he ever was.

Leaning up against the door frame, motorcycle helmet held loosely in hand. Everyone in here is looking at him, but his attention is entirely devoted to Eli and Dani.

In some of my pettier moments I had hoped he would be one of those men that didn't age well, with a round belly and thinning hair on top. That isn't the case though. He is impossibly handsome. Tall and lean with cords of muscle flowing down his arms. Broad shoulders, full lips, and a sharp jawline. Thick dark curls framing grey eyes that refuse to look over at me.

I know I am looking at him too intently. It's just that after so long my eyes feel parched. He's just standing there, as if he's completely oblivious to the way everyone in this room is watching him.

It's one of the things I liked most about him.

He can stand in the fire, but he doesn't burn.

I'm nearly there and he still hasn't looked at me. I know him well enough to know that means he doesn't want to talk to me. It hurts, but honestly, it's the simplest option. I decide I'll acknowledge him with a little wave and just keep walking out into the hallway, but Dani sees me coming. She pulls me in and asks me if I can believe my own eyes.

I can't, or I don't want to anyway.

She's talking quickly, excitement pouring out of her at the sight of him. I just nod and give a little shrug. Camden looks over at me with a blank expression, "It's good to see you, Emma."

^^^^^^

Camden

Coming back here was always going to be a risk. I was just hoping I had stayed gone long enough that the risk was all my own.

Judging by the way every face in this room is turned in my direction with near murderous expressions in place, I would have to assume I'm wrong. I see her walking toward me. I can't not see her, but I don't look at her.

It's the only defense I have to offer.

Dani is still talking. I make sure to keep my eyes pointed in her direction, but I can see the way Emma is starting to question her decision to come over. Her insecurity makes my hand twitch at my side. I want to reach out and grab her. To pull her into a dark corner where no one else can see us. I want to drink in every detail of her.

I can't do that though. It wouldn't be fair… to her.

Eli lifts his hand in the air, and even though I'm not really a high five sort of guy I take the opportunity to pull my head up, stealing an unobstructed glance at her, as his hand slaps against my own. She doesn't mean to do it, I can tell by the way the corners of her lips quiver a bit as she fights to pull them back down, but she smiles.

Nothing hits quite like her smile. I've drawn a million different versions of it, but none of them are as painful as the one I'm staring at right now. It's tinged with a sadness I've never seen in her before and I feel so convicted my chest hollows out.

I did that. I know I did, and now she's going to walk right past me. I can see it in her eyes, and I know I deserve it, but a stark heaviness settles in my gut.

I picture myself reaching out for her, feeling the softness of her skin up against my own. God, I want that, but I know it won't go the way I want it to. She won't reach up and wrap her fingers in mine. The rest of them won't turn away. They'll watch me even closer, wondering if Emma will do the right thing. If she'll push me away.

I let my head drop and accept that she doesn't want to talk to me. Remind myself that she shouldn't want to talk to me. I left her. She has no reason to come back. No reason to trust me, or hope, the way I do that forgiveness is real. That sorry might matter because I only know one truth in this whole world, and it's that nothing matters without her.

She's close enough now that I can let my gaze travel up her legs. Dani must realize she's not going to stop because she reaches out for her. Emma stiffens and my eyes dart in her direction, but her expression is too painful to look at.

I don't know what to do, but I know I have less than a moment to figure it out, so I just say the first thing that comes to mind, and I know immediately... it's not the right thing.

^^^^^^

Emma

Of all the things I hoped he'd say when he finally came home, *good to see you* was not one of them. It's so blasé. Like we're old college buddies that met at a party once and had a really good chat about the weather. It holds none of the pain or longing I've felt every day since he left. It says what I already know to be true. I loved him much more than he ever loved me.

"Camden?" I'll admit it's not poetry, but it's not *good to see you* either.

"Yeah, It's me." He reaches up to run his hand through his hair and I can tell he's nervous. I'm sure it's not because of me. It's because of them, and since I know that half the town will take its cue from Tatumn, and Tatumn will definitely take her cue from me. I do my best not to look bothered.

Camden shifts his helmet to his other hand and stands up taller. I pull the inside of my lower lip in with my teeth and bite down.

As far as cosmic things go, I feel like this is unfair. He's the one that left me. Didn't I at least deserve a warning? *Then? Now?* Shouldn't I be allowed a time out, a moment to gather my thoughts, come up with a plan before having to sacrifice myself to save him.

I wonder how long I have to stand here.

How many seconds of torture do I have to endure in order to ensure his safety?

Dani is still talking. I have no idea what she's saying because everything in here sounds like an echo. I am having a hard time meeting his eyes, not that he's trying to meet mine. It's just that I know I should look at him. Directly.

If I was in better control of my emotions. I would just say something casual to him, like he did to me, and then I could walk away.

His eyes trail all over my body, "You look good. I've seen you dancing over there." I look up at him and his cheeks flush. It's disarming. I ask him how long he's been here. "Long enough to know that puddle of wine on the floor came from your glass."

I give him a noncommittal quirk of my lips and then Tatumn walks up and rests her hand on my shoulder. I look over at it, and then up at her. She may have invited him here, but right now she's come to save me.

Her hand drops to my back, and she gives me a little push toward the hallway. As I'm walking away, I hear Dani chastise him for leaving the way he did, and he says, "I know. I shouldn't have done that."

4

Ten years ago

Tatumn and I had always kept in touch over the year, but this year was the most we'd ever spoken. I'd started face timing her every night before bed in hopes of catching a glimpse of Camden in the background. I never did though. She always took the calls in her bedroom, and he definitely wasn't allowed in there.

I knew he was still with them because my mom called Dani too, and unlike Tatumn she didn't sneak off when the phone rang. Anytime I heard his name mentioned my ears perked up. I'd overheard her talking about things like they were tragic.

She'd get this look on her face while she was listening to Dani and then she'd say something like, "Well he did spend a lot of time in foster care, it's probably going to take him some time to adjust."

I had to look up what foster care was. He was an orphan, apparently, except I also heard them mention his mother. So, she definitely wasn't dead. If I'd been braver, I would have asked Tatumn about it, about him. I couldn't though, because even the thought of saying his name out loud to her made my palms sweat.

She did talk about him sometimes, mostly out of frustration. I knew he had started in Tae Kwon Do because he had used his breaking skills to dismantle the kitchen counter in her playhouse out back.

She was really upset about it. I knew I was supposed to be upset too, but for some reason the thought of him breaking through wood with his bare hands was much more intriguing than upsetting to me.

When we got to the ranch that year, I could barely wait for the car to stop to hop out. Tatumn was walking across the top of the fence. I didn't even bother to close the car door before I ran her way. I knew I shouldn't, Tatumn had made it very clear that we were not friends with her cousin, but I couldn't help but scan the horizon for his dark head.

"Emma!" Tatumn yelled as I ran across the yard, "Watch this." She put her hands into the air and then bent backward and did a walkover on the fence. When she stood up and turned my way, I could tell that she was waiting for me to say something. "That was really cool, Tate." Her bright blue eyes lit up as she hopped down and ran toward me. "I know. I can teach you if you want."

"That's okay, I'll just watch you do it." I said, taking another look around the yard.

Eli ran up behind us. "Where's Camden?" He asked, and even though I was a little jealous of the easy way he'd said his name, anticipation bubbled up in my belly. "I don't know, he was out by the garage earlier."

Eli didn't even wait for her to finish before he took off. I wanted to follow him, at least with my eyes, but Tatumn was still talking, and I knew better than to turn away.

My skin itched with the need to look for him. I was completely consumed with thoughts of Eli finding him, worried that they may just take off. It could be hours before we saw them again. The thought made my stomach drop.

Tate's face wrinkled up in this hopeful expression and I realized she was still trying to convince me to get up on the fence with her. "Tate, I can barely walk a straight line on the ground. I don't think back walkovers on the fence are in my future. I can watch you do them though."

"Watch me? That sounds so boring. I don't want you to watch me. I want you to do it with me." I didn't know what to say. I wasn't being modest. I really couldn't see myself turning any kind of flip with any amount of success. "It won't be boring. I'll just go grab my book."

"Oh, did you bring it?"

I knew what she was talking about. My teacher had nominated me for NaNo RiMo, and I had written a book that I was really proud of, but the thought of Camden Pierce reading it made a wave of panic and humiliation rush over me like a waterfall.

"I did, but I don't want the boys to see it so maybe we can look at it later." Her face twisted and she looked at me like she didn't understand the words coming out of my mouth. "What boys? Eli and Camden? What do they matter?"

Eli didn't matter. He had made merciless fun of me for it already, but that was just him. He would sooner die than admit he liked something I'd made. Camden though, that was a different story. One I had no idea how to tell Tatumn. I shrugged, "You know how they are."

"You know how who is?"

Everything in me tightened around the sound of his voice. I had spent hours, or maybe even days, wondering what it would be like when I got to see him again. I had written his name in the corner of all of my notebooks for school and every time I opened one, I stared at it for a moment and thought of him.

I watched Tatumn's entire disposition change as he came closer. Mine did too, but I was hoping my infatuation wasn't as obvious as her irritation.

My heart was beating too fast, thrumming in the tips of my fingers. He stopped right beside me, and Tatumn said, "You." in this scornful tone that made my skin feel too tight.

Camden cocked his head to the side and lifted his chin in this very cool way that made me wonder what it would look like if someone else did it. I could tell he wasn't really bothered by Tatumn's slight. He seemed almost indifferent.

"You know a lot less than you think Tate, and I'm not bothering anyone… am I Emma?"

I'm sure I was just making it up, but it seemed like he'd lingered on my name just a moment longer than was necessary. He turned to me as he spoke, and his eyes caught mine. I felt all the blood in my body rush into my cheeks, but I couldn't look away.

I was like a fly trapped in honey.

He was just standing there, not really doing anything, but my mind was busy taking note of all the ways he'd changed. His face was different, still boyish, but the edges seemed a little sharper. His hair had been cut short. It was cropped on the sides, but the top was left longer so when he spoke it fell forward and rested on his brow.

"I brought you something." He lifted his hand into the air and opened his palm.

I knew what it was. You don't spend years trekking across the mountains in Montana and not know what a handful of elk scat looks like. "Oh yeah, what is that supposed to be?" Tatumn asked in that same irritated tone.

"Chocolate covered blueberries." He looked up at me again. My memory hadn't done those grey eyes justice. They were still stormy, but right now they had a little bit of mischief in them too.

"I know how much you like chocolate, Emma." He said it like it was just for me, and even though he was actually holding a handful of elk scat, I didn't want to disappoint him. I took one from his hand and lifted it toward my mouth.

"Did you make these?"

He gave me a slow nod, and I noted the bit of apprehension that floated through his eyes, "Yep." he said without blinking.

I didn't take my eyes off of his, but I still saw Tatumn roll hers. "He did not. Don't believe a word he says. Those are…" I gave her a brief look, just to let her know that I knew what I was holding, and then I turned back to him.

His mouth was held in a tight line. It was obvious that he'd read the subtext of the look between Tatumn and me. His eyes darted toward my hand and then he looked back up at me expectantly.

This was a game that we both knew we were playing. I knew this wasn't chocolate and he knew that I knew, so the game wasn't about that. It was a challenge. A question as to how far I was willing to go to please him, and how far he was willing to let me.

"I do love chocolate." I mused.

"Yep, and these have a little bit of a nutty flavor. You like nuts?" he asked with his big grey eyes boring into mine. "No, not really, but you made them… all by yourself?" There was a small twitch at the corner of his left eye, but he nodded.

I pretended to believe him and pulled my hand closer to my lips. His eyes widened. I opened my mouth. The intrigue in his eyes was absolutely intoxicating. Until I realized it meant he was actually going to let me do this. I dragged it out as long as I could but when his eyes darted away from my lips, I let my hand drop.

I told him I guessed that made sense since he was obviously full of crap, and Tatumn laughed so loud that Dani came out on the porch.

"Everything alright over there?" She yelled out across the yard.

Tatumn looked over at Camden, "You're so dead now. Mom's going to freak when she finds out you tried to feed Emma elk poop." Camden's hand fell and his palm emptied. "Tatumn don't." he said in a warning tone. "Don't what, tell her you're acting up again?"

When none of us answered, Dani left the porch and walked over to us. I saw her eyes scan the ground as she walked up. "Camden what'd you do?" she asked like she already knew the answer. Tatumn was looking at him like she'd just won another gold medal, and something about the disappointment in Dani's eyes and the joy in hers made the words tumble out of my mouth. "Nothing. He didn't do anything."

Tatumn's stare went cold, and her mouth dropped open. Camden looked every bit as shocked as she did. I gave Tatumn a look that said *none of us need the moms hovering* and did my best not to meet Camden's eyes.

"Nothing huh?" Dani asked as her gaze fell to the ground and passed over the small pile of scat at Camden's heels.

"Nope, just saying hi before Eli and I head down to the river." His eyes darted to mine. I could tell he wasn't used to having anyone on his side. What I couldn't tell was whether or not he liked it.

Dani looked at him, and then she turned to me. I knew, she knew I was lying. "Mom, Emma didn't do anything." Tatumn said. It wasn't necessary. I could tell it wasn't me she was upset with.

I had just surprised her.

^^^^^^

The river was always cold, but the sun was shining bright so the rocks beneath our feet had a little bit of warmth in them. The boys had their fishing poles and waders, and the moment we got to the water they took off downstream. Tate and I climbed up on Long Rock. She jumped in, and I laid my towel out and picked up my book to read in the sunshine.

Tatumn talked the whole time, but luckily for me I didn't have to pay much attention to know what she was saying. At

33

the end of each chapter, I would look up and find her diving in and out of the water. "Are you going to come in?" she asked. "Maybe." I answered before flipping over and diving back into my book.

The boys had been gone a while. I assumed they'd left us. Eli usually did. So, when Camden climbed up on the rock and sat down beside me, I nearly jumped out of my skin.

Eli was right behind him. He stepped over me and shook the nasty river water off onto my back as he passed. Eli was a lot like Tate, he never looked before he jumped. His splash was a lot bigger than hers though and a bit of it landed on the pages of my book.

"Dammit Eli." I yelled out at him.

Camden looked over at me. "Are you allowed to talk like that?" he asked sounding a little stunned.

"What? Dammit? He deserved it." I pulled the corner of my towel up to blot the water from the page, and he continued to watch me. I was too aware of his eyes on me. It made me feel like I was doing it wrong, even though there wasn't really a wrong way to do it.

"What are you reading?" His voice was soft, *inquisitive*. I could tell he actually wanted to know, but I absolutely did not want to tell him. It was a good book. One of my favorites but admitting that *The Sisterhood of the Golden Locket* was my sort of thing seemed so childish when I had to say it to Camden Pierce.

"Nothing. Just an easy read." I said in an offhanded manner, hoping he would hear the disinterest in my voice and lose interest himself.

It didn't work. His brows rose and he pinned me with those grey eyes of his. "It doesn't look like nothing. You were pissed when Eli got water on it." I felt my eyes roll around in my head, "Well yeah, but that's because he did a cannonball like five feet from me. He was trying to splash me."

"Fair enough." He reached over and plucked the book from my hand. "*The Sisterhood of the Golden Locket.*" He read aloud, much slower than was necessary, and I felt my cheeks blaze with embarrassment.

"Camden, give that back."

"I will. I just want to read a page first."

I reached out for the book and felt the warmth of his forearm rub up against mine as he yanked it away. His skin had this very specific texture. His forearms were covered in coarse hair and the effect was a slight roughness that sent something unfamiliar running through me. It wasn't really unpleasant, but it was uncomfortable, so I pulled my arm in and sat back down.

"I'm serious Camden. Give it back."

He rose up to his knees and the sunlight caught on all the droplets of water as they ran down his torso. I don't think he was doing it on purpose. He was just trying to keep me from taking the book from him, but the way he looked towering over me with the sunlight glistening off his chest made me need to look away.

"I'm serious too, just give me a moment. I want to know what kind of stuff these sisters get up to." I pulled my lip in between my teeth and watched a slow smile spread over his face as he read.

"See. That's why I didn't want you to read it." He looked down at me. "You're going to make fun of me now, aren't you?" Disappointment pulled at the corners of his lips.

"I wouldn't dare make fun of the Sisterhood." He said with so much sincerity that I couldn't help but laugh. The hint of smile spread out over his face. "Look who's laughing now. Are you making fun of me?"

I knew we were still talking about the book, but it felt like he was asking me something else. Like he wanted to know if I liked him. Or if I found him laughable. It was such a ludicrous thought that only a very serious answer would do. "No, I wouldn't do that."

He held my gaze for a moment, and I thought he was going to say something else, but then he handed me my book and looked out at the water.

"Are you getting in?" I looked over at Tate and Eli who were splashing around below us. "I don't know. The water's pretty cold."

Camden turned toward them, and I got a moment to stare at his profile before he looked back over at me. "Yeah, it is. This rocks pretty warm though." He laid back and closed his eyes. I knew that meant that he was done talking, and I knew I shouldn't be watching him lay there the way I was, but I found it nearly impossible to look away from him.

Especially if he wasn't looking at me.

It wasn't just the way he looked either. Camden Pierce was without a doubt the most attractive boy I had ever laid eyes on, and the way his tanned unblemished skin stretched out over his body as he lay there in the sun was fascinating. It just wasn't the most fascinating thing about him.

He was the only person I had ever met that had a past. A real one, the kind you don't really want to talk about. All the fractured bits of him that I had gathered over the year made me feel so curious.

I contemplated just asking him about it. I pictured myself saying something like *so, tell me about your mother and why she's never around* and immediately dismissed the idea. I didn't know if we were friends, or if he just thought of me as an extension of Tatumn, but I knew that no matter what I wondered. He didn't want to tell me, and I didn't want to ask.

∧∧∧∧∧∧

I turned away and picked up my book again. He didn't move or speak for a long time. The shadows from the trees above moved over us and I had to change position to get my legs back in the sunshine. It was nice, lying there with the sun on my back and him beside me.

It was so nice that I had all but forgotten that Tate and Eli were below us. Until Eli screamed her name and Camden leaped into the water. I stood up, dropped my book, and watched as Eli panicked and Camden swam downstream.

I caught a flash of her bright orange bikini underneath the water and jumped in myself. The current carried me toward him, and I dove under. Her foot was stuck. Camden was struggling to lift the rock that held her down.

I wrapped my arms around her waist and pulled. She didn't move. The rocks she was stuck between were literal boulders. Camden wasn't weak, but he wasn't that strong either. Eli dove down to help us and I felt an undeniable pressure building in my chest.

I looked over at Camden and I couldn't tell if his lips were blue from lack of oxygen or if it was just an effect of the freezing water running over them. Either way I was running out of air, and he'd been under longer than I had.

I reached out to tap his shoulder and his head jerked to the side. His eyes were so full of fear that I turned away from him and looked back at Tatumn. I knew he wouldn't be able to help her if he passed out too. I pointed to the surface. He didn't even look up. Eli joined him and the two of them pushed against the rock together.

I swam up and took in a huge gulp of air before diving back down. By the time I'd made it back to them, they seemed to have realized that the rock couldn't be moved, because both of their hands were wrapped around her leg. I grabbed ahold of her shoulders, and we pulled.

When she broke free, Camden wrapped his arm around her waist and swam upward. By the time I'd made it up he was already kneeling over her with his cheek held close to her lips. I watched as he reached down and pressed his fingers over her wrist and then he bent back over her and breathed into her mouth.

"Is she dead?"

Eli always had a way of cutting straight to the point, but hearing him say that, even though it was exactly what I was thinking made my mouth go dry with fear for her. Camden didn't answer. He was still leaning over her body, breathing out and watching for her chest to rise.

Eli pushed past me and fell down beside him. I joined them and took her hand in mine. It was so cold that a chill ran down my spine. Camden put his cheek over her lips again, "It's not working. She's not breathing."

I didn't know the first thing about saving a life, but it made sense to me that drowning was really just choking on too much water. I told them this and Eli rose to his knees and pressed on her belly.

Water rushed out from her lips and Camden picked her up and started running.

When we got back to the ranch Tate was still limp in Camden's arms. Eli called out, and Dani came rushing out onto the porch, "What happened? What'd you do?" She said in this accusatory tone as she looked down at Camden.

He didn't even bother to deny it. Instead, he said, "She needs a doctor." Dani's eyes were wide with panic. My mom ran out the back door and told Dani that the ambulance was on the way.

It was a strange moment, and I knew that he was right. Tatumn did need a doctor, but not because of something he'd done. "Dani, it wasn't Camden. She got stuck between some rocks. He found her, we got her out, and then he saved her."

Dani was still looking down at Tatumn, "Did he?" My mom stepped up behind her and gave me a reproving look.

∧∧∧∧∧∧

Later that night Camden climbed into the bunk beside me. Tate and the moms had all gone to the hospital. They put her on a stretcher and left us all behind. The house was too big and too empty.

Everything was quiet, including Eli, which just made the whole thing that much scarier. I kept telling myself she was fine. That a girl with as much life as Tatumn had couldn't die young. Surely the universe didn't allow such things to happen, but it had been hours, and we were still alone.

"You're scared, aren't you?" His voice was barely above a whisper. It made me feel like he was really listening, or maybe he was even confessing something himself. I nodded and he turned away.

"You saved her, right?"

"Did I?" He asked, and I heard the echo of Dani's words from earlier woven into his own. There was nothing about this situation that I liked, but it really bothered me that he felt like the villain even when he was the hero.

"That wasn't fair, what Dani said." He rolled his head to the side and looked toward the window. "Sure, it was. She was worried and I was there."

"So what? I was there, she wasn't, and I'm telling you if Tatumn lives it's because you saved her."

He looked over at me with an openness in his eyes that I hadn't seen before. "You really are scared, aren't you?" I held his gaze, but I didn't say anything.

"She's going to be alright, Emma." He said it like he knew, and not in the loose sense of things you just hope will come true. He said it like he really knew, like he'd seen this kind of thing before.

"How did you know how to do that anyway?" His eyes shifted away from mine.

At first, I thought he wasn't going to answer, but then he said, "My mom." like those two words were an entire explanation all on their own. "She taught you?" Somehow, I knew that wasn't the case, but it seemed like the right thing to say. He shook his head, "No, but I had to do that for her sometimes."

Another long list of questions I wasn't sure I should ask formed in my mind. He pushed the covers back and laid his hand down on his chest. "She's an… well, anyway she passed out a lot. I learned to check her pulse and breathe for her. It was better if I could help her at home. If I had to call the ambulance they took me away for a while."

"Took you where?"

"Anywhere, to another family, to an elderly couple, to a home with other children. It didn't matter, I just couldn't go back with her. At least not for a while."

"Where is she now?" He looked over at me, but I didn't look at him. I didn't want him to see the sadness in my eyes and mistake it for pity.

"I don't know."

He said it like a fact, but I didn't know if he was telling the truth or if he just didn't want to answer. A gust of wind blew the curtains open, and the cool breeze hit my legs. Camden reached down and pulled the blanket up over me.

I wasn't going to ask him any more questions, but something about the way he kept looking at me and then looking away again made me feel like he had some questions of his own.

I turned back to my book, just to have something to look at that wasn't him, and he asked me where my dad was.

I told him he was back home. "Why doesn't he come to the ranch with you?" I wasn't sure how to answer him. I leaned my head back on the wall, and he said, "Do your parents not like each other?"

It wasn't a thought that was fully formed in my mind but when I heard him say it. I knew it was true. My parents didn't really like each other. I thought about telling him that they did. Just so I wouldn't have to say it out loud, but something about the way he was lying beside me so still and quiet, made it seem like it was okay to tell the truth.

"No, not really. Dad travels a lot for work, but even when he's home, they don't spend much time together."

Camden rolled toward me and propped himself up on his elbow. I put my book down on my lap and he said, "That was really nice, what you did for me."

"I didn't do anything."

He seemed to think about it for a moment. "Sure, you did. You did more than anyone else ever has, but you know you don't need to, right?" I knew he was talking about what I'd said to Dani, but it really didn't seem like much, so I just looked at him and said, "She's going to be alright, isn't she?"

He gave me this look, like he knew what I was doing, and he was trying to decide whether or not to allow it. He turned his cheek away from me and when the curtains blew open again the moonlight spilled over his features. I liked being this close to him. Close enough to see the way the light illuminated his eyes and shadowed his lips.

Enough time passed that I was pretty sure he wasn't going to answer, but then he said, "Yeah. Tate's a tough little bird. She'll be alright."

∧∧∧∧∧∧

Roger's farm was down the hill from the ranch. He had a few sets of twins this season and the moms abandoned the weaker ones. He called Dani and asked if we'd be interested in feeding them. The babies were cute, with fluffy coats and wet noses, and they were smaller than the others, but they didn't look weak to me.

Tate grabbed one of the bottles and hopped the fence without a thought. I was always the one that looked both ways for us. Even though Roger had the babies in their own pen, I still made sure the moms knew we were coming as I followed her in.

"Do you think it tastes good?" Tate asked as she stood on her crate watching one of the fluffy little boys slurp up the milk. "It's cow's milk. We know it tastes good." Her eyes poked to the side. "I know, but do you think it tastes different like this?"

"I don't know. It seems warmer." The look on her face morphed from contemplative to intrigued and I knew she was about to ask me to taste it. I wasn't going to do it, but then I saw the boys go into the woods just as she said, "I dare you to taste it."

It wasn't the milk I was thinking about while she was waiting for my answer. She didn't know that though. "If you do it, I'll owe you a dare." I was still staring off into the trees. "Anything I want?" She sounded reluctant, but she said, "Sure."

The milk was warm and delicious. Tate stared at me in wide eyed amusement the entire time I drank it. I made a show of swallowing the last bit and wiping the warm cream off my lips so that she wouldn't be able to back out of her end of the deal.

When I told her she had to go into the woods and scare the boys, she looked over toward the trees. "I don't know Emma. We aren't supposed to go in there."

She wasn't wrong. The moms had never let us wander into the woods.

"Well, neither are they."

They were whispering when we found them. Which seemed odd since they didn't know anyone else was out there. Tate ducked down and motioned for me to do the same. Eli looked up and released a big cloud of smoke, and then Camden reached over and took something from his hand.

"Oh my God. Mom is going to kill him." Tatumn whispered.

She looked over at me with our dare still dancing in her eyes and I shook my head, *no*. This wasn't a good idea. I only dared to her to do it because I was curious about what they were doing out here, but now that I knew. I didn't want to be here.

I reached over to try and stop her, but it just wasn't in Tate's nature to back down from a dare. The way she screamed when she jumped over the log scared me as much as it scared the boys.

Eli let out a string of curse words like I'd never heard before. Whatever they were smoking dropped to the ground and Tatumn stood there laughing as Eli searched for it.

Camden turned away from them. "Where's Emma?" he asked as he bent over to pick something up. Smoke traveled all around his fingers as he twisted his foot into the ground below him.

"She's over there, and she saw you too." Tate taunted.

"I bet she did." His tone sounded so sure that it made me wonder if he was implying something about the way I watched him. He walked over and sat down on the log behind me, "What are you doing over here, Emma?"

"Nothing. Just sitting here." I didn't look up at him. I wanted to act as if I hadn't seen him, or maybe I wanted to acknowledge the fact that I had but act as unaffected by his presence as he was by mine. He leaned forward. His shoulders slumped over his lap, and he took another drag.

"You want to try it?"

He was looking at me so intently that I felt like there was only one right answer. I asked him what *it* was. "It's just weed." he said offhandedly, trying to put me at ease, but making me feel incredibly awkward instead. I shook my head, *no*, and turned away.

I was sure I had answered wrong. Which made me feel anxious about looking over at him, but then he said, "You're a good girl, Emma." The words sounded encouraging on their own, but the way he said them made me feel like being good was a bad thing.

My eyes shot toward his, and he let out a breath rough enough to move his shoulders. It felt like he was laughing at me, so I turned away.

"You don't need to get upset, it's not a bad thing to be a good girl."

I wanted to believe him, or really, I wanted to believe that he liked good girls. That he liked me, but even though there was just a veil of smoke between us, it felt like a continental divide.

He took another puff and when he exhaled the smoke floated toward me. I lifted my hand and waved it away. "Are you going to tell the moms?" Somehow, that was the most insulting thing he'd ever said to me. Humiliation tightened my chest, and I answered with a gruff, "No."

He reached down and snubbed the joint out on the log beneath him. I couldn't help but watch the expert way his fingers twisted around it.

"Do you do that a lot?" He shrugged in this really causal way that said *no not really*, but I knew what he actually meant was *yes*, or *sometimes*, or *maybe*.

"You shouldn't." He looked at me like I was a child. I looked at him like he should know better. "People do things they shouldn't all the time, Emma."

"That doesn't mean you have to."

He looked down at the ground with a reluctant nod. "You are going to tell the moms, aren't you?" I shook my head, *no*. "You think Tate will?"

"I don't know. Tate sort of does her own thing."

∧∧∧∧∧∧

The engine was already started. Camden was sitting in front of me and even though there were handles at the back, I wanted to wrap my arms around him. "You scared, Emma?" He taunted, turning his face toward mine as he reached up to

46

fasten the button on his helmet. I was, but I didn't want him to know that. "No."

Summers in Montana were perfect. The sun was warm, and the air was cool. We usually drove the ATVs on Sunset Hill, right beside the ranch, but today we were headed down the hill toward the creek.

As soon as we were out of eye shot of the moms, Tate demanded Eli stop and let her drive. He slowed down and hopped off while Camden pulled us up beside them. "You owe me." Eli said.

Camden nodded in this very inconsequential sort of way and turned around to ask me if I wanted to drive. I told him, *no,* and he looked down at the space between us. It was probably just my imagination, but it seemed like he liked it even less than I did. Our eyes met and my cheeks warmed. "You can hold onto me if you want. These hills get pretty steep."

I held out as long as I could. Mostly because I really wanted to hold on to him and I was sure he knew that. Tate was a wild woman though. She tore through fields, drove us in and out of puddles, over rocks, and through the shallower parts of the creek. When she took us up the hill, I felt like I was going to fall off and my arms wrapped around him.

His body was solid. He felt like a hot coal and a firm anchor. He smelled like the woods dusted in smoke. I found it very hard not to press my nose into his jacket and breathe him in. Not that he would have noticed. Tate was completely fearless, and it felt like we were flying through the trees.

The ATVs were made for this sort of thing. I knew that, but it still felt dangerous. I had my arms held very loosely around him, but the angle of the hill pressed his back into my chest. We hit a bump, and my arms tightened. It was all very natural. Holding him like this. He felt sturdy. Like even though the world was flying by us way too fast, I could count on him to keep me safe.

Tatumn screamed, and a bolt of anxiety shot through me. I poked my head over Camden's shoulder to look ahead. She screamed again, but as I watched her long blond hair trail out behind her, I realized she wasn't scared or hurt.

Her scream didn't come from a place of fear or pain. It came from joy. Pure unbridled joy like only Tate knew how to harness. "She's alright." I heard Camden yell out, "just having a good time."

I nodded and let my head tuck back behind his shoulder. Tate and Eli were both hollering now. She sped up over a hill and we all caught some air. I threw my head back, laughter bellowing out of me. Camden sped up and we caught more air than Tatumn did on the last jump.

We didn't land it though.

We hit hard.

I flew up off the seat and Camden kept going. I could tell he didn't have control of the ATV anymore. He was just trying to stay upright. I was lying on the ground with all the air knocked out of me, but for some reason I'd never felt so happy in all my life.

^^^^^^

"What are you reading this time?" Camden asked as he climbed into the bunk beside me. "*The Hunger Games.*" I said, continuing to trace the words on the page with my eyes. "Still into the sisterhood, huh?" He nudged my shoulder teasingly. "It's more than a sisterhood."

"I know. I've seen the movie." I turned the page. "The book's better." He pulled out his sketch pad and opened it up. "I'm sure it is." His pencil moved over the paper. I still wasn't sure what we were, or if we were anything at all, but I knew I liked him sitting beside me more than I liked anything else.

He was good at it too. Whenever I tried to read around Tatumn or Eli, they never could keep quiet. He could though. I read and he drew and even though we were both lost in our own worlds, it felt like we were lost together. After a while he picked his head up and put his pencil down to stretch out his hand.

"Does it hurt?" I asked as I watched his long fingers spread out beside me. "Sometimes, after a while." He reached into his pocket and pulled out a chocolate. "I brought this for you."

"Why'd you do that?"

"Because you didn't tell, and because I threw you off the back of the ATV."

A small laugh escaped my lips. "You did, but it's no big deal. I already told you that." He held his palm out and looked at me pleadingly. "Take it, please."

It was chocolate, and I was never opposed to chocolate, but the way he was handing it out like an offering made it feel like more.

"Fine, but I'm still mad at you for smoking."

"I know you are." He picked up his pencil and began drawing again. "I'm really glad you didn't tell." I turned another page, "I wouldn't do that." He looked over at me and I could tell he was trying to decide something. I just didn't know what it was. "I know." He said it like he believed me. Like he trusted me, which made me feel like I was betraying him.

"You should stop doing it though."

"I know." He wiggled his pencil in his hand and turned away from me. I liked the way the contours of his face softened when he drew. I went back to reading my book, but I couldn't help but look over at him sometimes. The drawing he was working on was impressive.

"Is that me?" I asked even though I thought it probably wasn't. He looked over at me, pulling the drawing in toward his chest.

"Yeah, but it's not done yet."

I could tell he was self-conscious about it, "It's really good." His eyes softened. He started drawing again. The soft sounds of pencil dragging over paper filled the room. He leaned into me, and I just sat there thinking about how much I liked him.

5

Now

Emma

The ladies' room is really fancy. The walls are papered in an elaborate print of deep purple and gray. The sinks are marble with golden handles and the towels feel like you could dry off with them after a shower.

I lean over the sink and fill my palms with cold water. My reflection in the mirror doesn't look right. My skin is pale, and my eyes are too wide. I splash the water on my face and let the drops run down over my neck and chest.

The door swings open and Tatumn gives me a look that very clearly asks if I'm losing it. I am. I know I am, maybe if I tell her that she'll let me leave. Her face falls, and she walks in the room, "You handled it well."

I nod and she gives me a careful look, "He's here for the wedding. Mom invited him. Are you okay?"

I nod again, but it feels like a lie, and I can tell that she can see straight through it. "I ordered the death by chocolate for dessert. I know it's your favorite. Alan said they were about to bring it out."

I turn away from the mirror and she walks over to me. She picks up one of the plush towels and puts it under the running water. "You're all blotchy. Are you sure you're alright?" I am not alright. I am freaking out, the blotches on my chest should say that for me, but I don't want her to worry so I just lie and tell her it's just the wine.

She looks up, and I know she doesn't believe me.

"Do you want to leave? He'll be here all week, but you could go now. Have a little more time to prepare before you have to see him again." She presses the towel over my temples and gives me a sympathetic look. I can't help it. I don't want to ask, but I need to know.

"He's only staying for the week?"

Her eyes dart back and forth, the way they always do when she's nervous. "I don't know actually. Mom said he might come. She didn't say how long he'd be here though. I assume he'll leave again."

I assume that too.

I turn back around and catch another glimpse of myself in the mirror. I *don't* like what I see, so I say, "I'll stay." and she gives me a questioning look.

I tell her I really want to go, but I can't have him thinking I left on his account. She gives me a slow nod. "You know how toxic his ego can get. He'll be insufferable." I say it to make light of a heavy situation, but she gives me a hesitant look before stepping in and wrapping her arms around me.

"He's already insufferable. He always has been."

I don't want to argue with her, so I just say, "Really. I'm alright. I just need a moment." She pulls back and looks me in the eye. "You don't have to be alright. I know it's a lot… seeing him again."

She's right about that, but I do have to be alright. "Tatumn, I love you, but we both know that mental breakdowns are frowned upon at weddings." Her smile falters. "Well then we're both in trouble, because between my mother and my husband I'm definitely going to lose my mind."

"He's already your husband?"

"Close enough."

She reaches out and places her hand on my shoulder, "Are you ready now?" I'm not, but I also know I'm not going to be. I give her a nod which she seems to accept.

I should leave it at that, but I can't help but say, "I wish you would have warned me though." Her shoulders drop. "I would have. If I had known for certain that he was going to come. I've wanted to tell you about him so many times, but I just couldn't make myself do it. Not after the way things were when he left."

Her face has fallen, her eyes are tight and she's speaking too quickly, but I still ask, "What do you mean so many times?" Her eyes dart away from mine. "Mom found him. A year ago. They talk a lot. I was forbidden from telling you."

"Why?"

Her eyes close and her head falls back, "Because he lives with someone."

I know exactly what she means by someone, but I ask anyway.

She looks like she would rather swallow nails than have to say another word. It takes her a while, but she eventually tells me that he lives with a girl named Gabby. He's in school for social work and anthropology. He volunteers as a big brother for a little boy named Sam, and one of his drawings was featured at the Met.

As she's talking, I realize how much time has really passed. He has an entire life where I don't exist at all, and it sounds like a good one.

The more she talks the more I feel the nervous energy leave me to make room for all the pride I feel at what he's been able to accomplish. I don't love the bit about Gabby, but it's not really surprising either.

"So, are you mad at me?" I shake my head, *no*.

"Good, because I'm kind of the star of the show out there and I'm surprised Mom hasn't sent someone in to get me already." We both laugh at the truth of what she's said and then she asks me if I'm ready to go back out there again.

I don't know if ready is the right word, but I nod. She looks me in the eyes, "Just stick with me. I'll make sure he doesn't even look your way."

"That's probably not necessary. He barely looked at me when I was standing right in front of him." I don't mean to do it, but my voice is riddled with self-deprecation. Some of the light leaves Tatumn's eyes. She takes my shoulders in her hands and gives me a very stern look.

"Emma, he'll look at you. He already has. I saw him watching you as you walked away, and he didn't like it."

It shouldn't make me feel better, but it does. Tatumn notices and gives me a sad sort of smile. "He should notice you. You're the best thing that ever happened to him, and what you two had was real, but he left… and that means you really need to ignore him."

I know she's right. I just can't fathom actually being able to do that. I mean how do you ignore the other half of your own soul, especially after a couple glasses of wine? Tatumn doesn't give up easily though. She's waiting for me to acknowledge her. To admit that she's right, and we both know she is, so I nod.

"Yeah, complete indifference, the kind *T Swift* talks about."

She gives me a look full of solidarity.

"That's right, now let's go back out there and show him what he's missing."

6

The next summer when I came back, I really thought things would be different. My hair had grown out and Mom had let me start wearing makeup. Two of the boys at school had asked me out, but I'd told them both no. There was only one boy I wanted to notice me, and right now he was sitting on the porch with another girl.

A very pretty girl with long blonde hair and a smile that took up her whole face. Camden was sitting really close to her. I could tell that whatever he was saying was amusing, because she kept leaning in and letting her hand drop to his arm as she laughed about it.

Eli made a comment about how hot she was, and my skin went tight. Mom told him not to talk about women like that and he swore he meant no disrespect.

I felt so embarrassed. I woke up early this morning to fix my hair. I put on mascara and lip gloss. I picked out an outfit. I'd never done any of that before. I'd never even thought about it, but I knew I was going to see him, and I'd hoped he was going to see me too.

Mom pressed the button to open the hatch. Eli and I went to get our bags. I pulled the straps of my backpack on and grabbed the handle of my suitcase. Tatumn and Dani ran out to greet us. Camden didn't even look our way. Mom wrapped Dani up in a hug as Tatumn hopped down off the steps.

"My God, I'm glad you're here. I've been so bored."

I tried to smile. "Yeah, I'm glad I'm here too." I lied.

Mom dropped her arms, and Dani came to take my suitcase from me. She grabbed both of my shoulders and held me at arm's length. "Well, aren't you just the prettiest girl in Montana?"

She leaned down to place a kiss on my forehead. I mumbled a thank you, but my voice sounded too tight, and her gaze shot over to Camden. When she looked back at me it felt like I'd been caught doing something I shouldn't. She reached out to rub her hand across my back and I forced a smile.

Camden still hadn't looked up. He was too busy staring at her. I noticed Dani give them a look as we passed by on our way into the kitchen. Mom's brows rose, and Dani gave her a little nod in return.

I couldn't help but turn back to look out the window at them. His finger was on her thigh. Watching him touch her made my chest burn. His hand moved upward, and she squirmed a little. She pulled her lower lip in with her teeth and his head dropped to the side.

The kitchen was loud, everyone was talking. Dani poured Mom a glass of wine. Tatumn was telling them about her last season. Eli congratulated her on leveling up. Mom said she was proud of her too.

I could hear it all, but in a muffled sort of way that didn't make much sense. They were even closer now. He had his hand in her hair. Pulling at the ends as he wrapped them around his fingers.

Mom looked at me, and then out at him. She said Dani's name with a bit of weight and emphasis on the end and Dani's eyes shot toward mine. I did my best to feign indifference. She walked over to the door and told Camden to come inside and say hello.

His shoulders dropped in a huff of annoyance, and I realized he didn't want to see me at all.

The girl stood from the bench and pulled at the hem of her shorts. Her eyes shifted toward us and even from a distance I could tell they were brighter than mine. Her hair was longer too, her curls looked more natural, and her skin was smooth and tanned in a way mine never was.

She reached her hand out toward Camden, and he took it. His eyes rolled and his jaw flexed, but he stood just like she wanted him to. She began walking toward us, dragging him unwillingly behind her.

"Who is that?" I asked Tate, she and my mom were talking about cheer now. She was planning to try out for the team. "Oh, that's Jessica, Camden's girl."

Dani looked over at me with a remorseful expression. It made me feel even more pathetic than I already did. She turned to Tatumn, "Camden doesn't have a girl. Jessica lives down the hill. She's a nice girl, sings in the church choir."

When Jessica stepped inside her face lit up with a smile. She walked right over to me. "Hi. I'm Jessica." I already knew that. "Emma." I mumbled. She turned to Eli. He introduced himself, and when she turned to greet Mom, he gave Camden a look that said way more than I wanted to know.

Camden's already stoic face went smug. I bit my lower lip to redirect some of the pain that was building in my chest. "Camden why don't you walk Jessica home. We're going to make dinner soon, and you're going to join us." He looked over at Dani and nodded.

"You guys all go with him. It's getting late and he doesn't need to be walking home alone in the dark." It wasn't that late. The sun was right overhead. I could tell that's what Camden was thinking as he said, "Alright, sure."

He still hadn't looked at me, at least not directly, and the thought of having to watch him walk her home made me feel frantic for any excuse to get out of going with them.

"Shouldn't we go to Roger's, see if he needs any help this summer?" Tate nodded. I gave Dani the flattest look I could. Sadness, or disappointment, or maybe even pity flooded her eyes. It was obvious that she knew what I was doing, and worse she knew why. It didn't matter though because I simply couldn't go with them.

"Fine." Dani said. I released a breath I didn't know I was holding, but then she added, "Jessica lives right down the road from Roger. Eli, you can stay with him, but you boys wait for the girls before you walk back up the hill."

We walked in two groups. Eli and Camden were on either side of Jessica. They were several paces ahead of us. I tried, but I just couldn't pry my eyes away from the place where his skin met hers.

Eli was putting on a show. He always went overboard when girls were around. Normally it was somewhat entertaining. Watching him fumble over his overly lanky limbs to try and impress them, but this girl was actually laughing. Which sort of ruined the whole thing.

"What's with your mom?" I asked Tate. "Nothing really, she's just pissed at Camden. He got sent home from the school trip. Jessica did too…" It wasn't like Tatumn to leave out any details, so the fact that she'd let her words drop felt significant.

"Why did they get sent home?" I asked, hoping she was going to tell me they'd been served some bad lunch meat at the airport and had to fly home due to illness.

"He got caught fingering her in the stairwell."

I had no idea what that meant, but I could tell by the way she said it that it wasn't good. She kept talking about how upset Dani was. It was an expensive trip. He hadn't even made it to the second day. Everyone at school was talking about it. Camden wasn't bothered, but Jessica was.

I looked back over at him. Studying the way, he had his fingers wrapped around her palm. Wondering what it was he'd done with them to get sent home.

We all made it to Roger's farm and Eli turned back. "We'll meet you out front, just wait for us here when you finish up." I nodded and watched as they walked on. "Does Jessica live that way?" I asked. "No, she lives over there." Tate pointed at a little red farmhouse about halfway up the next hill.

"Then where are they going?"

"I don't know, but we could go find out."

It was stupid, following them into the woods like we did. We came across Eli first. He was smoking again. "Where's Camden?" Tate whispered. I shrugged, and we moved on. I suppose I deserved what I got. You shouldn't ask questions you don't want the answers to, but it still felt rotten.

"Oh God, what is he doing to her?" Tate said in a voice full of revulsion. "I can't watch this. I'm going back to find Eli." She turned away from me, but I just stood there, trapped by all the things I knew I wasn't supposed to be seeing.

It was the strangest thing I'd ever done before, and I knew it. I just couldn't look away. I was mesmerized. *Disgusted.* Mostly with myself. Jessica let out a little moan and Camden looked up at her. Seeing his eyes open startled me. The trees I was hiding behind weren't thick. I knew if either of them looked this way they would see me.

His fingers dug into her side and her lips parted. Watching him kiss her was like burning on a stake, intense, uncomfortable heat ignited within me. She let out a sound somewhere between a whimper and a moan and his eyes opened again.

The way he looked at her caused a searing pain to settle in the back of my throat. I didn't want to see this. I didn't want to know the way Camden Pierce looked when he looked at someone he wanted, because he'd never looked at me like that before.

Jessica made another noise. He looked my way.

I knew he'd seen me.

^^^^^^

The refuge the ranch usually offered completely vanished. I felt like an intruder in my own home. Like my perverse nature had put me firmly on the outside of things and I wasn't sure there was a safe way back in. Camden hadn't said anything, but I knew he knew, and that was enough to keep me away.

Tate finally convinced her mother that the river was as safe as it ever had been, and we were allowed back in the water. My favorite spot was a long way off from the ranch, a bend in the river that stayed shallow, but was still wide enough to let the sunshine down on us.

I did everything I could to banish the images of Camden and Jessica in the woods, but Tatumn kept bringing it up. Talking about the way he was kissing her. How gross it was, and how she felt like she should probably have her eyes baptized in holy water after having to see it.

"Tate, can we please talk about something else?" She gave me the same careful look she'd been giving me all summer. "Sure, but what's wrong with you? You freak out every time I mention it, and you're the one that stayed to watch."

I felt the weight of her words in my chest, and even though I knew I deserved it, I didn't like the way she said it like an accusation. I jumped off the back of the ATV and started walking toward the water.

"I didn't *stay to watch*. I just didn't know how to leave without them seeing me, and nothing's wrong. I just don't like talking about it. It was weird, and if you think you need your eyes baptized, I need mine replaced with prosthetics."

"If it was so weird, then why did you stay and watch?"

I had asked myself the same question so many times. I even understood why she wanted to know. If she had done something like that, I would have been full of questions.

"I don't know. I guess I'm a deviant." I let my shorts fall to the ground and pulled my shirt off over my head. "What's a deviant?" Tate asked. "Someone that likes things they shouldn't." I said it jokingly, but as I defined it for her, I realized I really was a deviant.

"Are you saying you liked watching them?" I shook my head. "No. I didn't, and I don't like talking about it either, so can we please talk about something else." She sat down and pulled her boots off her feet.

"Like what?" I walked into the water. It didn't really matter what time of year it was in Montana, the water was always cold. "I don't know, like anything." She gave me a bored look. I searched my mind for something that would occupy her. "Tell me about your gymnastics." Her eyes rolled to the top of her head, "No. Boring. Now do you think Jessica's still a virgin?"

She was taunting me. Begging for an explanation, but I couldn't give her one, at least not one she'd want to hear. "Tate, that's worse." Her eyes narrowed, "Why does it bother you so much?"

I could tell by the carful way she was watching me that she thought she knew. I couldn't tell her though, so I asked her if she had a crush.

It was risky. I knew that, but Tate was relentless, and I was tired of dodging her questions. I knew she liked a boy named Ethan. She'd told me about him before. She stood and pulled her shirt over her head. "Ethan, he's the captain of the football team now. At least three other girls want to date him, but I'm pretty sure he likes me."

I nodded, because why wouldn't he, and she said, "We went to the spring dance together. It was Hawaiian themed. He wore a grass skirt, and I wore a flower crown. We danced together twice."

I looked over at her. She was everything I wasn't, bright and alluring, with light blonde hair and bright blue eyes. She was beautiful, and she knew it. I was a little jealous of her for that.

"Did he kiss you?"

"No."

"Did you want him to?"

She stepped into the water and walked out toward the middle. The current split around her legs and she sat down and submerged herself up to her shoulders. "No. He's cute, but there was no way I was having my first kiss in the high school gym."

"What about you… do you have a crush?"

She said it like she knew I did, but I knew until I confirmed it for her, it was nothing more than speculation. It was an impossible question to answer anyway.

Tatumn was my best friend and Camden was her cousin. He lived with her, and I'd liked him from the first moment I saw him. Before Camden there weren't any secrets between us, but I knew she wouldn't approve, and it wasn't something I was capable of saying anyway.

I wasn't exactly sure why either. I knew I liked him, but it wasn't something I could see myself talking about.

It wasn't like it mattered anyway. He was older than me and he had a girlfriend. I knew even if he liked me, which he didn't. I couldn't be with him. Not the way things were. I wasn't sure why I thought that either. It wasn't like anyone ever told me I couldn't.

It was more implied by the way everyone treated it as a complete impossibility.

∧∧∧∧∧∧

Dani and Mom insisted we be home for dinner, but Camden was there, and he wouldn't stop looking at me. I ate as quickly as I could and told Mom I had a headache, and I was going to lie down.

She gave me a sympathetic look and offered to get me some Tylenol. I told her no, because I didn't have a headache, and Tylenol couldn't fix whatever was wrong with me.

I crawled into my bed, pulled the blankets up to my shoulders, and picked up my phone. I was the only one inside. The weather was nice, so we had dinner on the patio.

At first, I just scrolled through the internet looking for cute puppies and funny videos of people falling down, but I couldn't stop thinking about his fingers and it was driving me mad.

I don't know what I expected to find when I typed the word *fingered* into my search bar, but it wasn't this. I moved from one image to the next, each one more confusing than the last.

It looked rough. Intrusive, but the women seemed to like it. The men did too. I came across a video and pressed play.

The girl on the screen moaned louder than Jessica had. I looked around the room to make sure no one had come in while I wasn't watching. The door was closed, and I could hear them all talking and laughing with each other outside.

I turned back to the screen and watched as the woman in front of me writhed and said things like *yeah*, and *oh*, in this really sultry way.

It was really something I should have expected, him coming in to find me. I hadn't spoken to him once since I'd arrived, and he'd been watching me. Still, somehow, he was there. Climbing into bed beside me before I had time to register his presence.

"What are you doing, Emma?"

I threw my phone down on my chest and pressed my thumb over the speaker. He gave me a suspicious look and I felt my cheeks flush. He didn't say anything else, but he did look down at my phone. I could still hear the girl on the screen moaning.

I knew he could too.

He leaned in, propped himself up on one arm, and reached out to place his hand over mine. The look on his face changed from suspicion to intrigue. I had to close my eyes to get away from him.

"What do you want, Camden?"

I clutched the phone tighter to my chest. His hand was still touching mine, and I was so scared he was going to use it to peel mine away and take the phone from me.

"What are you doing, Emma?"

I knew he was only asking to give me a chance to answer. "Camden, leave." He didn't move. His fingers pressed into mine and I jerked away from him.

I pressed the volume down button as quickly as I could. "It's okay, Emma. You don't need to be embarrassed." I wasn't embarrassed. I was mortified. "I'm not kidding. I really want you to leave."

"Why won't you look at me, Emma?"

He wasn't upset. He just wanted to know. "Because I can't."

"Sure, you can."

I thought about it and very quickly decided I was right. I couldn't look at him. "No, I really can't. Now will you please leave?" He reached over and turned my face to his, "No, I'm not going to do that."

I know what goes around comes around. Karma and cosmic comeuppance and all that, but I had only seen him kissing her.

"Open your eyes, Emma."

I couldn't.

"Seriously. I don't care what you were looking at on your phone. I just want to talk to you." My eyes opened, but I didn't look at him. He reached out and took the phone from me. I watched as he turned the screen over and looked down at that woman with her legs spread wide. It was so humiliating that I had to pull the blanket up and hide my face beneath it.

"I had no idea you were into this sort of thing."

I pulled the covers back. "Oh my God Camden… I am not *into this sort of thing*." His brows rose on his head. "Shut up and give me my phone." I said, wishing I could turn into dust and settle into the cracks of this room for the rest of eternity. "Why? Were you not finished?" He teased. "Shut up, Camden. I just…" I didn't know how to tell him, but he looked at me like he already knew.

"Tatumn told you, didn't she?" He handed me my phone. I turned away from him. "Yes, and I just… I didn't know what it was."

He leaned back, letting his head rest up against the wall. "So, you looked it up online? Were you at least in private browsing mode?" I gave him a puzzled look. He took my phone and swiped across the screen several times. "There, I cleared your history."

It was so uncomfortable, sitting beside him with all of this between us. "You could have asked me." I looked over at him, "Asked you what? What fingering meant?" He shrugged in this cool way that said he wasn't bothered by the idea.

"Yeah, I would've told you." I pulled myself up and rested my back on the wall beside his, "Really?" He turned to face me. "Yeah, you can ask me anything you want. I'll always tell you the truth."

"Well then…" I said just to tease him, but he didn't flinch, and I realized he was serious. "You really would have?"

"Yeah." he said in this quiet offhanded way. "You shouldn't be watching stuff like that. I'm sorry Tatumn told you." I turned away from him.

"You must really like her?" I could tell he was uncomfortable, but he just lifted his chin. "Who, Jessica?" He knew who I was talking about, but for some reason he waited for me to nod. "I guess so, but it's not like I think about her much when she's not around."

The way he said it made it sound like there was someone he thought about, and it wasn't Jessica, but I wasn't naive enough to believe it was me either. He got quiet and turned toward the window.

"I know you saw us, and I know you don't want to talk about it. You've obviously been avoiding me ever since, but I don't like not talking to you, so I just want you to know. I'm not mad."

I knew exactly what he was talking about, but I still wanted to deny it. I wanted to say something like, *I don't know what you're talking about*, or *I didn't see anything*, and if he was asking me, *if I had seen them*, or *why I had watched*, I might have done it.

He wasn't though. He wasn't even upset. He said he didn't like not talking to me, and he sounded like he meant it.

I felt disappointed in myself all over again, "I'm really sorry about that."

His hand fell to his lap, "It's not that big a deal. It bothers me more that you won't talk to me." He looked over at me and I could tell he was hurt. I felt terrible. I wanted to apologize again. Do it better. I wasn't really sure what to say though. It wasn't like I could explain to him why I had been avoiding him. I didn't even want to admit that I had been.

"It's just been really weird. You know?"

I wasn't sure I did, but I nodded anyway.

"You usually watch me pretty close." His eyes darted in my direction, but I looked away. "but now it's like you can't look at me at all and I admit it was weird. Seeing you behind that tree while I was…"

His words dropped and I picked them up for him, "Kissing her." He nodded. "But it wasn't nearly as strange as

70

watching you turn away from me all those other times. I thought you were mad at me."

I shook my head, "No." He looked over at me, "but you are upset?" It was an honest question, and I was upset, but mostly with myself. "I'm not." He looked at me like he knew I was lying, so I said, "Not mad though."

He reached over and picked up the jar beside my bed. I watched as his hand gripped the lid and his fingers worked to spin it open. "Good. I don't want you to be." He reached in, pulled out a piece of chocolate, and held it out to me.

I looked down at his hand, "No thank you. Not from those fingers." He rolled his eyes, but I could tell he was amused. "Are you sure?" he asked in this deep voice that made my stomach clench tight. He was looking at me like he knew what he was doing, or like he knew what he was doing affected me.

"That's not fair." I said as I looked up at him.

"Why not?"

I could tell he thought his comment was every bit as entertaining as my own, but it wasn't. He peeled the thin foil away and held it out to me, "Take it." I wasn't really sure why, but I couldn't take it from him. He wasn't going to let it go though, so I reached over and dipped my fingers in the jar to pull out another.

"You want one?"

Mischief pulled at the corner of his lips, "Sure, can you unwrap it for me?"

I wasn't sure what the game was, but I unwrapped the chocolate and held it out for him. He leaned forward and took my fingers in his mouth, sucking the chocolate from between them. It felt like I'd malfunctioned. *Pleasure, disgust, intrigue, humiliation, curiosity, desire.* They all mingled within me.

I jerked away from him and let out a disgusted noise. He laughed and looked over at me. The way he was sucking on the chocolate in his mouth made a strange shiver run across my chest. I turned away to wipe my fingers on the blanket, and he said, "There, now we both have dirty fingers."

7

Now

Camden

I go after her as soon as I can. Dani is a very hard woman to shake though, and by the time I make it to the hallway she's nowhere to be found.

I shouldn't have let her walk away. I should have asked her to stay, told Dani I needed a moment, but I didn't do that because the look on Emma's face was one I'd never seen before, and I didn't know what to do.

I assume she's left, so I run upstairs to the lobby, where there are lots of people standing around with bored looks on their faces waiting for their tables. I go outside and walk along the cars in the parking lot until I find her Corolla.

Empty.

I go back in and rush down the stairs. A quick peek into the bar just to make sure she's not back, and then I walk down the hallway in search of the ladies' room.

I consider peeking inside. It would be nice to get her alone, and everyone here already thinks I'm a heathen anyway. I don't do it though, because I hear Tatumn say, "*He should notice you. You're the best thing that ever happened to him, and what you two had was real, but he left… and that means you really need to ignore him.*"

I linger there for a moment, hoping Emma is going to say something. Hoping she knows that I didn't leave her, not really. I mean I did leave, but it was for her, not because of her. There's a difference. At least that's what I tell myself. I don't hear her though, and eventually I leave.

I go back outside and consider leaving for good. I shouldn't have come back, or actually I shouldn't have left because she never used to look at me like that.

^^^^^^

Emma

Eli has definitely been taking advantage of the open bar because the moment we walk back in the room he comes barreling through the crowd with his arms spread wide. I do my best to dodge his embrace, and he insists we follow him onto the dance floor.

I don't know where he's gone but Camden's not here anymore. I feel a surprisingly large pang of disappointment hit me, and then Tatumn whispers something in Ethan's ear and he makes his way to the stage.

Cash walks up, puts his arm around my shoulders, and looks over at Tatumn. "I take it she didn't know." Her eyes narrow and she shakes her head, *no.* "Well then, there's really only one thing to do."

He squeezes me tighter up against him and waves his hand in the air. The waitress appears and he asks Amy to bring us a round of shots, wedding cake for the bride and tequila for the rest of us. He tells her it's going to be a long night and the way he says it makes her cheeks flush.

When she walks off, I ask him how he knew her name and he tells me, "I know all their names." with a roguish glint in his eye.

Ethan makes his way back over and gives Tatumn a look that puts a smile on her face. The band starts playing something with a beat. Tatumn takes my hands in hers and pulls them to the rhythm of the music.

I know what they're doing, and I am trying to pretend he doesn't exist, or more so I'm just trying not to gawk in his direction when I see him enter the room and walk over to the bar. He takes a seat next to my mom. Dani leans forward to talk to him.

I know I'm not supposed to be looking at him, but he is really hard not to see. Amy comes back with a tray full of drinks and Cash takes me away from Tatumn. We both tilt our heads back. He gives Amy a little smile and tells her to keep them coming.

Tequila is not my favorite, but right now I'm just thankful that I don't have to decide what to do with myself while he just sits there, cocktail in hand and serene expression on his face.

After several songs, and a few more shots of tequila, the lights get dimmer, and the band slows down. Cash takes my hand and wraps his arm around my waist. He pulls me in tight and I lean my head on his chest.

"You alright, Sweetness?"

I'm not, not really, but I tell him I'm always alright. He gives me a look that says he knows that's not true, but he doesn't say anything else. He is very warm, and his shirt is just a little damp. He leans in and I feel his chin up against the side of my head.

Every time we make a round, I look over toward the bar. Camden is still sitting next to Mom and Dani, the three of them seem to be having a good time. I watch as he lifts his drink to his lips, and then Cash turns me away from him.

^^^^^^

Camden

I see her before I even walk in the room, but she's surrounded by a crowd of people that I know don't want me around, so I act like I haven't seen her at all and take a seat at the bar. Dani and Amber are talking. I hope I can manage to avoid interrupting their conversation and angle my chair toward the dance floor.

I can tell that whatever is happening out there, it's not Emma's idea, but she looks happy enough to go along with it. The band picks up and I watch as she and Tatumn sway beneath the lights. Dani leans in and asks me how my trip was. I tell her it was fine, and then I get the bartender's attention and order a club soda and lime.

When I look back out at the dance floor, I see Emma tilt her head back. Her face contorts and she forces herself to swallow. I stifle a laugh and lift my drink to my lips. Several songs play as Dani does her best to include me in their conversation, and I do my best to pay attention, while I watch Emma take a few more shots and get a little looser on the dance floor.

She's different.

Not in an obvious way. She's still the most beautiful girl I've ever seen. She still smiles like she means it and listens as others talk. It's subtle. Evident in the way she holds her shoulders straighter and lifts her chin in this playful way while she speaks.

I watch as she leans in to say something to Cash. Her head tilts back in a laugh and I'm desperate to know what she thinks is so funny. The lights dim and the music slows. Cash gives her a look I could have gone my whole life without seeing and then he wraps his arm around her waist.

When I received the invitation and thought about coming back here. I only thought of her. It's not like I didn't know she would have moved on. It would have been really upsetting if she hadn't, but I didn't know to expect him.

Cash Alexander is the one man in the world that I am absolutely certain does not deserve her. He's two dimensional. She's the entire universe.

I watch as he pulls her in. She lays her head on his chest and my throat gets tight. He releases her hand and runs his fingers over her back. Her eyes dart in my direction and I quickly look away, pretending to be interested in what Amber is saying.

When I look back up, Cash's head is tilted into hers. Her entire body is molded to his. It's like ancient Chinese water torture. I can feel every move he makes and every time she responds to his touch, I feel a pressure build up in my head and move down into my chest.

Amber sees me looking. "You know she published a book." I tell her I did, I've read it, and it was really good. She says, "She's doing really well. She's just been accepted into an MFA program at MSU, and she finally seems to have found some happiness." My mind catches on the word *finally*. I look over at her to see that she means exactly what I think she does.

Dani senses the tension between us and tells Amber about the work I've been doing with my little brother, Sam. Amber's eyes sweep over me, "I'll bet you're really good at it." I know she means that I'd be good at it because of how bad I was when I was his age, *but I am actually good at it*, and Sam's a good kid. I tell her that and hope she'll stop talking to me.

Don and his wife walk up and Dani thanks them for coming. I can still hear them talking, but I take the opportunity to look away and find Emma again.

The band is done playing. Emma is standing at the dessert table with no shoes on, picking up pieces of chocolate cake and shoving them in her mouth. Cash is standing beside her and the two of them are laughing in between bites. Emma looks up with a wide smile on her face and Cash reaches out to wipe some chocolate from her chin.

I decide I've seen enough and stand up to pull a few dollars out to leave on the bar. Don turns my way, "It's been a while." I tell him I know it has and look over toward the door. He says, "Bozeman's been a pretty sleepy town since you left.

Should I be expecting that to change?" I look up at him, "If it does, it wouldn't have anything to do with me."

He follows my eyes over to Emma. She's walking out the door with Cash beside her and her heels dangling from her hand. I don't want to be rude, but Don is blocking my way, and I really don't want her to leave before I get a chance to talk to her.

I turn to Dani, wrap my arm around her shoulders, and tell her I'll see her soon. She smiles, Amber waves, and I walk away. Don and his wife follow me out. I look over at Emma. She's fumbling with the handle of her car door. Don gives one of those throaty chuckles, "That sure looks like trouble."

I agree and start walking her way.

^^^^^^

Emma

I walk out of the room without so much as glancing in his direction. I regret it immediately, but Cash is walking with me, and I can't think of a good enough reason to turn back. When we get outside, Cash asks me where I'm parked and tells me to toss him my keys.

I have admittedly had too much to drink, but so has he, and I just don't want to give them to him. I tell him I'm fine, not to worry about it, but he gives me a reproachful look, "I'm driving you home, Sweetness, so you'd better toss them over or I'll come find them myself."

I laugh and tell him that's not necessary. He gives me a look that says he doesn't agree. "Really, I'm fine. The chocolate soaked up all the alcohol." He does this thing with his face that tells me he's trying to decide whether or not to leave me here, so I say, "If you want me to, I'll say the alphabet backwards." He laughs, and then leans in to give me a hug. "Fine, but if you need me, call. I'll come get you."

He leaves and I fumble through my purse to find my keys. I push the unlock button, pull the handle, and climb into the driver's seat.

It feels like relief wrapped up in anguish, being away from him again.

The image of his face in my mind forces my eyes closed and I hear the sounds of conversations fading and car doors closing all around me. When I open my eyes and lean forward to push the ignition button, my head falls to the steering wheel for just a moment, and then I turn around to pull the seat belt on.

I don't know how long he's been there, but the sight of him startles me. I turn away and he knocks on the window. I look in my rearview mirror and place my hand on the gearshift, ready to pull it into reverse, but he knocks again.

It's a very strange feeling, needing him to come closer and wanting to push him away. I don't really want to see him, but I look at him anyway. "Emma, roll the window down." He says like I actually have to do what he tells me.

I remove my hand from the gearshift and ask, "What do you want?" A splinter of pain, or maybe frustration, *probably frustration*, passes through his eyes. "Open the door." He says in that same authoritative tone, and I wonder what it is about the way I'm glaring at him that makes him think I'll listen.

He leans down. The glow of the streetlamp above us illuminates his face. It's very unsettling, the simultaneous familiarity and strangeness of it. He's staring right at me, but I have to turn away, because looking at him is like driving into the sunset. Beautiful, but blindingly painful.

"Please Emma, open the door."

It sounds more like a plea than a command this time. I look over into his concerned eyes and it irks me, seeing him look at me like that. "What do you want?" His eyes pull in at the corners and I can tell he's upset. I just don't know if it's with me or himself.

"I just want to talk to you."

"Well, I don't want to talk to you." I mean it, but I also don't mean it. I want to talk to him, but I've wanted to talk to him for a very long time and he's been… unavailable. I lean over and pretend to mess with the controls of my heater.

"I know. I know you don't, but Emma, please open the door."

I have a choice. I know I do. I don't have to open it. I can just put the car in reverse and leave. The same way he did. I think about it. The way he left without a word. The way the mountains seemed to grow in his absence, blocking out all the sunshine. I could have handled anything… but that. I didn't handle that well.

I'm still not handling that well.

I know what I should do, but something about the defeat in his voice makes me reach over and pull the lock. He hears the click and stands up. We look at each other through the window for a moment and then he pulls the handle.

"Scoot over."

"No."

"I mean it. You've been drinking. You're not driving, now scoot over."

"How do you know I don't drive drunk all the time?" His face hardens. "Do you?" He asks like he knows I don't. "No, but I could, and you wouldn't know a thing about it."

"Scoot over, Emma. If you don't, I'll pick you up and move you myself."

∧∧∧∧∧∧

Camden

I climb into her car feeling equal parts relief and apprehension. The light sweet scent of strawberries and vanilla lingers in the driver's seat as I sit down and look over at her.

She's so close, but the way she's looking at me makes her feel very far away. I reach over and pull the door closed. She picks her phone up and presses play. The music starts and she gives me a bored look, "Are you going to drive or not?"

Her voice is full of spite and I'm not sure what to do with it. Should I just lead with an apology? Say something like, *look I know you're mad but…* but what? I'm an asshole and I shouldn't have left like that? You're the best thing that ever happened to me? I know I screwed up, but please forgive me… take me back, tell me you still love me, because I do, and I am desperate. *Lonely. Scared.* I don't want to go one more day without you, and it's not something I need to think about. I don't need time to decide because I know I shouldn't have left, but I did… and distance puts everything in perspective.

I am firmly seated, belted in, but I feel untethered. Like I'm floating in space without a cord, low on oxygen, knowing I'm the man that blew up the ship.

My palms feel slick on the wheel as I put the car in reverse and pull out of the parking lot. Bozeman Montana isn't really a sleepy town, especially on a Saturday night. People are gathered on patios and huddled on corners all over town. I pull up to the stop sign. Two girls in jeans and boots start walking across.

I still haven't said anything, and every second that passes makes it more difficult to speak.

Emma rolls her window down to let her arm dangle out and I reach over and turn the heater up. I could just start simple, *apologize*, but not for everything. Maybe just for tonight, for forcing her to climb over the console. Even though that felt like instant karma. *Long legs. Short skirt.* I wouldn't say that. I'd just say, "Sorry, for earlier." She picks her hand up and rests her fingers against the top of the window.

She is impenetrable. Completely off limits. Distant in a whole new way.

I know it's pointless, but I try again. "It was a nice party." She scowls in my direction, the same way she did earlier. "Yeah, and the weather's been really nice too."

It's a harmless comment, but she says it like an insult. I let my foot off the brake and the car pulls forward. I don't know what I've done, but when she picks up the hem of her dress and starts nervously running her finger over it, I almost beg her to tell me what she's thinking. I thought she planned the party. She certainly ran it. I meant it as a compliment, but she seems to have taken it badly.

I hate this. Not knowing what to say or how to act. Five years of repressed anger is a lot colder than I thought it would be. She turns the music up and I say, "You and Cash huh?" That gets her attention. I don't know whether to celebrate or recoil.

"What about Cash?"

"I don't know, just looked like you two were pretty close."

She shakes her head and presses the volume up button again. I've waited too long for this. I know she doesn't want to talk to me, but I don't care. I want to talk to her. I want to know everything about her, even the things I won't like. I have to yell it, but I say, "Sorry, am I not supposed to talk about that either?"

She pretends not to hear. Or maybe she really didn't. The music is so loud that people on the streets are turning our way, watching us go by. I reach over to turn the volume down and before she has a chance to turn it back up, I say, "It's okay if you are. I left so you could be happy."

Her face explodes with emotion and then goes stock still.

Everything I've said to her so far has been wrong, but this feels worse. Like I've said *the* wrong thing. The thing that will turn her against me forever. I panic, "Emma please, talk to me."

She says, "You don't get to do that."

I nod like I understand, but I don't. "Do what?"

She waves her hand in the air, "Act like you did this for me." I did, and when I left that really is what I was thinking about, but I know now I also did it for me. "Okay... yeah, I'm sorry I said that. That wasn't fair." Her eyes narrow, "I don't owe you an explanation." I shake my head, "No, of course not. I owe you one."

"Well, I don't want it."

This is what I was most afraid of. Not that I wouldn't ever see her again. That when I did, she wouldn't see me. I say the only thing I can think of, and it feels weird, off topic and too deep for a night like this, but she's made it clear that she's not interested in small talk and anything real is off the table. "What's the most beautiful thing you've ever seen?"

Her eyes dart in my direction, "Sorry, that was stupid." One corner of her lips pick up, "No that's alright. I'll play, but you have to go first."

I don't have to think about it. It's her face right before she comes, but I can't tell her that, so I shrug and say, "I don't know."

Her eyes narrow in on me, "What was that look about?" I tell her I didn't make a look. "Yes, you did" I'm sure she's right. It's hard not to make a face when I'm picturing hers twisted up it the perfect mix of agony and ecstasy, *cheeks flushed, lips parted, eyes closing tight*, but I say, "No, I didn't."

She looks at me like she knows I'm lying. "Tell me."

"No, I can't." Her eyes roll, "Whatever, you're the one that wanted to talk." I can tell by the slope of her shoulders and the angle of her chin that she isn't going to say anything else.

I really can't start off with preorgasmic bliss. It would send, not exactly the wrong message, I am hoping to get to see that again someday, but that's not what I'm after right now and I don't want her thinking that's why I forced my way into her car.

I let my foot off the brake and ease us through the intersection. She's staring out the window, watching the silhouettes of the shadowy buildings go by like they're the most interesting things she's ever seen.

We pull up to a stop light and her skin is cast in a red glow that makes her look both ominous and alluring. I'm sure she can feel me watching her, hear the sound of my finger tapping against the wheel, but she doesn't show it.

She just sits there, looking away from me. My finger taps quicker. The light turns green, and we start moving again. I can't go the whole rest of the car ride without talking to her, so I say, "I assume we're not talking about the obvious things?"

Her head shoots toward mine, the nervous expression on her face tells me she doesn't know what I'm going to say next, but whatever it is she's not ready to hear it. I do my best to make my arms relax, finger stop tapping, shoulders fall. "Like the sunrise over the mountains?"

Her eyes settle and the corners of her lips pick up. "I don't know, do you see beauty in anything that isn't obvious?" At the moment, no. Right now all I see is her, and she is so obviously beautiful that it's difficult to look away from her. I take too long to answer and her face falls.

I want to say, *no, give me another chance*, but she says, "It really doesn't need to be this serious. I'll tell you some of mine first."

I put my foot on the brake. "Some?" She gives me an impatient look. "Yeah, I have three, now do you want to hear them, or should I just stop talking?" I shake my head, "No, I want to hear them."

She goes quiet for a moment, and I can hear the chatter of all the people fading as we pull across the street.

"One time, when I was at the zoo, watching the monkeys pick bugs off of each other and eat them." I look over and say, "Naturally." She gets this little smile on her face, and it feels like I've won the lottery. "I know… quality entertainment, but when they were done, the one on the ground stood up, turned around, and gave the other monkey a hug."

I shrug, "Yeah, we studied that actually, it's a sign of good will."

Her eyes fall to her lap, "Well it looked like more than that." I can tell I've upset her again, so I say, "I've never seen it, just read about it." She looks over at me. "What did it look like to you?" She looks out the windshield, "It looked like they meant it. Like they really loved each other."

I nod, "I bet that was beautiful." She nods and says it was. The song changes and for a moment it's silent in the car. "So, what else do you have?" Her head tilts to the side. "The sign they put up in front of the fields when they burn the grass around the lake that says revegetation in process." The car in front of us pulls to a stop. I veer left to get around them.

"That's one of the most beautiful things you've ever seen?"

She gives me an irritated look, "Well, it's not the image. It's the sentiment." I can't help but smile. "It's striking really. The ground is scorched, *black and lifeless*. It's really ugly and when you first look at it you feel bad, like something bad must have happened there, but then you read the sign."

I put my blinker on and say, "Revegetation in process?" She nods enthusiastically, "Yes, exactly." I tell her I'm sorry, but I'm still not getting it.

She looks away from me, quiet for a moment, "Sometimes bad things happen for a reason, sometimes things have to burn before they can grow." I tell her I know exactly what she means, I've been burning for years, and she says, "Yeah, me too."

The air in the car thickens, but I don't want her to stop talking, so I say, "So, we have heartfelt monkeys and sentimental signs, what's your third one?"

She hesitates and I say, "I saw a homeless man sharing his blanket with another homeless man in the dead of winter." She smiles like she approves, and I feel the pressure in my chest release.

"Tatumn's face the first time she saw Agatha." I nod, and she says, "I know that sounds really obvious… but Agatha was the ugliest baby I've ever seen. Her head was pointed. Her hair was caked in blood and her face was bruised and swollen in all these weird places, but when the nurse handed her to Tatumn. She looked at her like she was the most beautiful thing she had ever seen."

I can tell she's reliving the moment, looking over in my direction, but her eyes are lit up, dancing in the memory. I turn onto the highway that leads to the ranch and tell her I don't think that seems obvious at all, not all mothers love their children like that.

Her lashes fall to her cheeks, and I know I've said something wrong again. Made it too serious, veered into territory she's not ready to enter yet. I say, "Agatha's a lucky girl." She nods, "Do you have anymore?"

I have to think about it, because most of mine are really obvious, and they all involve her. Flashes of her riding my bike in a field, hair blowing back, sunshine on her shoulders, apprehensive but excited expression on her face. Her sitting at the end of my bed with a chocolate kiss in her hand. Her hands wrapped around my waist as we tore through the forest on the ATV's. Her lying on a rock beside the river, reading, watching me draw.

Her lips after I've kissed them.

The way she used to look at me like I was everything she'd ever wanted. Like I was already enough. Her sitting next to me on the couch. Lying in her bed, dark hair spread out on the pillow above her. The way her eyes pull in and her cheeks flush when she's embarrassed. The way even when she's scared, she'll still say the thing that no one else will. Her legs wrapped around me, *eyes closed tight, cheeks flushed, head pushing into the pillow, shoulders falling, arms reaching out, fingers digging into me.*

I cannot answer her.

"No, nothing that isn't obvious." She gets this expectant look on her face.

"Then tell me the obvious things."

I shrug and say, *no,* and she asks why. The road curves and I pull the wheel to the side. The way she's looking at me like she really wants to know makes me need to look away from her. I keep my eyes on the road, but I say, "It's your fault. I don't have anything nearly as good as your heartfelt monkeys." One proud corner of her lips pick up.

"Well, obviously… you're never going to beat that, but it's okay if you're boring now. Most people only see beauty in the obvious things."

I let my eyes dart in her direction, "They're not boring, just obvious."

She looks over at me and I can tell she wants me to say more. I tell her that I don't think that's true, at least not for everyone. She looks intrigued so I say, "You've always been able to see beauty where no one else can."

The lids of her eyes drop. "Maybe, but I'm usually wrong." I shake my head, *no*, and say, "I've never known you to be wrong before."

She looks right at me. "I was wrong about you."

It stings, but I say, "That's still a pretty good record."

She nods. "I've learned though." I'm not sure I want to know but I ask, "Learned what?" She looks over at me, "That when something looks broken, it is." I tell her I don't believe that either, but it's not true.

I turn back to the road, but I can feel her gaze as it travels from my cheek to my jawline and lands somewhere on my upper arm. I don't want her to look away, so I say, "I actually think you're right, if it looks broken it probably is, but I don't think that being broken is always a bad thing."

She doesn't say anything, so I tell her that in Japan there's an artform called *Kintsugi* where they put broken pottery pieces back together with ribbons of gold. "It's meant to represent the beauty in imperfection. They highlight the flaws instead of hiding them, and honestly the broken pieces are much more interesting than the original works were."

She asks me if that's the kind of art I do now and I say, "No, but I have seen it and it's lovely." Her chin drops, "I'm sure it is, but in Bozeman when something breaks, we usually just throw it away." I don't know why it bothers me so much to hear her talk like that, but I don't like it. I tell her that not everyone in Bozeman is the same and she gives me a playful look.

"Have you gotten wise in your old age?"

"I'm only two years older than you."

"Yeah, but you've aged at least a dozen since the last time I saw you."

I feel it as she digs into me, but it still doesn't feel like the time to bring up anything real, so I just tell her she doesn't look like she's aged a day. She lets out a laugh and it's like winning the biggest prize at the fair. I can't help but smile, but when I turn her way she says, "You're not actually flirting with me are you?"

I was, but the way she says it, like it's the most ridiculous thing she's ever heard makes me shake my head, *no,* and turn away from her. She leans over and lays her head down on the edge of the door. Her hair blows back in the wind and even though I know she doesn't want me to, I watch her reflection in the rearview mirror as I drive.

^^^^^^

Emma

I can feel him looking at me, so I close my eyes and lean forward to let the wind hit my face. The warmth of summer is finally creeping back in and right now the breeze is this perfect mix of moist heat and coolness. I feel tired, and too drunk to keep talking to him, so I let my head fall back to rest in the open window.

I can feel the curve of the road as Camden turns the wheel and my stomach's not quite ready for that, so I open my eyes and look up at the night sky.

His head darts in my direction, and I feel the need to pull at the hem of my dress. He turns away quickly, like he's been caught doing something he shouldn't, and I say, "I think we'd both be safer if you just kept your eyes on the road."

He makes this low hum of a noise and looks back over at me. I feel myself smile and even though it's probably not the best, I like the way he can't seem to look away.

I readjust myself in the seat so that I'm facing him. His hand falls to the gearshift, and I notice the way the muscles in his thigh seem to grow when he presses down on the gas. He tilts his head in my direction, "I heard you wrote a book." I did, but I don't want to talk to him about it, so I just say, *yeah*, and hope he'll move on.

He gives me a quick look. "Actually, that's not true. I mean your mom did tell me about it, but I already knew. I read it."

I feel myself wince, "Well, that's embarrassing."

He lets off the gas a bit to accommodate another curve in the road and asks, why. "I don't know, it just is. It always has been." His face hardens, "Always?" I nod, "Yeah, the thought of you reading anything I've ever written is the most mortifying thing I can think of."

"But I don't understand, you published it. Everyone can read it."

"I know, but everyone reading it doesn't bother me." His brow wrinkles, "But it bothers you that I read it?" I nod and he shakes his head. "Well, I thought it was really good, and I'm sorry. I didn't know you didn't want me to read it."

"Well, it's not like I could have told you." His eyes pull in at the corners, and I can tell I've hurt him. I don't like it, but for some reason it feels like maybe I should, and I'm not sure if I like that either.

"I heard about you too."

His gaze shifts from the road. "Oh yeah, what'd you hear?" I let my head fall to the side. "Oh, just that you're a famous artist now, and a decent person to boot." He looks at me and I can tell he's trying to fight a smile. "Well, I'm sorry to tell you, but someone lied to you."

"You mean you didn't have a piece at the Met?" His eyes dart my way. "No, I did." I look over at him. "So, it's the bit about being a decent person then?" The beginning of a laugh leaves his lips. "Yeah, that's definitely not true. I'm still as rotten as I ever was." I shake my head, "I hate it when you talk about yourself like that." His hand falls to his thigh.

"Well, I don't particularly like that you didn't want me to read your book." I roll my eyes at him. "You didn't want me to see your art."

He looks at me like I'm ridiculous. "That's not true. You're the only person I wanted to see it." I know that's not true. "Really, the only one. Not even Gabby?" His eyes widen infinitesimally. "How do you know about Gabby?"

I pull my lower lip in, "Tatumn told me." I can tell he's irritated but he says, "Well, sure Gabby saw it, but that doesn't mean I didn't want you to." My chin lifts. "No, but it does mean I'm not the only person you wanted to see it."

His jaw tightens. "I don't know what you think you know about Gabby." I cut him off and tell him that I don't know anything really, just that they live together.

He shakes his head in this slow meaningful way. "Yeah, we do. She's my roommate. We've lived together for years, but there's nothing between us outside of friendship."

I can tell by the way he's looking at me that he's telling the truth, but I say, "Would Gabby also say you're only roommates?" His eyes narrow and he reaches into his pocket. "I don't know, maybe we should call her and ask. Or better yet, let's call Jordan, her fiancé and see what he has to say about it."

He holds his phone out to me. I shake my head, "No, that's not necessary." He puts the phone down in the cup holder and runs his hand through his hair. I feel like I should apologize, but instead I just look away. I hear him sigh, and it sounds like disappointment.

"Emma, I'm sorry. I don't know why I said it like that. I'm just really nervous."

He reaches up to place both hands on the wheel and I watch all the muscles in his arm tighten as he grips it. "Yeah, well you shouldn't be. I've had enough tequila tonight to tranquilize a horse. I probably won't remember any of this in the morning."

He gives me a look that says he knows that's not true, and I do my best not to look away from him. It's not until he's turning into the driveway of the ranch that I realize I never told him where I lived. I let him pull all the way up to the garage and then I ask, "Did my mom tell you I live here too?" He leans forward and pushes the ignition button to turn the car off. "No, but Dani did."

I open the door and put my feet down on the ground. The rocks poke into my skin, but I stand up and start walking toward the porch. I can hear the sounds of his boots on the gravel behind me, so I ask where he's staying and tell him I'll call an Uber for him. He stops. I step onto the steps and turn around to face him.

He gives me this funny look, "Alright, thanks." I open the app on my phone and find a driver in the area that can be here in fourteen minutes. It's too long, but it's the best I've got. "So where are you staying?" I ask again. He shifts his weight from one leg to the other, "It's 3547 Bear Creek Rd, Gallatin Gateway." I look up from my phone, and he has this infuriatingly smug look on his face.

"You're staying here?" I ask, even though he's already told me he is.

He drops the smug look. "Yeah, Dani said there would be plenty of room." I try not to panic, but I feel like this is something someone should have mentioned. I look back at the house behind me and feel a deep sense of betrayal. "Is that alright?" He asks in this voice that sounds very far away.

It's not alright. Nothing that has happened between us is *alright*, and he cannot actually think I would be okay with him staying here with me. *Alone.* This isn't my house though. It's Dani's. "Sure, yeah. It's not a problem. It's a big house."

He steps away from the car and starts walking my way. My skin tingles with every step he takes in my direction, and I turn around and climb the rest of the steps to get away from him.

"I'm tired though. I'm going in." My voice shakes, and I move toward the door. He follows me. I can hear his shoes as they slide over the loose gravel, his steps as they land on the porch behind me, and the sound of him opening and closing the door.

"Emma, what are you doing?" He asks in this irritated tone as he tries to catch up with me.

"I'm tired. I'm going to bed." I say without turning around to face him.

"Look at me." he begs.

"You can have the Indian room. Agatha stays in *ours*." The word tastes like bile in my mouth, and I have to shake my head to get rid of the shock of pain it causes.

"Emma, I know you're upset. You have every right to be, but please look at me."

I stop about halfway up the stairs and think about turning around. I think of seeing him. In this house. Looking up at me. I explore a thousand possibilities of the outcome, but none of them seem desirable.

In the time it takes me to decide not to turn around he makes his way to the stairs and climbs up to meet me. I am still picturing him over there looking up at me when I feel his hand on my elbow. His touch is like a taser, a jolt of extremely concentrated pain courses through me and settles in my chest. I jerk away from him, "Don't touch me."

His hand drops, and his breath deepens. "Emma, I don't want to hurt you. I promise I'm not here to hurt you." He's too close to me, so I take another step up and ask, "Then why are you here?"

He takes a moment to answer, "The wedding. I'm here for the wedding."

I turn around and he looks up at me with a stricken expression. I want to say, *how dare you come this close only to tell me you'd rather not be here at all. How can you be so cruel, so clueless, don't you know what this is doing to me?* I nod, "It was really good of you to come. I'm sure Dani is really excited to see you."

His shoulders drop and his eyes hold mine.

"Yeah, seemed like she was."

8

Tatumn had a boyfriend now. She was only a few months older than me, and my mom still wouldn't let me date.

Ethan came from a good family though. He was one of those pretty boys that lived on the right side of town. He was still the captain of the football team and Dani was friends with his mom. So, when he invited Tatumn out, I got to go with her.

The moms dropped us off at Lindley Park and Ethan ran over to us. The two of them looked at each other in this way that made me feel like I should look away.

He asked her how long her mom said she could stay out and she popped up on her tip toes and wrapped her arms around his neck. It was easy to see how much she liked him, and I could tell he liked her too. Tatumn told him she'd talked her mom into letting the boys bring us home later, and Ethan said, "Cool."

His friends were yelling at him, so he gave her a quick kiss and ran back out onto the field. When he left, she said "Isn't he hot?" in a way that let me know she didn't actually want me to answer.

We sat down on the grass, and I asked her who the other guys were. Tatumn lifted her finger in the air. "That's Cash Alexander, he's got rizz, but you can't believe a word he says, and that's Peyton and Logan Harris they're brothers and they're totally hot, but they both have girlfriends already."

I didn't like the way she'd said that last bit like I was asking. "Okay, good for them." She looked over at me. "No need to be catty, I was just letting you know not to waste your time with them later."

"Later? What's happening later?"

"Nothing really, we're going to the trench. They'll all be there."

^^^^^^

The trench was nothing more than a really big hole in the ground out in the middle of nowhere. There was a trail of rocks that you could walk down, but almost everyone slid in. I was wearing a white dress, so I took the rocks.

When I walked up to the group Tatumn and Ethan were talking about Camden and I couldn't help but listen. She told him she thought he'd be here soon, and he said, "Soon, when's that going to be?" Tatumn looked over at me.

"I don't know what they think I can do about it. You know how Camden is."

I did. I knew exactly how he was, and I was just as impatient for him to get here as Ethan was. She took my hand in hers and led me to the other side of the trench. We climbed up a rocky path and then she pulled me down beside her.

"You can ask. I know you want to."

I turned away from her and stared out at the mountains. The sun was low in the sky, and they were separated into stacks of indigo and grey. "I don't know what you're talking about." She looked at me, and I could tell we were both thinking the same thing, but she said, "Sure, Emma. We don't have to talk about it."

I should have let it drop, but I was actually curious why Ethan was so anxious for Camden to get here, so I said, "Talk about what?"

"About Camden."

"What about him?"

"I don't know, I think you're the one who's curious." She sounded like she knew exactly how curious I really was, and even though she was right, I still felt exposed. "I'm not curious." I said in a firm tone meant to make her believe me. "Emma, I know. I've known for a very long time. You like him. It's okay, weird... but okay."

"I don't know what you're talking about, I don't *like* Camden."

Her brows rose in this *you're a really terrible liar* sort of way.

"Fine, but he doesn't like me. Not like that, and he already has a girlfriend so it wouldn't matter even if he did." She leaned back on her hands. "Camden doesn't have a girlfriend, he has girls... lots of them, but he doesn't date, everyone knows that."

The sound of engines roaring tore through the air and we turned around to see Camden and a few other guys on motorcycles pull up to the trench. "Thank God, Ethan is so annoying before his first beer." I laughed and she stood up and reached out for me. "So that's why everyone's waiting on him, he's bringing the beer?"

Tatumn shrugged. "Well, that… and other things."

^^^^^^

The sun was past the horizon and the trench was in full shadow. The guys Camden rode up with were all sitting in a circle, passing a bottle around, and listening to music I didn't recognize. Tatumn was sitting on Ethan's lap, and I was standing at the edge of the group all alone.

I knew I was here with Tatumn, and I should be paying attention to whatever it was she was talking about, but there was a girl in Camden's lap and his hand was resting on her thigh. I tried to look away, it really wasn't something I wanted to see, but every time I did, he would make a noise or move just enough to get my attention again.

I was watching him when Cash walked up and asked what I was doing over here all alone. I wasn't expecting anyone to talk to me, so the sound of his voice made my shoulders jump. Camden's lips twitched and I knew he'd seen me staring. My cheeks got warm, and I turned away from him to look at Cash.

He was one of those guys that looked pretty good from a distance, but up close he was stunning. He had full lips and hair that looked like he'd just finished running his fingers through it. I told him I wasn't doing anything, and he asked me if I wanted a drink.

He had one in his hand already, as if he was sure I was going to accept it. In fact, everything about him seemed sure. He stood tall and straight. He didn't avoid eye contact. That bothered me a bit, but I tried not to look away.

He held the drink out to me, and I took it, even though I didn't really want it. "So, you're Tatumn's friend?" His eyes traveled blatantly from my legs to my chest. "I am… and she already warned me about you." I said just to see how he would react.

His eyes darted in her direction, "Did she?"

A playful smile rested on his lips.

He leaned in and asked, "What kind of warning was it?"

His breath was hot on my neck, and I could tell that he liked the fact that he was the kind of guy that came with a warning. He lifted his bottle to his lips, and I watched as the glass rim pressed into them.

His smile widened and he wrapped his finger around my wrist. No one had ever looked at me the way he was, and it made me feel like I should be doing something different with my hands. I pulled away from him and he said, "I wouldn't believe everything you hear."

I shook my head, "No, I don't, but I definitely believe this."

He laughed. A big genuine laugh, and then he stepped in even closer. "Are you going to tell me your name, or do you want me to guess."

I told him to call me Emma and he said, "You don't look like the kind of girl that likes to play games, Emma. So, I'll just tell you. I think you look real pretty in that white dress, and I hope I get to take it off of you later."

I could tell he was being honest, but it was so ridiculous that I couldn't help but laugh. He pressed his hand to his chest, feigning heartbreak.

"I can't believe you're laughing at me."

I told him I couldn't believe he'd said that, and he looked at me like I was the strange one. I realized that as ridiculous as it was, he was serious, "Did you actually expect that to work?" He shrugged. "No, not really, but it's not usually much harder than that." I laughed again. "Emma, you're hurting my feelings."

"Whatever, guys like you don't have feelings." He gave me a wounded look and said, "Well aren't you the judgy type." I grimaced. "I'm sorry. I didn't mean that. I'm sure you're *full* of feelings." A small amount of pain or discomfort still polluted his eyes so, I placed my hand on his chest in an effort to comfort him and he said, "Well, I am right now." as he looked down at it.

I looked him in the eyes, *dark blue and surrounded by hordes of lashes*, "You bounce back quickly." He got this cocky grin on his face, "I sure do." He leaned in and I realized he was going to kiss me.

I had never been kissed before, and I wasn't about to kiss this boy I'd just met while we were standing in a pile of dirt surrounded by a bunch of strangers. I pulled away from him, but he caught my chin with his thumb. "Come on, Emma. I just want to know what you taste like."

I leaned back a little more and tried to come up with something teasing to say, but before I could get it out, Camden was telling him to leave me alone.

"Does she want me to leave her alone?" Cash asked, and even though I knew he was talking to Camden, it felt like he was still talking to me. Camden stepped in closer and said, "Yeah, she does." like he knew my mind better than I did.

"Actually... I don't."

They both looked over at me. Camden with a troubled expression. Cash with a smirk. Camden's eyes narrowed and he looked at me very carefully. Like he was waiting for me to take it back or change my mind.

"Really, I don't need your help. I can handle myself."

∧∧∧∧∧∧

Camden had always been gorgeous, and I had always had a hard time looking away from him, but now that he was all sharp lines and lean muscle it felt nearly impossible.

When we were at the ranch it seemed like he was avoiding me, but I knew that wasn't actually true. He was just too busy with his own things to notice I was there. So, when he showed up at the river and walked past all the others to kneel down beside me, I felt like maybe I was missing something.

Until I realized, I was the one holding the joint. Everyone was looking at me and I couldn't tell if that was because of some weird face I was making in response to him, or if it was because they wanted me to do something with the joint in my hand.

Camden reached out. His fingers brushed against mine and I froze. Our hands were suspended in midair, smoke trailing over our fingers, and for a split second it was all I could see.

Our hands, entwined, his fingers touching mine.

105

He leaned in, confidence lifted the corner of his lips. "I'll take that."

I looked back down at my hand, *the joint, his hand*. I looked up and realized everyone was still watching me. Tate's brows rose, and I knew she was about to say something I wasn't going to like. I shook my head, and she smiled in this *I knew it* sort of way. I held it out to him, "Sure." He took it from me and looked over at Cash as he took a hit.

There was definitely something happening, some unspoken aggression passing between them. Cash leaned forward and held his hand out. He said, "Didn't know you were coming today, Pierce?" but it sounded more like *I wish you weren't here*, or *don't you have anywhere else to be*. Camden handed him the joint and turned back to me. He sat down and his legs pressed into mine.

"I didn't either. It was Eli's idea."

Eli had never, and I do mean never, volunteered to hang out with me. I looked over at him and he looked as confused as I did. Ethan asked if they were up for a game of ball and Eli blew out a cloud of smoke. "Sure, so long as it's in the water. It's too hot to run around out here."

Camden's hand fell to his knee and the back of his palm grazed my thigh. My skin buzzed and my muscles tightened. He gave me a knowing glance, "I'll sit out with you. I know you don't like the cold water."

Cash stood up and took his shirt off. I don't know if it was to get me to look at him or not, but I did, and oh my God... abs. He held his hand out to me. "Come on Emma, I know you don't want to miss out on the game, and if you get too cold... I'll warm you up."

Camden's jaw tightened. Tatumn stood up with a laugh. Camden told Cash that I didn't really play sports and Cash said, "I'm pretty sure she'd like this game." Tatumn's smile was so wide when she said, "Come on, Emma. I'll keep you warm." I didn't really want to go with her. I liked the idea of sitting on the bank of the river with Camden by my side, but I could tell by the way Cash was still looking at him that we wouldn't be alone.

The two of us climbed up on Long Rock and just before we jumped in, she looked at me and said, "You know it wouldn't hurt you to want something you could actually have." The sting of her words was still pulsing through me when the cold water hit my skin.

Camden swam up beside me, but I was too embarrassed to look at him. "So, what are we playing?" he asked. "How about a game of capture the flag." Cash answered.

Eli turned to him. "We don't have any flags?"

Cash looked over at me. "The girls could take their tops off." He said it like he meant it, and I'm sure he would have let us do it, but I could tell what he really wanted was to provoke Camden.

"Hard pass, that's my sister." Eli said.

Camden looked really irritated, but he didn't give in to him. "Well, you guys don't have to stay." Cash said in this really condescending tone. Camden's eyes darted in my direction. I wasn't sure what was happening, but he was obviously upset. He looked back over at Eli, who gave him a slight nod, and then he looked at Cash.

"We're not leaving. Pick something else."

^^^^^^

It turned out all of Tatumn's friends liked to play games. We were at the trench again and I was sitting next to Cash. He had come out with Ethan every time we'd met up over the last few weeks and I was actually starting to like him.

Tatumn had been watching us all evening, so when she got everyone to agree to a game of truth or dare without looking away from me. I felt a little nervous.

Ethan said he would go first. He dared Cash to climb to the top of the trench and moon everyone. I thought surely, he would say, *no*, or *pass*, but he just looked over at me and said, "Hold my beer." before he took off.

Camden had been this strange mix of closeness and distance all summer. He was right next to me, and I couldn't help but look at him when Cash turned around and pulled his shorts down for all of us to see.

I knew he didn't like Cash. I just couldn't tell if his dislike had anything to do with me. It felt like it did, but it wasn't because he liked me himself. I watched as his eyes rolled upward and his head shook in this dismissive manner. The girl he was holding leaned over and pressed her lips into his, and I turned back around.

When Cash made it back, he asked, "Did you like what you saw, Sweetness?" and I had to look away from him too. He reached out and plucked his drink from my hand. "Alright who should I collect my pound of flesh from?" I shrugged. "I don't know, but hopefully not me."

He nodded and then looked across the circle and dared Cynthia to take her top off. She did it just as quickly and easily as he had, and I felt like I was playing a game I couldn't win.

When it was Tate's turn, she looked over at me, and a huge knot of anxiety formed in my gut. I wanted to get up and walk away, but there was nowhere to go. Her eyes darted toward Cash and then she looked back at me. After the things I'd just seen, *Cash's ass*, and *Cynthia's tits*, I was definitely looking for the chicken exit.

Tate's eyes narrowed and I almost said, *I'm not taking my dress off, or lifting it up. I'm really not even okay with foot stuff so no shoes either*, but then she looked at me like I could trust her, and I relaxed. A little. Until she said, "I dare you to kiss Cash."

Tatumn knew I had never been kissed before and even though she had asked if I would kiss him, if he tried, and I had given her a very loose *I don't know, maybe*. She had to know that this is not what I meant.

Cash didn't seem upset at all. He leaned over and turned my face to his. I thought about turning away. Declining him, even though everyone was watching, but then he said, "Don't worry, Sweetness. I'll be gentle." and I leaned into him.

His lips were even softer than they looked. He moved them over mine in a way that seemed almost practiced, as if he knew exactly what to do with his lips to get a response out of mine. I didn't have any idea what I was doing, but I could tell this was easy for him.

It lasted longer than I thought it would. When he pulled away, he asked, "Better than expected?" as he looked down into my eyes. I knew everyone was still watching us, but he said it quietly, like it was just for me… and then he was gone.

For a moment I felt really exposed, but then I realized he hadn't left. Camden had pulled him off of me. Cash said, "What the fuck is wrong with you, Pierce? Don't you have enough girls of your own?"

Camden's eyes darted to mine, and he said, "Don't." Cash stepped in closer, pushing Camden back with his chest. "Don't what? Kiss her? She liked it you fucking loser."

Camden looked over at me. I didn't know what to do. I tried to stop him, saying things like s*top*, and *you don't need to do this*, but he wasn't listening. His eyes swept over mine and a wave of shame and embarrassment like I'd never felt before moved through me.

He said, "I knew it." and then he hit him.

^^^^^^

Tatumn was meeting up with Ethan at the coffee shop and I simply couldn't risk running into Cash after what had happened. So even though she had literally begged, I declined the invitation and walked to the river.

I was lying on my back in the sunshine watching the breeze move the branches above me and trying not to think about Camden, when he showed up.

I hadn't said a single word to him since we'd left the trench, and I knew it was bothering him. I just didn't know what to say. I didn't understand what was happening between us, why he was so quiet when we were alone and so attentive when we were around others.

It didn't make any sense and even though I knew he thought he'd done something good, protecting me from Cash. What he'd actually done was humiliate me to the point of tears.

I had come out here to get away from him, but I didn't want to have to tell him that, so I turned over and picked up my book.

He sat down beside me and asked me what I was reading. I didn't answer him, *because I didn't want to talk to him*, but then he pulled out his sketch pad and I felt really irritated that he'd been able to let it go so easily. I asked him if he'd really come all the way out here just to ignore me some more.

He looked at me like I was a petulant child and waved his pencil in the air like I should be able to derive the true meaning of his existence from the sharpened graphite he chose to work with. "No, I came out here to draw." He said, and I felt foolish for thinking he'd come looking for me. "Fine, I'll go then." I closed my book and sat up to pull my shirt on. He reached out and put his hand on my arm.

It was a gentle touch, barely enough pressure to hold on, but he didn't touch me much and I felt stunned. It was like a match had been lit. I could feel the warmth from his fingertips seeping into me and I knew that any moment now it would go out.

"I didn't come out here to draw. I just knew you were mad, and it bothered me when you didn't answer me, so I said that, but I didn't mean it. I don't want you to go."

The way he was staring at me was really unsettling. "Why are you out here then?" I don't know what I wanted him to say, perhaps that he'd come to find me. Or that he was sorry for the strange way he'd been acting, but he didn't say either of those things.

"He's just not a good guy, Emma."

I couldn't detect even the hint of remorse in his voice, and that made me feel like he didn't care that he'd hurt me.

"And you are?"

It wasn't a real question. I knew Camden was a good guy.

He shook his head and looked away from me. "No, I'm not. I'm definitely not, but I'm also not trying to mess with you." I don't think he meant to hurt me, but he did. I looked away from him and ran my finger over the smooth edge of my book.

"Aren't you though?"

He looked up at me nervously. "No… Emma. It's not like that." I knew what he meant. He didn't like me *like that*, but that's not what I'd meant at all.

"What is it like then?"

His eyes pulled together, and I could see him carefully trying to choose his next words. His pencil dropped and he rubbed his thumb over the callus on his forefinger. "I don't know really. I guess it's just that I don't want to see you get hurt, and Cash isn't who you think he is."

In all honesty, I didn't think of Cash that much. He was fun to be around, and it was flattering that he seemed to like me, but it wasn't like I was sitting here feeling a terrible loss because he wasn't here with me. I felt more upset that Camden had spent all summer ignoring me unless I was with him.

"What do you think I think about Cash?"

His eyes darted nervously in my direction, "Well, you like him, don't you?" I did like him. Cash was easy to like, but

Camden said it like it meant something more, so I just shrugged.

"He's really not who you think he is."

"Well then, who is he?"

He hesitated and I said, "That's what I thought."

He looked up at me, "What?"

I pressed my hand into the cover of my book and shook my head, "I don't know what's going on with you, or why you care so much, but it seems like Cash is a decent guy and you're the one with the problem."

His shoulders pulled tight. "I'm full of problems. That's not really up for debate here, but I'm also not pretending like I don't have them. I'm not chasing nice girls around acting like I have good intentions. He is, and no one ever sees it, because his dad is a lawyer and his mom is on the school board, and he plays football and smiles at all the right times."

I could hear what he was saying. I knew that he'd had a hard life, and that it bothered him that he had to live with his aunt, but what it sounded like was that he was jealous. Of Cash. Of his easy life and ability to be charming.

What it didn't sound like was that he was jealous of me, with Cash. In fact, other than his skewed perception of me as a *nice girl,* it didn't sound like this had anything to do with me.

"I assume I'm the nice girl?" He nodded.

"Well, if that's all it is then I don't think you need to worry, because Cash has never led me to believe he has good intentions. He's actually really up front about what he wants from me."

Camden looked back at me with a shocked expression, "And what is it?" I thought about lying to him. Telling him that

Cash wanted to be my boyfriend, that he'd asked me out and I was considering it, but I decided against it. "Not much really, he mostly talks about wanting to kiss me… or take my clothes off."

He gave me a thoughtful look, "And you like that?" I did, or maybe I didn't. I wasn't really sure, but I knew I liked it better than being ignored.

"I do. I mean at least he pays attention to me."

Camden scoffed. "Of course he does. Look at you. You're exactly the kind of girl a guy like him wants." His dismissive tone made my skin tingle with disappointment.

I looked away from him and let the pages of my book fall from my thumb repeatedly, but I could still feel him watching me. He let out a frustrated sigh.

"It's just a game to him, Emma."

"Yeah, well maybe it's game I want to play."

He shook his head. "No, it's not."

^^^^^^

When Camden and I got back to the ranch. Cash was sitting on the porch with Tatumn and Ethan. My first instinct was to run. Or turn around and pretend I hadn't seen him, but he was looking right at me, and Camden was standing too close for me to go anywhere anyway.

I climbed the steps and Cash looked up at me, "There you are, Sweetness." I had no idea why he was being so nice to me, but I couldn't help but wince at the sight of his eye. His gaze drifted from me to Camden. "I was hoping to see you at the coffee shop, but it looks like maybe you were busy."

I resisted the urge to look back over my shoulder. "Yeah, I went to the river to read." Cash nodded and looked down at the book in my hand. "Well, if you're all done with that, maybe I could talk you into coming to the arcade with us now."

I could feel Camden watching me and I knew he'd want me to say no. "Sure, just give me a minute to get changed."

I put on my white dress and Tatumn fixed my hair and makeup. She talked the whole time about how much she thought Cash liked me.

She said Ethan was giving him a hard time about it this morning at the coffee shop, but she thought it was cute, and Cash didn't even seem to mind. "He insisted we come back here to get you before we headed into town… and Emma, he doesn't do that sort of thing for other girls."

When I came back out, Camden was sitting with the guys. His eyes moved over me in a way that made me feel like I didn't have enough on. Cash stood up and offered me his hand and I took it. Camden went inside and we all climbed into Ethan's BMW.

When we arrived at the arcade, which turned out to be some guy named Finn's basement with a gaming console and few pinball machines in the back corner, Cash pulled me down beside him.

He asked me if I wanted a drink. I shook my head, *no*, and he asked me what I liked to do for fun. My shoulders pulled up. "Not much really. I read, sit very still, and eat a lot of chocolate."

He laughed like I was joking, but it was the truth, so I just shrugged and let him have his fun. He told me he didn't read much, but his sister did. She was in fourth grade, her name was

Adeline, and she liked mysteries. I told him I liked a little bit of everything, but I guessed romance was probably my favorite.

He stood up to get himself a drink and brought me back a soda. When he sat back down, he said, "I like romance too." and I knew he wasn't talking about books.

He had this confident but slightly apprehensive expression on his face. He leaned in, his bottle bumped my knee. I looked down and he caught my chin with his thumb and kissed me.

He was really good at it. His hand held me steady. His lips moved in this slow way that coaxed mine open. His cool fingertips caressed my knee.

I knew we were in a room full of people that I didn't know, and most of them were probably doing their own thing, but some of them were undoubtedly watching us.

I tried not to mind, not to think about it while his tongue was licking mine, but then I heard the door open, and felt vibrations on the stairs. I pulled away and Camden and Eli were standing above us.

Eli made a comment about us needing a room, "Emma, you know they're all watching you, don't you?"

I looked down at my lap.

Cash said, "You going to hit me again, Pierce?" in this cocky way that sounded like he actually wanted him to. I looked up at Camden. Alarmed and ready to beg him not to, but he just shook his head dismissively and said, "Why would I do that?"

I became very aware of the way everyone seemed to be staring at us and turned my knees to the side to let them pass. Cash picked my hand up and led me across the room to where Tatumn and Ethan were. She looked at me with this proud little smile on her face and I knew she had seen me kissing him.

I was embarrassed, but not ashamed of what I'd done. People were always making out at these things. I knew it wasn't a big deal. No one really cared. It was the pride in Tate's smile and the cool indifference in Camden's eyes that made me feel uncomfortable.

Cash didn't seem to notice. He pulled me in closer, wrapped his arm around my waist, and continued talking to Ethan. I didn't mean to do it, but I looked over at Camden. I was trying to pay attention to what Cash was saying, but it was impossible not to notice the way he was sitting all alone. Camden was never alone at these things. Several girls had come over to him. He wasn't being rude, just inattentive enough to frustrate them and make them move on.

Cash noticed me looking at him. He leaned in, moved the hair off my shoulder, and pressed his lips to the curve of my neck. When he pulled back, Camden looked over at us, and he said, "Is there something going on between you and Pierce?"

I shook my head, *no*, "Camden and I are just friends." He pressed his lips just below my ear, "Well, he doesn't look at you like a friend." I nodded, "Yeah, you're right. He hasn't been very friendly lately, maybe we aren't friends at all."

Ethan asked if anyone was up for a game of beer pong and Cash said, "Sure, I'd be happy to kick your ass in a game or two." Ethan and Tatumn took one side of the table and Cash dragged me to the other. I told him I didn't want to play. "Don't worry, Sweetness, I'll do all the drinking. You just need to get the ball in the cup."

I told him that I couldn't aim a ball at a canyon much less a cup, but he just shrugged. "Well then, I hope you're okay carrying me home later."

I missed my first three shots, but Cash was good, so we were still ahead. I didn't really care who won, but Tatumn was competitive. She told Ethan if they lost, she was going to kick him off her team and take Cash for the next round.

Ethan wasn't bad but he didn't seem to care the way Cash or Tatumn did, so when the game ended Cash went to her side of the table and I went outside.

I could still hear the noises of the party, *music playing, people talking, bottles clanking against one another as they were thrown into the bin*, but the sky was covered in soft white clouds, and the moonlight was reflecting off of them in a way that made it seem quiet.

I walked over to the edge of the yard and wrapped my hands around a fence post. I heard the door open, but I didn't turn around. There was no reason to believe that whoever it was was looking for me.

I knew it was him before he got to me though. It was in the slow cadence of his walk and the way he'd stopped twice before asking if I'd liked the game. I could tell he knew I didn't, he probably knew I wouldn't before I even started playing. I told him it wasn't really my thing, and he asked me if I'd met Finn.

I could tell he didn't really care if I'd met Finn or not, he just didn't know what else to say. I told him I hadn't and asked, "Why?" He leaned back on the fence. "I don't know Emma… because it's his basement?" His shoulders dropped in a way that looked like surrender, *or maybe defeat.*

"Oh… well, no I didn't meet him." His chin lifted and I could tell he hated this as much as I did. I asked him if he was alright. "Yeah, Emma. I'm great." I knew he was upset with me. I just wasn't sure why. He looked back at the house. "So, are you two dating now?" I shook my head *no*, and he said, *oh*, like it didn't matter to him either way.

He looked down at his feet and I asked, "Why?" He didn't look up, but I could tell he was annoyed with me by the way he said, "Am I not allowed to ask you that sort of thing?" I told him, no, he could, but it didn't seem like it should matter to him. His lips lifted and he looked at me like I didn't know anything at all. I turned away.

"Why would you think it wouldn't matter to me?"

The wind picked up and I pressed my hands to my thighs to keep my dress down. His gaze traveled down my body. The look in his eyes was one I hadn't seen before, and I stumbled over my reply. "I guess that's not what I meant. It's just that it seems like maybe I'm the only girl in Montana that you don't want to date, so it shouldn't really matter if someone else does… want to."

The moonlight caught in his eyes. "You think you're the only one, huh?" My mind sifted through dozens of girls that I'd seen him with. "Well maybe not the only one, but definitely, yes, I do think that." He nodded. "That's interesting."

He reached up to run his fingers through his hair and a small sliver of his torso was exposed. I didn't know what he'd been doing that had caused such a change in him, but he looked tired and frustrated. His body was leaner than it was at the beginning of the summer. I wanted to ask him what was going on, because something was going on, and I didn't believe that all of this was really about me and Cash.

He shook his head and shoved his hands in his pockets. I asked him what he'd meant by that. "Nothing," he mumbled, but then he looked up, "Actually, I don't want to date any of the girls in Montana, so I don't know why you would think that."

My eyes rolled, "That can't be true. I've never known you to do anything you don't want to, and you seem to be dating quite a few of them already."

"No, I'm not."

"Well then what are you doing with them?" He gave me a sharp look. I didn't want to know what he was thinking.

"The same thing Cash wants to do with you."

∧∧∧∧∧∧

Camden had hurt my feelings before, but never so intentionally. For the first time in my life, I absolutely hated that we all shared a room. Tatumn and Eli were both passed out drunk, snoring loudly and keeping me from sleep.

Even though he didn't sleep above me, I felt him move from his bed. It had been hot this week, and the windows were all propped open. The moonlight silhouetted him as he moved across the room. I turned around to face the wall.

He pulled the blanket back, and I felt the mattress give under his weight as he climbed in beside me. "Go away, Camden." He shifted a bit, "No, I don't want to." I could feel him staring at the back of my head and it made me feel helpless and alone.

120

He put his hand on my shoulder. My arm tensed, but he didn't let go. "I'm sorry, Emma. I know I've been off lately." I tried to pull away from him. "I'm tired of you being mean to me, Camden. I don't even know what I've done. Just that you don't like me anymore."

He moved in closer, "I like you, Emma."

"It really doesn't seem like you do." I scooted further away.

"There's just a lot going on right now and I'm not handling it well. I know I overstepped. I shouldn't have hit him. I shouldn't have said anything, if you like him. Fine. I'll drop it."

I turned to look back at him and he coaxed my body over so that we were facing each other. "What's really going on, because there's no way all of this is about Cash." He didn't answer me, but he was so close that I couldn't stop talking. "You're wrong anyway. Cash isn't better than you, and you need to get that out of your head."

He nodded like he knew what I was saying was true, but then he said, "He has more money than I ever will." I told him he didn't know that, and even if that were true, it didn't matter. Money doesn't matter. He looked at me like I didn't understand anything at all.

"Money matters a whole lot to the people that don't have it."

I felt bad, like I'd said something terribly wrong. "That's not what I meant. Of course, it matters if you don't have it, but you have plenty." He scoffed. "Camden, you have two homes, and your second home is nicer than my first."

"This isn't my house. It's Dani's."

"Yeah, but it's yours too."

He shook his head and pulled his hands up over his face. I told him he could tell me what was actually bothering him, or he could go back to his own bed, because I was tired of whatever this was.

His eyes searched mine like he was looking for something in me that he couldn't find in himself. He rolled over on his back and I thought he was going to leave. He looked so lost that I almost took it back, told him he could stay, and he didn't have to talk. Not if he didn't want to.

"It's my mom actually."

Tatumn mentioned that his mom had moved closer. I hadn't thought of it much because it seemed like a good thing, "Your mom?" He shrugged, "She lives here now." I could tell by the way he'd said it, that it wasn't a good thing, but I asked anyway. He shook his head, "No, it's not." I wanted to ask him why, but it didn't seem like he really wanted to say more.

He looked out the window, and I said, "I don't like Cash that much, but I do wish you hadn't hit him. It was pretty awful getting my first kiss in a game of truth or dare, but it was absolutely horrendous having to watch the guy's face get smashed in after."

He looked back at me. "That was your first kiss?"

I nodded.

"It shouldn't have been like that."

I agreed, but said, "Well, it was." and he leaned over and pressed his lips into mine.

At first it felt like I was dreaming. Like there was no way this was real, but then he put his hand on my cheek, fingers running down my jawline, thumb catching on my chin. My lips parted and he pressed into them, pushed his hand back up into my hair and pulled me closer.

I felt the echo of his touch in every cell of my body. His tongue swiped across my lip and my eyes fluttered open. A needy sound escaped from somewhere deep inside me and the look he gave me was almost feral, *pained, reverent, hungry, and filled with desire like I'd never seen before.*

His lips never left mine but when my eyes closed again his fist tightened in my hair and he pulled, just enough to make my head tilt back. He kissed the corner of my lips, crest of my jawline, curve of my neck. I could still feel the vibration of his touch on my cheek when he was running his fingers over my chest. I moaned and he brought his lips back up to mine, scooted in closer, and pressed into me.

I was afraid to move. Afraid that if I did, he would realize what he was doing and disappear. He wasn't though. His hand wrapped around my hip, fingers digging into me.

Every part of me was tangled up in him, but he pulled at me like he needed me closer. I needed that too, but I wasn't brave enough to press into him or put my hand on his hip the way he had mine.

He reached around and pulled me tight up against him. I could feel his heartbeat in my chest. His breath on my neck as he licked and nibbled his way down.

He ran his fingers over my lips, and I whimpered into his hand and pressed a kiss to the tips of them. He looked up at me. Regret, fear, remorse all passed through his eyes. He pulled himself up beside me and wrapped his arms around my back.

I knew he was about to apologize so I said, "Don't." He grabbed a bit of my hair and rubbed it between his fingers. His expression was still stark, *shaken and unsure*, but he said, "I hate it when you're mad at me."

His thumb ran over my lower lip. "I'm not mad at you."

He looked back up at me, "Not even a little bit?" I shook my head. "No, at least right now I'm not." He kissed me again, slowly, softly, parting my lips with his own. I felt a wave of relief wash through me. My eyes closed, shoulders relaxed, breath slowed.

When he pulled back, he said, "You're really important to me, Emma."

I told him he was really important to me too. "Yeah, but you're the most important person in my life. You're the only person I actually like."

I laughed and he brushed the hair away from my eyes and gave me a tentative look. "I know you like me. I'm just not sure if it's the same for you as it is for me." He sounded so unsure of himself. "I don't know how it is for you, but I'm pretty sure it's not the same."

He looked at me like he didn't understand so I said, "I obviously like you a lot more than you like me."

He shook his head, "That's not possible."

I nodded, "I think it is."

He looked down for a moment, and I couldn't help but appreciate the perfect way his cheeks faded into his jaw line. "It's not like that, Emma." He said without looking up.

"Isn't it though?"

His eyes held mine, "No, it's not. I like you. I just know I shouldn't."

9

Now

Emma

When Tatumn was planning her wedding week, it seemed like a lot, but she had this grand vision of the perfect welcome home for Ethan and farewell for herself. She said it wasn't just a ceremony, it couldn't be.

She wanted the first few days to be small. Just close family and friends. Alissa was the best wedding planner in Montana and she and Tatumn had come up with the idea of turning the ranch into a sort of retreat.

I was standing at the window, watching Alissa direct the men and wishing I had a cup of coffee in my hands. Today was a catered lunch and archery tag competition. Alissa had all the obstacles and retaining walls custom made, and they were being strategically placed all over the yard.

Tatumn walked in and the instant our eyes met I knew she'd seen him. She handed me a cup of coffee and whisper yelled, "Is he staying here?" like I'd invited him.

"Yeah… apparently."

She looked at me like I'd lost my mind, "Did you know?" A deep expression of disbelief settled on my face. She shook her head, "No, of course not. How did you find out?"

I took a slow drink of coffee and contemplated the best way to say this. I knew there was no way to tell her that he'd driven me here… in my car, which I let him in, without it sounding like I'd planned it.

Like I wanted him here. Which I don't. Not at all. Not even a little bit. I want him gone. I want him to be as far away from me as humanly possible. I would rather him be on Mars than sitting downstairs in my living room.

The thought of having to ignore him is terrifying. How do I act like I don't know he's here? I'm good at a lot of things, but hiding my emotions isn't one of them. One look and he'll know. Or worse, I will. He'll look at me like he looks at everything else, and I'll know in a fraction of a second exactly how little I meant to him.

How do I pretend he didn't matter?

Act like it was just a bad case of childhood infatuation. That he was just a steppingstone on my path, and not the entire road.

How do I just walk by, without feeling him everywhere?

He'll see everything I've tried to keep hidden. Everything I repressed when he left will come bubbling out in awkward conversation or embarrassingly long pauses. Everyone here will see it. How do I keep that from happening?

I look over at Tatumn, "He drove me home last night."

Astonishment followed by complete disbelief washes over her face, "Oh my God, did you…"

I want to thump her, "No, of course not. I'm not a masochist. I offered to call him an Uber, and when he said he was staying here, I panicked and ran up to my room as fast as I could."

"And he just let you go?"

My head falls back in exasperation, "No, he followed me up the stairs like he didn't know why I was running, and then he told me he wasn't here to hurt me. He was just here for the wedding." She grimaces and I shake my head, "No… it's good. It's what I want. I just wish he wasn't staying here."

She nods, "Yeah, my mother's a real piece of work." Her eyes widen like she's just realized the implication on herself, and she turns to me, "I didn't know. I swear. I would have told her no because this is an epically bad idea… and this is my wedding, so she should've asked me."

I shake my head, "No, it's not Dani's fault. She just wanted to see him, and it's a big house and a free place to stay so why would he turn it down?"

She gives me an incredulous look. "Oh, I don't know, maybe because he walked out on you five years ago without even bothering to say goodbye and smashed your heart to smithereens. I mean honestly, he has some nerve… and my mother is not stupid, she knows how hard having him here would be for you, so no. Not okay, on either account."

I take another drink of my coffee. "Well okay or not, he's here now. I'll just have to avoid him."

She gives me a doubtful look, "Is that your whole plan?"

I bite my lip, "Currently… yes."

She sits down on the bed and looks over at the window. "You could come stay in our suite." I shake my head, "No, I'm not going to do that."

"Then you're going to need a really big distraction."

^^^^^^

Agatha is a whole lot of happiness wrapped up in a little bit of human. The first thing she says to me when I come downstairs is that she thinks my hair looks like tangles, and she wants a strawberry pop tart.

I get it for her and when we're eating, she tells me that she is going to shoot an arrow today, that she's never done it before, but she already knows how because she has a sling shot and she figures it's probably not much different from that.

Camden is sitting on the couch, drinking coffee, and looking at his phone. I can tell he's listening to us though, because when Agatha pivots to the cake she wants to eat for lunch and asks if I'll eat it with her, his lips lift at the corner.

I tell her I'd love to eat cake for lunch, but we'd better ask her mother if that's okay first. She says we don't need to. Her mother told her she could have whatever she wanted, just so long as she promised to stay off the field when we're all shooting at each other.

I nod and she tells me that she's done and ready to go outside to shoot her arrows. I grab both of our jackets, and we head out to find Alissa.

Agatha loves Alissa, she thinks she's pretty and likes that she always brings treats with her. Alissa releases the glove she has clipped to the top of her board and hands it to Agatha.

She tells her it's a real archery glove. Agatha says she likes that it's pink and pulls it on her tiny hand. Alissa walks us over to the edge of the field and Agatha runs to grab her bow from beside the target.

I tell Alissa I can't wait to see how this all turns out and she says, "I know. I'm not usually jealous of my clients' events, but this place is so beautiful, and the course looks like such a good time." I tell her she should play. She can be on my team, and she says, "Can't, I have to get the lunch set up inside while you all are out here."

Agatha, like her mother, is fearless and strangely capable. She shoots the arrow several times over and never really misses. Tatumn comes over to tell us that it's almost go time, and Agatha hits the bullseye.

We all head back inside, and Alissa gives us all this thick black armor to put over our chests. She goes over the rules, no faces, she will not have any black eyes in her wedding photos. No close range, she is not interested in taking anyone in for open wounds and having to miss lunch.

When she's done Tatumn and Ethan split up and pick teams. Tatumn picks me, Eli, April, Cynthia, and Jess. Ethan ends up with Cash, Camden, Dani, Josh, and Gabe.

We all split up and Tatumn goes over the course with us. She tells us all that Ethan and his friends will be the easiest targets, because they're too big to hide, and sets Cynthia, Jess, and April on them. Eli, she picked to take out Cash, who she knows will be gunning for her, and she will go for Camden and Dani.

She looks at me. "Emma, you're our easiest target so take the tunnel at the far edge of the field and try not to let them see you climb in."

When the game starts, we all run off in different directions. I do my best to climb in the tunnel undetected. Ethan's team seems to be working in pairs, but he's alone and obviously looking for Tatumn.

I watch as April fires at Gabe and Josh gets Cynthia out. Dani runs across the field to get behind another wall and Tatumn pops out and tags her. Ethan sees it happen and runs toward them, but Tate is quicker than him. She escapes through a tunnel he can't fit in and ducks behind the next wall. Jess fires in his direction and he throws his hands up and walks off the field.

Jess is doing this victorious wiggle, when Josh stands up from behind his half wall and shoots her. I notice Eli creeping around the edge of a row of tunnels and figure that's where Cash is hiding.

Eli's not really paying attention, or actually he's paying an incredible amount of attention to the end of the tunnel he's expecting Cash to climb out of, but Camden walks up behind him and takes him out.

The two of them run off toward the edge of the field. I see Tatumn and April pull their bows back and aim them at Josh. He looks like he knows it's over, but he shoots at April and manages to get her out. Tatumn's arrow hits him, and he lets out a bit of a yelp. Tatumn looks around the field. I can tell she can't see anyone, but she runs off anyway.

I hear their footsteps just outside the tunnel I'm in and pull the string of my bow back. They both step around opposite edges and I don't know which way to turn first.

Cash says, "Hey Emma." In this sticky sweet tone that says he knows he's got me. Camden doesn't say anything, but he does have an arrow pointed in my direction. I look between the two of them and Cash says, "I brought you something." as he raises his brow and points it in Camden's direction.

Camden's eyes widen in surprise and then he puts his bow down and Cash says, "Go ahead. I know you want to." A flash of pain or disappointment runs through Camden's eyes and then he washes his face of all emotion and looks at me like he expects me to take the shot.

I don't know if it's the way he surrenders to me so easily, or the way he accepts Cash's betrayal like he should have expected it all along, but when I look back over my shoulder and realize Cash still has his bow loaded and ready. I know that the moment I take Camden out. Cash will shoot me in the back.

I do a quick pivot from one knee to the other and take Cash out instead. He falls back and makes a pained noise, and I load another arrow. When I turn back to Camden there's a bit too much satisfaction in his smirk.

I hear Tatumn running in our direction and I know he can hear her too. He doesn't turn away from me though, instead he climbs inside the tunnel with me. I start backing out the other side.

I tell him not to come closer, that it's only going to hurt that much worse when I shoot him. He looks at me like he doesn't think I'll do it. I step out of the tunnel and pull the bow string back.

Cash is sitting in the grass looking up at me like I betrayed him. Tatumn sees that I have him in sight and stops running. I realize that they're all watching me, but the only person I'm concerned with at the moment is him.

He steps out of the tunnel, and I release my arrow.

^^^^^^

Lunch turns into dinner, and dinner turns into drinks by the fire pit outside. Dani takes Agatha back with her and the rest of us sit around talking and listening to music.

Cash sits by me, and even though I have apologized for shooting him and explained that I only did it because I knew he was going to shoot me. He's still upset. Tatumn isn't though. I don't think she's ever been prouder of me than she was today.

It makes me feel happy, to see her so effervescently settled in Ethans lap. Tatumn is very competitive and winning always makes her cheeks glow, but tonight it's more than that. It's this place, and all of us in it. I know she thinks that this goodbye is all her own, but the ranch might as well not exist without her here.

There is a lot of talk about Seattle, the *fresh markets, coffee shops, boutique shopping,* and of course the rain. I can tell that Ethan knows Tate's not thrilled about moving to the Pacific Northwest and the way his voice changes when he talks about it tells me that he desperately wants her there with him.

132

April and Jess are competing for Gabe's attention, but it's obvious that he's not here for that. Cynthia keeps looking over at Cash, but he won't stop staring at me.

Gabe played college ball with Ethan and when April brings up Ethan's new contract with the Seahawks to try to get Gabe to talk to her more. Ethan's eyes dart to Tate, and he says he doesn't really want to talk about work.

Gabe isn't going professional, he says he wasn't good enough for that, and Josh looks over at him. "You were offered a contract." Gabe's eyes pull in at the corners, but he doesn't say anything.

April asks him what kind of contract, and he tells her it was to play with the Broncos, but he didn't really want that sort of life, so he turned it down. Jess asks him what sort of life he does want, and he says, "A simple one." Jess's eyes light up and April turns to Josh.

Cash looks over at Camden. "What about you, Pierce. Any big plans for the future?" I can tell he doesn't actually want to know. He's just trying to goad him into joining in on the conversation.

I feel a bit of apprehension, but I want to know what his answer will be, so I look over at him. He is impossibly cool, sitting there with both hands resting on the armrests, shoulders held loose and low.

Camden looks back at Cash. "No, not really." I can tell it bothers Cash that it doesn't bother Camden to answer. He leans forward, pulls another beer from the bucket, and twists the top off. "So where have you been?"

Camden's eyes narrow slightly, and he looks over at me. "New York." I feel my own eyes open wider to let the information in. Cash says, "City?" Camden nods and tells him that he lived in Jersey.

Instead of waiting for Cash's next question, which he's obviously going to ask, Camden tells him that he went to Montclair, and he just graduated with a degree in social work and anthropology.

Cash nods, "Oh yeah, what are you going to do with that?" His tone is condescending, but Camden just shrugs, "You know man I'm not sure." The ease with which Camden answers pulls Cash's jaw tight. "You didn't think about that while you were in college?"

Camden's chin tilts up, and I say, "Not everyone wants to be a lawyer, Cash." He takes a drink and looks over at me with an irritated expression. "No, but everyone's got bills to pay."

Camden says, "You went to work in your dad's firm?" It doesn't' sound like an insult, but Cash says, "Yeah, well, we're pretty big on financial stability in my family, but I understand if that's not the case for you."

I shoot Cash a look. He shakes his head at me. I turn to Tatumn, whose eyes are shifting from side to side and realize everyone's staring at us. I don't know what I'm doing, or why I'm bothering to intervene, but I say, "There's more to life than financial stability, and pursuing a career that you find emotionally fulfilling is worth more than a paycheck."

Cash scoffs and looks over at me. "Says the girl who's never had to pay her own rent."

I can tell I've upset him again, and I know he doesn't mean it, but the way Camden's eyes darken on my behalf makes me nervous.

"True," I give him, "but I still think there's merit to doing something just because you want to do it. America is obsessed with this idea of success that can only be defined in monetary terms, and I just don't think it really works. Money can't buy happiness, they've proven that already, and with the way the world is today. We can't keep diminishing the value of true fulfillment, because while the world has plenty of lawyers, *happiness, peace, acceptance,* all seem to be in short supply."

Cash scoffs, "Man would I love to live in your world for a day."

My eyes roll and Gabe says, "I don't know, I think she's right."

"Obviously." Jess says, "Is that why you turned down the Broncos?" He nods, "More or less."

April turns to him, "Yeah, but you come from money, right?"

Gabe's lips press together, "My parents do alright."

She gives Cash a look of solidarity. "Only someone with money would turn down a multimillion-dollar contract to live the simple life. The rest of us would willingly claw someone's eyes out for a million dollars."

I laugh and Josh says, "I think you just proved her point."

Camden's eyes dart to mine and I turn away. Cash seems to notice and gives me a strange look, "Alright fine, but even if I concede that money can't buy happiness, I'd still argue for some form of financial stability because you can't wipe your ass with happiness."

Cynthia laughs and Cash nods like he knows he's right.

I give him an incredulous look. He shakes his head in annoyance, muttering something about lofty ideals and then he says, "I mean how happy do you think homeless people really are?" Camden turns his way, "Actually, a lot of homeless people are satisfied in their lives."

Cash gives a derisive nod, "Oh yeah, did you read a study on that one, Pierce?"

Camden shrugs, "Yeah, a few, and a surprising amount of homeless people are satisfied in their lives, and the ones that aren't have other problems like substance abuse and mental health disorders. Homelessness for those people is more of a symptom of their illness, but you're right, most studies show that people with higher incomes are happier. There's a limit to it though, and after basic needs are met it really doesn't make a difference."

Cash looks back over at April, "Well, I've never thought of my needs as basic, but I guess we'll have to go with his answer since he's the expert." Her eyes dart to mine. Tatumn stands from Ethan's lap and looks down at him with a pointed expression. He stands up and says, "I don't know about the rest of you but I'm pretty tired."

I walk Tatumn to her car, and she asks if I want to come with them. I shake my head and tell her, *no,* "I'm tired. I'm just going to clean up a bit and then head to bed." She gives me a tight hug, "I don't want to leave you here." I tell her I'll be fine, and then Ethan drags her away and they all leave.

Camden's inside, standing over the table looking at the remnants of the charcuterie board like he doesn't know what to do with them. I go to the cabinet and pull out a stack of Tupperware. The two of us put everything that looks edible into the containers and then place them in the fridge.

He's too quiet, and it makes me feel uncomfortable, so I say, "I'm sorry about Cash, he was upset with me, not you, and he shouldn't have said all that." His eyes cut to mine, "It didn't bother me. Guys like Cash never do know when to stop." I tell him I guess that's true, and then turn to go upstairs.

He says, "Hey, Emma?" I turn around and he looks at me like he doesn't want me to go. I don't know what to do with that, so I just say, "Yeah?" like I didn't see anything at all. His eyes pull in and then he shakes his head at himself. He looks up, face cleared of emotion, and says, "Do you know what time we're supposed to meet at the river in the morning?"

I know that's not what he wanted to say, but I just nod, and say, "Nine." as I push the disappointment away.

His eyes light up but his face falls, and that confuses me, so I start walking away again. He hasn't moved, but I can feel him watching me. I put my foot down on the last step and he says "Emma…" I stop and turn around.

I don't know what I want him to say, or why I want him to say anything at all, but when I look at him, he looks so young, *nervous, vulnerable,* that I can't help but listen.

"You know you don't need to do that, right?"

I give him a questioning look. "I know what you were doing, and I appreciate it, but you don't need to worry about me. I'm used to handling a lot worse than Cash Alexander." His lips pick up at the corners, settling into a sad smile, and I tell him I don't know what he's talking about.

He says, "Sure, okay." and I say "I'm serious. I wasn't just saying those things, I really do believe them." His eyes light up and something stumbles in my chest. "Oh, I know you do. It's just that…" He looks away from me and I ask him what he means.

He shakes his head, like he's trying to talk himself out of saying more, but I say, "Camden?" and he looks up at me. "It's just confusing. You're obviously upset with me, and you don't want to talk to me, but then you step in like you used to… and I guess I just don't know what that means."

I shrug, sadness picks up the corner of my lips. "It doesn't mean anything, Camden. Not everything has to mean something. You're the one who taught me that."

10

Seven years ago

The summer I turned seventeen was the best summer of my life. Camden was graduating so we got to come to the ranch early. They called out his name and we all jumped to our feet.

I'd spent all year cycling through elation and regret and I had no idea what to expect when I saw him. One moment I would be lost in the memory of his lips on mine. Absolutely certain that when I came back, he would be there waiting for me, but then I would realize that months had passed and he hadn't called, texted, or sent a homing pigeon.

I would hear him saying, *I like you, I just know I shouldn't,* and then the thought of coming back here would send me into a panic because is this really the time to grow a conscience, and what does that even mean?

Why shouldn't he like me? What makes me so different from all those other girls, the ones he kisses in public and pulls down onto his lap? Am I really that bad, *boring, ugly,* and wasn't he the one that told me that people do things they shouldn't all the time anyway? Does that not apply to me? Am I the only line he's not willing to cross?

What if he only kissed me because he felt bad for me?

What if he hadn't thought about me once since I'd left?

What if he had another girlfriend? One he liked and felt like he should be with.

Standing in that crowd, watching him cross that stage felt like a reckoning. I was equal parts hope and dread, but when he took his diploma in his hand and looked out over the crowd. His eyes didn't stop until they landed on mine.

I wanted to wait for him, or find him in the crowd before we left, but when I suggested it, Mom said, "Absolutely not, we've got to beat the traffic, and you'll see him at the ranch anyway."

I knew she was right, but I also knew that Dani had organized a party back at the ranch, and that by the time he got there it would be full of people that would pull his attention away from me. I couldn't protest though. That would be too obvious, so I just nodded and followed her out to the car.

The ranch was decorated with silver banners and black balloons. There was a big cake on the table that said, *Congratulations Camden*, in puffy white script. When he walked in, Dani ran over and threw her arms around him. His eyes found mine and I could tell he was uncomfortable. There were people everywhere, most of them looking at him, and even though they were all smiling I could tell he didn't like it.

I watched as he moved from one person to the next, nodding and accepting handshakes as he went. He kept looking over at me and I had to bite my smile to keep it in check. Dani was really proud of him. I was too, but when she told him that, he said, "It's really not that big a deal." She gave him a playful slap on the chest, "It most certainly is." Camden wasn't good at accepting praise, but I could tell that it made him happy, to make her proud.

My mom walked over and handed Tatumn and I a piece of cake. It was chocolate with chocolate icing, and I had to lick my lips to get the frosting off with every bite. When he finally made it over to me, he said, "You've got something." as he pointed to his lower lip.

I felt my cheeks warm with embarrassment and told him I'd done it on purpose, to make it last longer. A splinter of something I was hoping to see much more of ran through his eyes, "Well, I don't mind if you leave it there." His tone was suggestive.

It made me think about the way it would feel to let him lick it off.

My cheeks went from warm to hot. He watched as I tried to wipe the mess away with my fingers. It wasn't working. I could feel the chocolate as it smeared across my chin. One corner of his lips picked up and he reached over and handed me a napkin.

He asked if Tate and I were going out. "Yeah. I don't know where though." His voice was hesitant, *quieter than usual.* It wasn't like we never talked at the ranch, but he was different this time.

He told me I could ride with him, and I had to force myself to exhale before I could answer. He misread the gap in conversation as denial *or apprehension* and shifted his weight from one foot to the other.

"You know, if you want to. Or not, it doesn't really matter. I'm sure I'll run into you later." He was rambling. I wasn't really sure if he was trying to talk me into it or himself out of it, but I obviously wanted to go with him.

^^^^^^

I had never been on Camden's bike before, and I had no idea where we were going, but it didn't really matter. It was dark out and the sky glittered with stars. The roads were nearly empty, and my body was pressed tightly up against his.

He drove us up into the mountains and pulled his bike over on the side of the road. I don't know why I said it. I was thrilled to be alone with him but when he hopped off his bike I said, "I thought we were going to a party?"

He reached up to undo the strap on my helmet and pulled it off my head, "We are. I just wanted a little time with you before we got there."

I'd never thought about time much. Except for in reference to him. I'd certainly never thought of wanting it, but hearing him say he wanted time with me sounded better than anything I'd ever wasted my time wanting before.

He took my hand in his and led me through the trees to a small pond with a large rock beside it. He climbed up and leaned down to pull me up with him.

From up high you could see all the stars reflected on the surface of the water. It looked like if you dove in, it would feel like swimming in space. I told him that, and he asked if I wanted to find out if it did.

I looked over at him standing there in his black jeans, Vans, and t-shirt. Looking at me like he really expected an answer. "We don't have swimsuits." He shrugged in this *well I don't mind if you don't* sort of way.

"It's freezing, and we don't have any towels." He took off his shirt and my mouth watered at the sight of him. "You can dry off with this."

"Are you serious?"

He shrugged, and this time it said, *I am if you are.* I shook my head and even though he was the one standing there half naked with his smooth skin bathed in the moonlight. He looked at me like he could really see me.

All of me.

I felt exposed in a way I never had before, because now the secret I had been keeping for years was right out there in the open.

I liked him so much it scared me.

"You look a little nervous, Emma." I was sure he was right, so I tried to rein in my emotions. Tell myself this wasn't a mistake. He was here with me because he wanted to be, and just because I'd seen him brush off other girls like lint from a sweater. That didn't mean that he was going to do that to me.

He stepped in closer, and I couldn't stop my eyes from running over his sculpted chest.

"Come here, Emma."

Three words, that's how many licks it took to get to the center of my lollypop.

He reached out and pulled me in. I had to look away because my god he was warm, *hard, delicious.* I felt unhinged. Too close to the edge. To desperate for him to touch me and I knew desperation didn't look good on anyone, and it certainly wasn't a look I could pull off.

He lifted my chin and asked if there was something wrong. His lips were so close to mine I could barely focus.

I shook my head, "I don't know. I guess I'm just not sure how to act." Confusion pulled his eyes in, "Have I done something wrong?"

He hadn't. It was the opposite really, being this close to him felt right. *Too right.* Warning bells right, like if it seems too good to be true it probably is sort of right.

"No, I'm just not used to this, and since you didn't call." He interrupted me and asked, "Was I supposed to?" like he really didn't know. I felt silly for bringing it up. "No, you weren't, that's not what I meant. I guess I'm just a little confused, and I don't want to make this more than it is. If that's not what you want."

He leaned in closer, his lips nearly touching mine. "I thought I'd made it clear how I felt, and I didn't call because you didn't."

I nodded and he picked my chin up, "Emma, I'm serious. I think about you all the time."

It was everything I'd ever wanted to hear, but I didn't know what to do with it. He turned and looked back out at the water, "This is my favorite spot. I've never brought anyone else out here, but I wanted to bring you."

When he looked back down at me his eyes were filled with uncertainty, so I told him I thought of him too. He said, "Really?" My eyes rolled, "Yes, all the time."

He stepped in closer, "I wanted to call. I asked Tate for your number and held my thumb over the call button several times."

I looked up at him, *eyes wide and lips parted*, "Why didn't you?" He shrugged in this helpless sort of way, "I don't know, Tatumn and Dani kept talking about how busy you were. I didn't want to mess anything up for you."

I took his hand in mine. "I know you think pretty highly of yourself, but I don't think a phone call would have done that." His lips quirked, "I don't think highly of myself at all, but you don't seem to understand how intimidating it is to want you." I nearly laughed out loud, "I don't know. I think I might have some idea."

He shook his head, "No, I don't think you do."

I had spent four summers watching him navigate the world in a way I would never dare. He was confident, *cool*, and not even in that everyone wants to know you kind of way. He was the kind of cool that people wanted to emulate.

I was a quiet mousy girl on the outside of everything. People barely noticed me, so yes, I knew how intimidating it was to want him.

He lifted my hand to his lips, "You're so good, Emma. You do everything right, all the time. I don't. I never have and I don't even know if I'm capable of it, but I'm trying, because after last year..." A flicker of discomfort passed through his eyes.

"Camden?"

He looked down at me with a remorseful expression. "I can't watch that again, Emma. I know it's selfish and you'd probably be better off with an Alexander, but I want you all to myself."

I knew what I should say, you can have me, you already do. I am more yours than my own. You are the stars in my sky, the sun shining bright on all my darkest places. The mere thought of you is enough to keep me warm at night. Make me believe that all is not lost in this world. That there is hope and safety in small doses in the arms of the one you love. That I could see my entire life unfold in the lines of his face, *shoulders, hips,* but what I said was, "Camden, I'm really not that good."

A bit of humor entered his eyes, "You really don't know?"

He stepped in closer, and I felt my breath catch in my chest. "I'm very smart, and very self-aware, if anyone needs to be intimidated… it's me." His lips quirked and he leaned in to press them to the corner of my mouth, "You're perfect, but so oblivious."

I felt a lot of things at once and was just about to tell him about it, but then he said, "It's a real turn on." I nearly choked, or maybe I did choke but it was just on my own breath.

He ran his lips over mine and pressed them into the other side. "I heard about your poem." My eyes darted up to his, "It wasn't really a big deal, several other students had theirs published too." He kissed me. "Yeah, well, I've never had anything published, and anyway… I guess I just didn't know if you wanted me, in that part of your life."

I'd always felt like I could read him better than any book. Like every thought he had was written out in the soft grey of his irises. I could see them now too, but the hints of hesitation and fear that were layered with hope didn't make much sense to me.

His gaze dropped and I said, "The best parts of my life are the ones with you in it, Camden."

He looked back up at me, "Yeah, mine too."

He asked me if I was still confused and I shook my head, *no*. He tugged on my hand, "Come here, I want to make sure it's very clear for you." I climbed in his lap. He pushed the hair back away from my eyes and looked up at me, "I want you so bad it hurts, Emma."

His hand pressed into the small of my back, lips traveling over my neck, *chest, jaw line.*

It was like he was trying to consume me, one kiss at a time.

^^^^^^

By the time we made it to the party everyone was already drunk. The music was loud, and the air was smoky. Camden and I walked in together and I noticed more than a few people look our way. He leaned down and told me he'd find me in a minute.

I tried not to look bothered. He wasn't asking for my permission, and I knew he shouldn't feel like he needed it anyway.

It was surprising though, and I felt my face change when he said it. His eyes searched mine for a moment and then he kissed me. When he pulled back more people were watching, but he didn't seem to notice. He leaned down and whispered, "Don't get too lost in there. I want you back real soon."

I nodded, even though he was the one leaving and Tatumn walked up. "What was that?" she asked. "I don't know?" Her eyes narrowed, "So are you two like together now?" I

147

shrugged, "No, I don't think so anyway." Her brows rose, "Well, he kissed you, here, in front of everyone. So, I'd say you're something."

Before we'd arrived, I would have said the same thing, but when I saw Camden standing in the center of a group of girls that were obviously into him. I felt like maybe I was wrong.

"I don't know. You know how he is."

Tatumn turned around and followed my eyes over to where he stood, "Such a bloody idiot." she mumbled as she took my hand in hers and dragged me off into the crowd.

When we made it over to the group, Cash called me his summer sunshine and asked me how I was. I was, at the moment, sort of miffed, but I said, *good* and asked him how he'd been. He said, "Drunk. Mostly." and I couldn't help but laugh.

He told me I looked sober. "How would you know, you're too drunk to tell." He nodded in this loose happy way, "True, but I still think you need a drink." I nearly said no, but then I noticed Camden with another girl hanging off of him and remembered the way he'd said I was too good, that I did everything right… and changed my mind.

"Sure, I'll take one."

He took my hand in his and led me over to a line of coolers at the edge of the room. "What do you like, Sweetness?" I had no idea, "Not beer." He pulled out a can of lemonade and handed it to me.

When we made our way back over to the group. Tatumn took my hand and pulled me over to stand beside her, "Cash seems happy to see you."

I looked over at him. He was dancing, *alone*, on top of an end table. "Cash looks happy to see everyone, Tatumn." She shrugged. "So? He's a happy guy. You should still hang out with him later. I know he still likes you."

I took a drink of my lemonade, and even though I knew I shouldn't. I looked around the room to find Camden again. This one was blonde, tanned, and the way she draped her body across his definitely put her in the *I make wrong things right* category. Tatumn took my hand and dragged me outside.

Ethan led us over to the fire pit. We all took a seat on the ground and then Tatumn asked, "How about *Never Have I Ever?*" Ethan gave her a look, which she chose to ignore, and a guy I hadn't met yet said, "Never have I ever kissed a boy."

I watched as all the girls, and two of the boys lifted their cups to their lips. Cash turned to me. "Emma… I believe I qualify as a boy, or are you not drinking because you know I'm a man?"

"What?" I asked feeling confused.

A bright bit of laughter escaped from Tatumn's lips, and she told me if I'd done it, I had to drink. The next person said they'd never gone skinny dipping. I didn't drink, but Tatumn and Ethan did.

When it was my turn I said, "Never have I ever been in love."

Which was a lie. I'd been in love with Camden Pierce since I was thirteen years old, but I didn't take a drink. Tatumn and Ethan were the only ones who did, and it was really cute the way she leaned over and placed a small kiss on his lips when he pulled his cup away.

Camden came to sit beside me and asked what I was doing. I looked over at him, feelings of regret and relief mingling in my chest. His knee brushed against mine, and I pulled my legs in to wrap my arms around them. He gave me a strange look and I turned away.

A few more people took their turns, but I had no idea what they said. I was too focused on him to think about anything else. He leaned in, his lips brushed my ear. "You don't seem to be paying attention. Do you want to go somewhere else?"

I could feel the warmth of his breath as he spoke and when I turned around, he took my hand in his and pulled me up beside him.

As we were walking away, he said, "You seem a little off, are you mad at me?" I felt stupid for being upset about something he didn't even realize he'd done. I shook my head, "No, I'm fine."

He stopped walking and looked down at me, "I don't believe you." I felt like it was pointless. That if he didn't already know why I was upset, then my telling him wouldn't make a difference. He brushed the hair off my cheeks and tucked it behind my ears, looking down at me like I was a puzzle he couldn't solve.

He said, "Tell me, please." and it sounded like he really wanted to know. "It was that girl." He looked confused, "What girl?" I told him it was the one with blonde hair and really tiny shorts on and he said, "Emma, that's like every girl in there." It wasn't, but it was telling that he thought it was.

His eyes searched mine, "Wait, are you jealous?"

I told him I wasn't and tried to walk away, but he pulled me back and kissed me. We were standing in the middle of the yard. Everyone here could see us. I didn't know whether to lean into him or push him away. He seemed to sense my indecision and pressed his hand into the small of my back.

When he pulled away, he said, "I think I like it when you're jealous."

I pushed him away.

He pulled me back in. "No, I'm only kidding, but I do want to kiss you again."

∧∧∧∧∧∧

It was my birthday and all I wanted was some time alone with him. I woke to the sounds of all their voices, singing happy birthday over a plate of freshly made cinnamon rolls with a candle in them.

We all gathered around the table and Camden poured me a cup of coffee and gave me one of his secret smiles, before he turned away and got one for himself. Tatumn insisted on taking me shopping. Dani and Mom came with us, and we ended up spending the entire morning away from the ranch.

Camden was waiting for me when we got back. Sitting on the couch anxiously bouncing his leg. My mom looked over at him and he turned away. I went upstairs to our room to put all my new stuff down, and I knew he would follow me, but I thought he might wait longer than he did.

He closed the door behind him, and my mom called out my name. Both of our eyes went wide, "Put your swimsuit on. I want to take you out."

I nodded and he grabbed his sketchpad and opened the door again. I walked out to the landing at the top of the stairs, "Yeah, Mom?" Her eyes were trailing Camden as he grabbed his bag and headed out the door.

She looked back up at me. I could tell she didn't know what to say. She just didn't want Camden in that room with me. "Oh, just wondering what you wanted for dinner?" she asked, even though it was only noon and we'd just eaten lunch.

"I don't really care. I'm still pretty full right now."

She nodded, "Oh, okay. Well maybe we'll just order in."

My new swimsuit was creamy white with pink and purple flowers on it. I'd picked it out for him. I mean I liked it, but I'd thought about the way he would look at me in it when I tried it on.

He was waiting for me outside, sitting on his bike with the engine running. He took us back up into the mountains and we ended up in the same spot we'd gone to the night of his graduation. It looked different in the light of day. The mountains were always big enough to make me feel small, but they seemed even bigger from up here.

It was just the two of us.

He sat down and looked up at me. I pulled my dress off over my head.

His pupils dilated, and I felt a strange twinge of uncertainty mingle with a bit of desire. I bent over and pulled the sunscreen out of my bag, "Do you mind?"

He rubbed it in slowly, letting his fingers linger on my skin, and dip beneath the fabric of my swimsuit. "I really like this one." he said, and a smile spread out from somewhere deep inside me. When he stopped, I took the tube from him.

"Do you want me to do you?"

He did this cute little quirk with his eyebrows, and I shook my head, "Turn around."

His back was broad, filled with ridges and waves where muscles met skin. Goose bumps rose under my fingertips, and I thought about dragging my hand all the way down his spine, letting my fingers dip into his waistband and linger there for a moment. Feeling his muscles tense and his breath deeper.

I thought, if I was brave enough, I could wrap my fingers around the curve of his hip and pull, just a little. He would press into me, maybe reach over and grab my fingers with his own. He'd say something like, *you have no idea what you do to me, Emma,* and then he'd kiss me. Long and hard, letting his hands wander. I'd say, *yes, Camden, please.*

He looked back at me.

I let go and squeezed some more lotion into my palm. His lips caught mine and I fell forward. My hands pressed into his chest, rubbing across his pecs, and wandering down over his torso.

He had these delicious little stops in his breath.

I wanted to swallow every one of them.

I loved the way his mouth moved over mine. The instant heat that erupted from my center. I pulled away for a moment, just to get a breath, and he said, "Let me." as he picked up the tube of sunscreen and drizzled it on my legs.

He started at my ankles, running his hands over the tops of my feet, *calves, thighs.* The hungry way his eyes followed his hands left me breathless. He leaned over and pressed his lips into mine. I could feel the warmth of the sunshine in the rock beneath me, and his fingers pressing into my skin.

His breath came in slow bursts between kisses and when he pulled away, he said, "You need to prepare yourself, we're getting in there in a little bit." He gave me a look that I wasn't entirely sure how to read, and then he pulled back, reached into his bag, and took out his sketchpad. I turned away and picked up my book.

I loved the way he looked when he was drawing though. The way the muscles in his arms mimicked the movements of his hand. His face, *soft and contemplative*, as he slid the graphite over the paper. Every time the breeze blew the corner of my page up, I looked over at him, and I couldn't help the way my gaze kept lingering.

"You're doing it again." He said without looking up.

"Doing what?" I asked, even though I already knew.

"Staring." He lifted his pencil from the page and turned toward me.

I felt a flush of warmth in my face and turned away. He reached over and put his hand on my knee, "It's alright. I like looking at you too."

He asked me if I was ready to get in. "I don't know, how cold do you think is?" He shrugged. "It's freezing, Emma, but don't worry. I'll keep you warm."

The water was so cold it took my breath away. Camden swam up beside me and wrapped his arms around my waist. His skin always felt good up against mine, but right now with our bodies so wet and slick, pressed up against each other.

It felt nearly sinful.

"See it's not that bad, is it?" His eyes traveled all over my face, and I said, *no*. He leaned in and kissed the curve of my shoulder. "Thanks for getting in. I know you didn't want to."

A drop of water fell from his lashes onto my skin, "Well then, why'd you make me do it?" His hand trailed down my back and he pulled me in tighter, "Because I wanted to do this." A small, "Oh." fell from my lips. He reached down to wrap my legs around his waist and gave me a curious look.

"What is it?"

His eyes darted away from mine. "Really, what is it?" He looked up at me, *apprehension, curiosity, fear* danced in his eyes. I almost said, *Camden, stop you're making me nervous*, but then he asked, "Do you have a boyfriend back home?" I felt a literal shock, a jolt that made my muscles jump.

"No, of course not."

He shook his head, "I didn't mean right now. I know you wouldn't do something like that. I meant have you ever?" I shook my head, *no*. "So, you've never been with anyone else, except for Cash?"

"I wasn't with Cash."

He looked at me like I was lying, "Emma, I saw you kiss him."

"So? You've kissed a lot of other people too."

His eyes shifted away from mine, "Yeah, but that was different."

I asked him how, and he said, "Because it didn't mean anything." like it should have been obvious. I didn't know what he meant by that, but it sounded like he thought my kiss with Cash meant more to me than it had.

"Do you really think I want to be with Cash?"

It took him a moment to answer, but eventually he said, "No. Not really, but sometimes I wonder if maybe you should be. With a guy like him anyway."

"Why would you say that?"

He shook his head, "It's nothing, don't worry about it." It was too late for that, "What do you want to know?" He shrugged. "I don't know. You never really talk about home. I just wondered…"

"Wondered what, Camden?"

He shook his head and reached up to tuck a strand of wet hair behind my ear. "Nothing, really. It's not important." I leaned in closer, and he looked down at my lips. "Camden, tell me." He said, "Really, Emma, let's just drop it."

Disappointment pulled me away from him. I kicked my legs, and he said, "No, don't go." I looked back, "Tell me then." He shook his head, like he really didn't want to, but then he asked, "How much *experience* do you have, Emma?"

Embarrassment, shock, insecurity widened my eyes because the answer was none. I kicked my legs and let my hands skate across the water. "Are you asking me if I'm a virgin?"

He bit his bottom lip and looked at me like I knew exactly what he was asking me. I shook my head in disbelief, and his eyes widened.

"You're not?"

The astonishment in his voice made me say, "No, I am. Obviously I am, but I just can't believe you asked me that." Relief settled his expression, "Why would that be obvious?" I wanted to say, because you've never touched me and I'm not interested in anyone else, but he was really close, and I wasn't brave enough to say something like that anyway.

He moved in closer and wrapped his hands around my hips, "You really don't know how beautiful you are do you?" I shook my head. He leaned in and pressed his lips to the corner of my jaw. "Emma, what have you done to me?"

The way he looked in that moment, *pupil: blown out and dark hair dripping at the sides of his face* was so delicious that I would have done anything he asked. He said, "I want you so badly I can't think of anything else." His fingers dug into my sides, and I pulled my lip in and bit down.

"Don't do that." he begged.

The tone of his voice was so warm I wanted to crawl inside it. Another, *oh*, fell from my lips, this one more breath than sound. His eyes traveled all over my face. He looked down at my lips and I could almost taste him, feel him pressing into me. A swell of desire lifted my chest, and then he pulled away.

It was like ripping off a Band-Aid.

My skin burned from within. The longing in his eyes faded and shame washed over him. "I'm sorry, I shouldn't have said that." I didn't know what I'd done to turn him away. I was just about to say, *no, Camden, I want this*, but then he said, "We don't have to do anything you don't want to. I just want to be with you." and I felt too insecure to say anything at all.

His eyes narrowed in on my lips, and for one hopeful moment I thought he was going to kiss me, but he said, "We need to get out. Your lips are turning blue." I didn't know how that was possible. Embarrassment and desire burned from within me. He turned away and I felt a tremor run through my core.

"I'm serious, get out of there, you're shaking."

He held a towel out for me, and I walked into it. His arms wrapped tightly around my shoulders, and he ran his hands over my back. I nuzzled my face into his neck, and he took my hand in his and pulled me back up onto the rock.

We laid down beside each other and he said, "Come here, Emma. Let me warm you up." He wrapped his arms around me, and I laid my head on his chest. I could hear his heart beating quickly and wondered if he was as nervous as I was.

"Camden?"

"Yeah."

I knew what I wanted to say. I just didn't know how to do it. I felt very conscious of my own need and very wary of his. "What is it, Emma?" I placed my hand over the dip in his chest, feeling his heartbeat beneath my fingertips, "I want you." He squeezed me tighter, "Yeah, I know. I want you too."

My hand moved lower, and his abs tightened. His fingers trailed down my side, over my hip, and onto my leg. I had to close my eyes tight to let the words out, but eventually I said, "I mean right now." His fingers dug into my skin. He rolled me over onto my back and looked down at me.

I was afraid to blink.

His eyes were so intently focused on mine that it was hard to look at them. He ran his fingers over my cheek and tucked a strand of hair behind my ear.

"You're the most beautiful girl I've ever seen."

I wrapped my hand around his hip, "Please, Camden." He shook his head, "No, not like this." He kissed me, slowly, lips dragging over my chest, *shoulders, neck.*

I ran my hands through his hair, "But Camden, this is perfect."

He pulled back, "No, you're perfect, and you deserve better than this."

^^^^^^

The next few weeks passed in a heady daze of stolen touches and glances from across the room. We both knew my mom was watching, and that she didn't approve, but Camden couldn't seem to keep his hands off of me.

He did it discretely, by letting our hips touch when we were getting something from the fridge, or wrapping his finger around mine when I sat the spoon down after stirring my coffee.

We learned not to go upstairs together and spent our days on the couches or the chairs out front. Him with a sketchpad in hand, me with a book.

I started doing yoga with the moms in the morning and Camden sent me simi-lude texts about what positions were his favorite, or how he thought I had real potential as an acrobat. I'd look up from my phone and he would be watching me with this smile I had come to know as all my own.

In the evenings I would say I was going out, *to meet up with Tate, or to get something to eat*, but I would always end up with my arms wrapped around him as he drove or sitting in his lap as he talked with his friends. When we were out, he kissed me, a lot. It didn't matter if we were alone or surrounded by everyone else. He kept me close and when someone asked who I was he'd say, "This is my girl, Emma."

It was more than I ever imagined it could be. I had seen Camden with plenty of girls and then I'd heard the way he'd dismissed them as meaningless distractions. I'd never expected to be more than that. So, when he called me his girl, or let his hand rest on my knee as I sat in his lap and listened to the waves of conversation and music that surrounded us. It felt intoxicating.

I felt invincible with him by my side. Like even though I knew the world was a dangerous place, nothing could harm me so long as I had him.

At night, after Tate and Eli had gone to sleep. He would crawl in my bed and lay next to me. The room was dark, and we knew we had to be quiet, so everything we said came out in a whisper.

He asked me so many questions. He wanted to know about my friends, back home. I told him about Lanie, how we'd been friends since the second grade, and she was the funniest girl I'd ever known.

He said, "Funnier than Tate?" and I said, "Different, dirtier." He told me he didn't believe me. I was too good a girl to like that sort of thing, and I told him I wasn't nearly as good as he thought I was.

He liked to play with my hair. He rubbed the strands between his fingers, tucked it and untucked it from my ears. "Fine, then tell me one bad thing you've done." I had to think about it, and he said, "See." like he knew he had me.

"Hold on, I'm just sorting through them all." He leaned in and pressed his lips to the curve of my neck. "I like how good you are. There's no need to come up with something just to prove me wrong."

My lips pursed, "Once my mom made a pan of muffins for an assembly she was having at school. I ate one without knowing she hadn't made them for us and when she came into the kitchen, she blamed Eli, and I didn't say anything."

He laughed, "Emma, that's not even bad."

"I threw my brother under the bus for a muffin. How is that not bad?"

He ran his thumb over my lip, "You're right. I don't think I can do this anymore, you're just not who I thought you were." I pushed my lip out and he leaned in and kissed me.

Kissing in bed was different.

He could climb on top of me, press me into the mattress with the weight of his body, let his hands go everywhere. He didn't do that though.

He touched me, *kissed me, told me he thought I was beautiful, soft, that he wanted me,* but he never took me. I worried that he didn't want to, so I asked him if he had ever been *with* anyone before. His eyes pulled in at the corners and I could tell he didn't want to answer. I said, "It's okay, I know you have." but it hurt to think about, so I rolled away from him.

"Emma, look at me."

The moonlight was the only light in the room. "I have. Of course I have, but do you really want to hear about that?" I didn't, not really, but I did want to know what that meant for us.

He was so careful with me. So attentive, interested in everything I had to say, but I wanted to know that he wanted me. All of me. "No, I don't think I do, but why don't you want me like that?" He looked confused. "I do want you, but it's just not like that when I'm with you." I felt hurt and unwanted, so I pulled away.

He reached out and ran the back of his fingers over my cheek. "Emma, it's just that with you I want to take my time.

161

I'm not only interested in what comes next. I just like being with you."

I looked over at him, "What does come next?" He tucked a strand of hair behind my ear and let his fingers travel the length of it, "With us?" I nodded. He dragged his thumb over my lower lip and leaned in to kiss me.

"Everything."

I could tell he meant it. He was looking at me with this really serious expression on his face, and while I wanted to believe him. I was leaving in a few days.

"I'm serious. What's going to happen to us when I leave?"

His brows rose, "Nothing, the same thing that always happens when you leave." I told him I didn't want the same thing to happen. I didn't want to go months without speaking to him.

"Then we won't."

11

Now

Emma

I wake up early and head to the river on my own. Tatumn and Ethan are already there unloading the kayaks from the back of Cash's truck.

I ask them if I can help, but then Dani pulls up and tells me to come help her with the coffee and pastries she's brought for everyone.

Camden is sitting in the passenger seat. I do my best not to look at him as I walk up, but I can feel him watching me. I open the back door, and he hops out and opens the other, "This one's for you." he says with a hopeful look in his eyes, and I turn away. "It's a mocha, there's a chocolate croissant in there for you too."

I look back over at him, "Coffee and chocolate, huh?"

He shrugs. "I figured it was worth a shot." He's still looking at me with that same hopeful expression, but I wonder what it is he could be hoping for. He doesn't want me. I've known that for a long time. Is he hoping for friendship? Forgiveness?

I don't know, but I know he left me once and I can literally count the days until he'll do it again. If weren't for the fact that Dani's standing close enough to hear everything I say, I wouldn't be speaking to him at all.

I look away, "Yeah, well, coffee and chocolate only work for very small indiscretions."

He leans in a little closer. "That's okay, I'm willing to do much more."

I know he's trying to get me to look at him, but I just nod and say, "Dani's waiting on these." as I pick up the stack of boxes and turn to walk away.

"No, Emma wait."

I can hear the urgency in his voice, and I notice Dani's expression change, so I stop and look back at him. He tells me he just wants to talk to me. "We don't have anything to talk about, Camden."

It's a lie. I know it is, but I also know that he's leaving, and the less we talk the better off I'll be when that happens. His face falls and I have to fight the urge to comfort him. I tell myself it doesn't mean anything. He's here for the wedding, just like everyone else, and we don't have to do this.

He gives me a serious look, "So, you're just going to keep avoiding me all week then." I pretend to think about it for a moment, "Yeah, I am."

He says, "It's been two days." like that's long enough and I should just get over the fact that he walked out on me and never looked back. I feel the way my face contorts around the audacity of his comment. "Two days?"

The lids of his eyes drop and his jaw flexes, "I know that compared to how long it's been, that's not very long, but Emma… I can't be this close to you and not talk to you." There's a bit of pressure in his voice. Dani looks up at us.

I keep my voice low, "You don't need to stay so close."

"I can't help myself."

"You should try. For me, and for the sake of everyone else around us." He looks at me like I'm the one that broke his heart. I look back over toward Dani, she's pretending not to listen, but she's so close I know she heard.

"I don't think I can leave you alone, but if that's what you really want, I can try."

I think about it for a moment. I know that I don't actually want him to leave me alone, but I don't like the thought of being close to him either. It makes me feel weak. Vulnerable. I look back up at him, "Yeah, that's what I want, and we both know you're more than capable of it."

His eyes pull in and he looks away from me. I can tell he's hurt. That for some reason, even though we've spent years apart, the thought of having to stay away from me now hurts him. Or maybe it's not that he has to stay away. Maybe it's that I've asked him to, and that means he can't be the one to leave. It's much more likely to be a power struggle within himself than to actually have anything to do with me.

I step back and close the door with my hip. As I'm walking away, he comes up beside me and reaches over to take the boxes from my hands. "I'm fine. I don't need your help." He nods, "I know."

Dani offers me a chocolate doughnut and a sympathetic look. I take the doughnut and walk over to Tate. Her eyes light up and she asks for a bite. I hold the doughnut out for her, and she looks at my other hand, "Where's the coffee?" I look back over at Camden. He's leaning on the back of the truck looking at me. "I had to refuse it on principle." She gives me a puzzled look.

Camden walks over to us and his eyes dart to the doughnut in my hand. He says, "Here, take it. I know you want it." as he holds out the mocha latte for me. I tell him I really don't, and Tate says, "I'll take it." His eyes roll, but he says, "Fine." and hands it to her.

She takes one drink and looks over at me. "This is delicious, here Emma, taste it." I reach out and take it from her. "Yeah, that is pretty good." She looks back out at the boys. "You can have it. I'll go get one of my own in a minute."

Camden frustratedly bites his lower lip. "You know you could have just taken it. Dani's the one that bought it anyway." I shrug innocently, "I'm just trying not send any mixed signals." He shakes his head, "Believe me. You're not." Tatumn walks back over. "Emma, I brought you a croissant, let me have your doughnut, I know you like these better." I look away from Camden, "Yeah, sure."

He walks off with a sour look on his face, and Tate says, "This is going to be more fun than I thought." I tell her it's not fun, that I want to go home, and I'll just see her at the ceremony. She looks at me with a worried expression, "Don't." I tell her I'm not really going to, but I do want to, badly. She looks over at Camden. "This week isn't supposed to be about him, it's about us."

I give her a funny look, "You mean you and Ethan?" Her lips purse, "Well, that's what he thinks, but no. I mean you and me." She looks over at me and I say, "Well, isn't everything?" She nods and takes a bite of her doughnut. "You'll be with Eli on the float. It'll be like Camden's not even here." I know that's not true, but I say, alright, and she walks over to Ethan.

Our float guide shows up, and after Dani has plied him with coffee and doughnuts, he goes over the rules. They're pretty basic, don't fall in. If you do, get back out.

I finish my latte and throw it in the bin beside Dani's truck. We all put our life jackets on and then the guide tells us to line up next to our kayaks. I go stand at the front of one and wave Eli over. He says, "I'm not with you. Dani asked me to go with her." and walks right by me.

Everyone else is already walking to the water. Tatumn and Ethan already have their boat in. I stand there alone for a moment, hoping he'll just do the decent thing and sit this one out, but he walks up and says, "Looks like it's just you and me."

I think about walking away, maybe feigning a stomachache on account of the coffee and chocolate he brought for me. Tatumn looks back over her shoulder, and even though her eyes are wide with apology.

I know I have to go.

I pick up the front of the boat and Camden tells me to climb in first so he can hold it steady for me. I walk in the water and put my hands down on either side of the bow. I say, "Go ahead, get in."

He gives me a petulant look and puts his hands down on the stern, "Emma, just get in, this is ridiculous. We both know you're more likely to fall." I tell him he doesn't know anything about me, or what I'm more likely to do, and that I could be a professional kayaker for all he knows.

He looks at me skeptically. "A drunk driver and a professional kayaker, is there anything else I should know?"

"There's loads more."

"Well, I'm all ears."

I shake my head, tell him we don't have time for that, and he looks right at me, "I'm not getting in this boat until you're sitting down." There's enough determination in his voice to know that he means it. It makes me want to dig my heels in. Refuse him. Walk away and leave him standing there wondering where I've gone.

I get in the boat, but I don't do it for him. I do it for Tatumn. The lower half of my legs are cold and wet from being submerged in the river, but the sun is out and there's a bright spot of warmth on my upper arm that I focus on to keep myself from looking back at him.

He pushes his oar roughly against the shore to get us going. We had a decent winter, but it's still early in the season so the river is moving like it always does, but it's not rushing yet. I put my oar in and press back on it, helping him propel us forward.

He asks me if I've ever been on a plane before. I don't want to talk to him, but it seems rude not to answer, so I nod and tell him, *yes*. "You know in the beginning, before the plane takes off, when the stewardess stands in the aisle to give that safety presentation." I shrug. "They always tell you that if you're traveling with someone you need to put your air mask on first."

I think I know where he's going with this, but I don't want to hear it. "I didn't realize how badly I was suffocating here until after I'd been gone for a long time." The rawness in his voice makes me turn back to face him. "It was a really different place when you weren't here." I feel my eyes pull in and turn back around.

I want to tell him that I know, it's not the same place without him here either, but then he says, "When I first left, I could barely breathe. I couldn't sleep. Every time I closed my eyes I saw you, and I knew I'd let you down. I'd hurt you and I hated myself for it, but then I'd think about my mom and everything she was wrapped up in, and I knew I couldn't come back."

"It felt like my entire life changed in a single moment. I knew what I wanted, but you had a good life, and I wasn't going to be the one to take that from you. I was really angry about it though. It took a long time, and a lot of therapy, but I finally learned to breathe for myself."

"I made a life full of good things. Things I was proud of. I thought that would make it better. Prioritizing my own needs. Forgiving myself, and my mom, and it did, a little, but it also left all this empty space in my head, and all I had to fill it with was thoughts of you." I feel myself grimace and he says, "Being alone isn't all it's cracked up to be."

My head darts in his direction, "But you weren't alone. You had Gabby." He leans forward and pushes his oar back. "Yeah, I know, but that's not what I mean. In fact, sometimes I think I felt lonelier with her there, especially after she met Jordan. It just felt like I was in the way all the time."

I put my oar back in the water and press against it. "Yeah, I think I know what you mean. I feel like that with Tate sometimes." He catches the rhythm of my oar and we both move from one side to the other. "Yeah, but you've known

Tate your whole life. She loves you like a sister, and you have Dani and your mom too." I nod, "I know, but that doesn't mean I don't ever feel alone."

I hear the sound of his oar pressing against the water to slow us down, "Do you feel alone right now?" I don't, not when I'm with him, but I say, "Yeah, more than ever. Tate's leaving in a few days and Agatha's going with her." He says, "You like her, don't you?" I glance back and notice the way he's leaning in, waiting for my answer.

"Yeah, Agatha's really easy to love."

A slow press against his oar.

"You're really cute with her." He says quietly, like he knows he shouldn't say it at all. My chest tightens and it feels like a warning sign, a black flag on the beach telling me not to go further.

"Well, we spend a lot of time together." I hear the soft sound of his oar pressing into the water again. "Yeah, I can tell." We both press against our paddles, and the boat moves forward with the current. "So, you're nervous, about them leaving?" My shoulders tense and he says, "Never mind, you don't have to answer that."

It feels easier to talk to him like this, with his voice just floating up behind me. I can't see him, but I can tell by the caution in his voice that he feels how tenuous our situation is. I pull my paddle into my lap. "I am, but I'm also happy for them. I mean the ranch is going to feel really empty, but Tate's happier than she's been in years. So, I just try to think about that."

"You know it's okay to think about yourself sometimes too."

My nose wrinkles. "No, that doesn't sound right."

He says, "Emma." and the tone of his voice brings the tightness back. He pulls his oar into his lap and the boat slows.

"Why won't you look at me?"

I know what he means, but I tell him I can't, I have to watch the river. "I don't mean right now." I push my oar into the water to pull us forward. I don't want to answer him, but he says, "I know you're upset. You have every right to be, but Emma…" I shake my head and squeeze the oar so tight that it stings the skin of my palm, "It's just easier that way, Camden."

"It's not for me. I find it really hard not to look at you."

I can't help but turn to look back over my shoulder at him, just to see if he's serious. He is, but he's also just sitting there, coolly holding the end of his oar and looking at me like he knew I'd turn around.

"You can't say things like that to me anymore."

He leans in, "Yeah, well I can't not say them either."

I switch sides and do a couple of quick strokes to get us going again. It feels like I'm being swept away on a dangerous current and I don't like it.

I notice a group of rocks in the distance and try to get control of the direction the boat is going in. I tell him to be ready and he says, "I am." I can tell by the tone of his voice that he's not talking about the river. So, I say, "Seriously, Camden, let's just get through this." and he tells me that's what he's trying to do.

We hit the rocky area. I submerge my paddle in the water to steer us through. He leans away from me and puts his oar in on the other side. Our boat is swaying with the current, but the water is moving just fast enough to make maneuvering difficult.

I tell him there's a small drop off up ahead, and he tells me to pull my oar up. I do it, but not quickly enough, and when we go over the edge our boat tilts and I fall out.

At first all I feel is cold and wet, but then a wave of humiliation washes over me. I kick my legs and press off the rocks behind me.

When I break through, I hear him shouting my name. He sounds panicked, so I wave my hand in the air, and he swims over to me. He takes my hand in his and pulls me out of the rolling current beside the rocks.

When we're free of all the rough waves and no longer in danger of going under, he turns around and says, "You scared me." I feel bad for it, but I shrug and say, "I did that on purpose. It was too hot in the boat."

He swims in closer. "Oh yeah, is that a trick of the trade?"

I nod, "Yeah, all the best kayakers use it."

The corner of his lips pick up, and I say, "You know you didn't have to jump in after me." He gives me a thoughtful look. "Yeah, I did."

His voice is too sincere, body too close, eyes too open. Why does he have to be so attractive? Wet lips and sparkling eyes. He's wearing a bloody lifejacket, and all I can see is the bulge of his bicep and the water dripping down his neck. I want to lick it off of him and I hate myself for it.

He has no right to look at me like that. No right to stand so close or be so bloody sincere. He jumped out of the boat to rescue me. He shouldn't have done that.

"Well, it was a rookie mistake because now we don't have a boat." His eyes go wide for a moment, but I can tell he already knew that.

He gets this really serious expression on his face, like he's planning something, or maybe he's acting out something he's already planned and tells me he did it on purpose.

I know what he's doing. Standing so close, smirking, disarming me with his smile. I ignore it. "Really, is that a trick of the trade?"

He reaches up and brushes the hair off my cheek. My traitorous body reacts accordingly, warmth and tension moving out from his fingertips to my toes.

I'm still trying to work out how his touch can feel so foreign and familiar all at the same time when he says, "Yeah, it's common knowledge, but only the best know how to use it to their advantage."

He looks up. The sunshine catches in the droplets of water on his lashes. I say, "I feel like it's a disadvantage." and he wraps his arm around my waist.

"No. It's not."

I know I should push him away, but I can feel the warmth radiating from his body to mine, and it feels good. *Right. Natural.* I feel the moments of indecision between us and tell myself not to do anything stupid. Not to kiss him. Or let him kiss me, but then he looks down at my lips and I forget.

Everything.

He smells like river water and sunshine. His skin is slick, and his lips are parted. He looks at me, and I can see him trying to decide. Struggling with what the right thing to do is, but then his eyes close, and I'm not sure which one of us leans in first.

His lips move over mine as he pulls me tight up against him. I feel his hand in my hair. Fingertips on my neck, dragging along my arms, gripping at my hips.

He's so wet and delicious that I can't stop. I don't want to, but then he pulls back and runs his thumb over my lower lip. It's a hungry move and I love it, but it gives me just enough room to think. I ask, "What are we doing?"

His breath is heavy.

I can feel my pulse in my fingertips.

He leans in again. Our lips press together, and I let him kiss me because for the first time in a long time I don't feel hollow inside, but then I realize that I have felt hollow, and that he's leaving again.

There's a ripping sensation in my core as I pull away from him and swim toward the shore.

He follows me saying things like, *Emma wait, what happened, is something wrong?* I don't look back, but I tell him everything's wrong, "Don't you know that already?"

"I do, but Emma I've tried staying away from you and I can't do it anymore."

My eyes fill with angry tears, and I reach up to wipe them away.

"How can you say that? You know you're leaving."

I hear all the water rush off of him as he stands to follow me out. I tell him, "Don't. I can't do this." He asks me what I mean, and only because I know it's the only way to stop him. I tell him the truth.

"I can't handle losing you twice, Camden."

He stops. "You never lost me. You don't have to lose me, Emma."

I turn around to look at him. It's a mistake. His face is tortured, lips in a pout. His body wet and glistening in the sunshine, ripples of water lapping against his legs.

I nod, "Yeah, I did, and I already have."

^^^^^^

Camden

I watch as she gets out of the water and takes off her life jacket. The shirt she has on beneath it clings to her body, and she strips it off and stands there before me in nothing but a light pink bikini top and a pair of shorts. I know I'm staring, but the way the sun is glistening off her skin is hard to look away from.

Her eyes are red, and I can tell she's panicking, but she just looks down the river and says, "We should probably get going. It's going to take a lot longer to walk to the end than it would have to float." I tell her we don't need a boat. We can just float down on our life jackets. She looks down river, "Do you really think that'll work?"

I want to say, *stop, sit down with me, let's talk about this,* but her face is stony, and her eyes are cold, "Yeah, I know it will."

She looks down at her wet shirt lying on the ground like it's the biggest problem she has to solve, and she doesn't have the energy to deal with it. I say, "Just leave it off." and she gives me an incredulous look. "You should at least try not to sound so salacious when you speak to me." I nod, abashed, and look up at her.

"Trick of the trade... sorry, it just comes out like that."

Her face hardens. "You shouldn't have kissed me." I disagree. I think I should have kissed her *sooner, longer, more often.*

"I didn't."

She looks at me like she doesn't have the patience to deal with me. "Fine, but you did kiss me first." Her cheeks go pink. I want to run my fingers over them to feel the warmth beneath her skin. She looks away from me, "Well, it was a mistake, and it can't happen again."

She leans over to pick up her shirt, submerges it in the water to clean it off, steps in, and pulls her life jacket out in front of her. She lays the shirt down across it and then starts walking out into the river. "We really do need to go. They'll be worried if they find our boat before we do." I nod and swim over to her. I tell her she'd be safer if she put her life jacket on and she gives me an exasperated look.

"I don't know. I think I'd still be in a fair amount of danger."

I can tell by the way she says it that I'm the danger she's worried about. She lays down on her stomach and spreads her arms out in front of her. I reach out and take hold of her ankle and she turns back to face me.

I know she wants me to let her go, but I say, "I can't risk losing you to the current." She releases a small huff of air and turns back around.

Her skin feels so soft and slick in my palm that I have to make myself press into her just to keep my hand from wandering. Tension builds in her calf as she tries to pull away and panic rises up in my chest.

I say, "I don't think it was a mistake." and she doesn't even turn around before she begins chastising me. "Camden you're leaving, and you only came for Tatumn's wedding anyway so let's just try not to ruin that."

I want to tell her that she's wrong. I didn't come for the wedding, and I'll stay if she wants me to. She's too upset to hear it though, and I really don't think it was a mistake.

I let go of her leg and swim up beside her, reach out to take her hand, and tell her, her leg's too slick to hold onto. She says, "You don't have to hold onto me. I'll be fine on my own." I know it's true. She is fine. I can tell by the way she holds herself, but I'm not.

There hasn't been a single day in the last five years that I haven't thought of her. Every time something good happened to me, I wanted to tell her about it. When I had a bad day at work, or an assignment really frustrated me, I wished she was there to help me through it. I missed her in my bed, at the breakfast table, on the sidewalk.

The last year's been the hardest. Talking to Dani so much, hearing about her. I couldn't help but ask, but everything she told me just made me miss her more.

I know she doesn't want to talk to me, but I also know that every time I walk in the room she looks away. Before I got here, I told myself that whatever happened between us would be her choice, and I know it's a ridiculous reason to hope, but it feels like she's *trying* to avoid me. Like there's a reason she has to look away. I can tell she's hurt, and I know I shouldn't have left her, but if after all this time she still has to try, *to look away, to avoid me.*

That has to mean something.

I haven't let go of her hand, but she won't look over at me. She's kicking her legs too hard, trying to pull away without ever letting go. She's going to get tired, and I know she won't talk to me if she can see me looking at her, so I tell her to roll over on her back and give me her other hand.

She looks at me skeptically, "No, we won't be able to see the rapids." I look out at the smooth expanse of water before us and say, "I'm pretty sure we've made it through the rockiest part."

She gives me a doubtful look, obviously about to say, *no,* and pull her hand away from me, but I can't let that happen. She hasn't lost me, and I can't let her think that. I roll over on my back and let her hand twist through my fingers.

She looks down at our hands clasped together and flinches. It hurts, but I reach up and hold my other hand out for her to take. She looks at it like it's a lizard, about to flip over and come after her.

I don't know what to do. I can't let her go, but I have no idea how to make her stay. I tighten my hand around her other palm and close my eyes to let the sunshine warm my face.

I can feel the way she's watching me and the thought of looking back at her is so tempting it's hard to ignore. She says, "Did I really kiss you first?" Her voice is so full of shame and embarrassment that I want to tell her *no, it was all me,* but I need her to trust me, so I nod.

"Sorry about that."

The remorse in her voice turns my face toward her, "You don't need to apologize. I was definitely going to kiss you. You just beat me to it." Her cheeks lift and I can almost see the smile she's trying to hide.

I lift my hand out to her again and this time she flips over. Her fingers twist in mine and she reaches out to take it. I pull her in closer and we float along with our hands intwined and our heads resting next to one another's.

I want to reach over, turn her face to mine and kiss her again, but the current in the river is tortuous and we seem to be floating too close to the edge. She says, "I don't understand."

I kick my legs and steer us back toward the center. "Sure, you do." She shakes her head, "No, I really don't. You left, and you're not coming back." She says it like a fact, and it takes all of my self-control not to tell her she's wrong. That I would never leave again if I thought she still wanted me here.

"I'm here now, and you know why I left."

"I'm not sure if I do."

"Well, it wasn't because I wanted to leave you, so I hope you don't think that." Pain pulls her face in, "What else am I supposed to think?" There's a really vulnerable look in her eyes and I hate that I put it there.

"Emma, things were so bad back then. I wasn't myself, and when everything happened, all I could think about was you. I didn't want to hurt you, or leave you, but I had to. It was the only way I knew to keep you safe."

She says, "Safe from what?" and I tell her, *me... mostly*. She nods, like she understands, but I can tell she doesn't like it. "Am I safe now?" I look up at the clouds, "I don't know, but you're not in the same sort of danger you were back then." She tilts her head, and a bit of her hair brushes up against my skin.

"Was it always New York?"

I look over at her, "No, I spent the night in Minneapolis and stayed at a hostel in Cleveland for a while." She turns to look at me, "But you never lived anywhere else?" I shake my head and feel the slick heat from her cheek up against mine.

"Does it feel like home?"

I press my arms out further, feeling the way her fingers grip onto mine. I want to tell her she's the only thing that's ever felt like home, but I know better than that. "New York's not home." She gives me a questioning look, "But you do like it there?" I can tell by the measured tone of her voice that she's trying to work something out.

"It seemed like a good place to disappear."

She leans her head back and I watch as she chews on her lower lip.

"You wanted to disappear?"

I can hear how much it hurts her to say that, so I tighten my hand around hers, "I didn't want to, but I needed to, at least for a little while." Her eyes close. "Is five years a little while?" I press my hand into hers, "No, five years is a really long time." She nods.

"I've wanted to come back ever since I left. I was just too scared to do it." She lets her head fall to the side and rests her cheek up against mine.

"What were you afraid of?"

I press my hand into hers and hold on tighter. "I don't know. Everything." She nods and I close my eyes to concentrate on the way her skin feels up against mine.

I know I'm living on borrowed time. That the moment we find the others, she'll walk away, and she won't look back.

Fear makes everything about this moment feel important.

I try to memorize the exact way her hand curves around my own. The feeling of her head next to mine and her body stretching out behind me. She's speaking in this low tone, filled with curiosity and uncertainty. I want to tell her she doesn't need to be so unsure of herself, *or me*, but trust isn't something you can ask for, so I just count myself lucky that she's this close and hold on a little tighter.

She presses her palm into mine, "What about now?" I think I know what she's asking, but I'm not sure she's ready to hear the truth. I think about telling her that I never want to leave. That I want to wake up with her by my side every day for the rest of my life, but I say, "What do you mean?"

She turns toward me and runs her teeth over her lower lip. "Do you want to disappear right now?" I don't, not unless I can disappear with her beside me.

"No."

"What about in a few days, are you going to disappear then?"

The water rushes over our hands. "I don't know Emma. Do you want me to?"

^^^^^^

Emma

I'm still pondering the true meaning of his question and whether or not I should answer honestly, when we hear the others. I roll over and see Tatumn jumping up and down on the riverbank. She starts walking toward me and I swim off and leave Camden behind.

Our boat is pulled up next to all the others. She tells me that they were just trying to decide who should stay here and who should go looking for us.

"Well, there's no need for that now, we're here." She looks at me like she can see his kiss on my lips, "You two looked pretty close." I shrug, "Yeah well, it must have been a mirage." She nods and we both walk out of the water.

I know she wants to say more, but I don't want to talk to her about him. Or actually I do, but I know she won't understand. He left me. *She told me to ignore him.* I can't.

I turn around and see the guys gather around Camden. He tells them that we fell in at the drop off and the boat floated away. Tatumn says, "You fell in way back there, no wonder it took you so long."

There's a hint of accusation in her voice, but I just say, "Really, did it?" and she gives me a suspicious look.

"What happened?"

I try to turn away and she grabs my arm, "Did you jump out of the boat to get away from him?" I suppress a smile, "No, I fell out." Her eyes narrow.

"What are you're not telling me?"

I don't mean to do it, but our kiss flashes through my mind, and I reach up to cover my lips.

Her eyes settle on the tips of my fingers and then she looks over at him. "Did something happen between you two?" She sounds genuinely curious, but her voice is too tense for me to answer honestly. Camden looks over at me with a tentative smile on his face.

"No, nothing happened."

She says, "Emma." in this authoritative tone that makes me look over at her. Her eyes search mine, "Isn't he leaving?" I shrug, "I don't know, maybe." She looks over at him and then turns back to me with an anxious expression on her face.

"I hope you know what you're doing."

"I have no idea what I'm doing. I didn't even know he was coming, but he's here now and so far, he's been pretty hard to avoid." Her eyes dart to the side, "But you still want to?" I don't. I know I don't, but I say, "Yeah, of course I do."

She gives me a careful look and I know I'm not going to like whatever it is she's about to say. I start walking off, toward the trailer where Alissa and the guys are loading up. She says, "You still love him." like she knows it's the truth.

I have always, and will always love him, but I say, "No. I don't."

12

Camden texted me before I'd even made it home. It was just three words, *miss you already*, but it felt big. We spent most evenings on the phone. Him telling me about how he was becoming the foremost barista in Gallatin Gateway, and me telling him the quickest way to a girl's heart was coffee and chocolate. He said he thought he could come up with something better, and I told him I couldn't wait to see what that was.

If Mom asked, I told her I was talking to Lanie or Grace and sometimes she believed me, but others I could tell she didn't.

Camden started making moody soundtracks for the coffee shop he worked at, and he sent me a new song every day. He said it didn't matter how far apart we were, he felt closer to me than he did to anyone else even when I was hundreds of miles away.

Lanie and Grace both started dating and they teased me that I was having a love affair with my phone. It didn't feel like that though. I had never had so much of him before, and it felt real.

I liked talking to him, hearing the energy in his voice when he'd just woken up and the fatigue after a long day of work. Sometimes when we were both tired, we would just lay in our own beds with our phones pressed to our ears, listening to each other breathe or saying things like, *I miss you* or *I wish you were here.*

My mom invited the Hamiltons over, obviously trying to set me up with their son. Jerimiah and I had gone to the same elementary school. He was tall with shaggy blonde curls, and his mother did Pilates with mine.

When they left, I asked, "So does that mean I can date now?" She got this far off look in her eyes and lifted one shoulder, "You can date, Jerimiah."

I didn't want to date him, and she knew that. "What if I want to date someone else?" She stood up from the table and walked into the kitchen. I followed her and she said, "Camden?" in this distasteful tone that made my jaw clench tight. I didn't answer.

She went over to the sink and turned the water on. "He's too old for you, Emma." I picked a platter up off the island and brought it over to her. "No, he's not." She took it from me. "He lives too far away. You'd never even see each other." I wanted to say, *then what are you worried about,* but I knew she wouldn't appreciate it.

"That's not true, and I plan to apply to MSU in the fall anyway." She dropped the fork she was holding, "Really?" She sounded so shocked I almost wanted to deny it, but I just nodded, "Yeah, Montana has always felt more like home than here."

When I told Camden about Jerimiah, he said, "I don't know maybe she's right." I told him no, she wasn't, and besides, I already had a boyfriend. He asked me if that's what he was. I hesitated, but I said, "Well, I thought so." and he went quiet.

"Camden, is something wrong?"

I could hear the careful way he was breathing through the phone. "No, not with us anyway." I asked him what he meant by that. "I don't really want to talk about it." The distance between us made me feel helpless and the distance in his voice made him feel very far away. I told him that whatever it was, he could tell me, and he said, "Emma, please. Let's just talk about something else."

My dad left in the spring. He sat Mom and I down and said, "She's old enough to know the truth." Mom gave him a shifty look. He said, "I'm in love with someone else. I have been for a long time, but your mother and I felt it was best to wait to tell you. We wanted to give you stability while you were growing up, but your brother's gone, and you're old enough to understand love now."

It felt like a mean thing to say to someone you were leaving and I tried not cry when he told me he was in love with a man named Josiah.

It was strange watching the easy way that my mother absorbed his words. Once he was gone and it was just us at the house, I asked her how long she'd known. Her eyes shifted away from mine, "A while." I told her that wasn't fair, that they shouldn't have pretended for us. She seemed to think about it, "Well, when you have children, you'll do better than we did."

187

I didn't know what she meant by that, but I asked her if she'd ever loved him. She picked up her book from the side table and started thumbing through the pages. "I still do. It's just that my definition of love has changed."

It shouldn't have been so heart breaking, hearing her talk about her husband like that, but it was. Eli had gone to college in California. Mom told him over the phone. I could hear the shock in his voice from my seat on the couch.

Josiah was a baker. He owned a shop in downtown Naperville. When I came over, he always had treats laid out on the counter for me. I decided I liked him, and it was obvious that Dad was happier with him than he ever was with us.

When I told Camden about it, he asked me if I was alright, and said "That sounds rough." I told him I was, most of the time, but sometimes I felt sad, for my dad. I wished that he hadn't left, or more so I wished that he hadn't wanted to, but I also hated that he'd felt like he had to stay. Camden said, "Yeah, families are hard sometimes." I asked him how his mom was, and his voice got quieter.

"Not good."

I went to prom with Jerimiah, and Camden asked for a photo of me in my dress. I propped my phone up on my dresser and stood in front of the window. He told me I looked too beautiful to be going out with another man. "We're just friends. Jerimiah has a girlfriend in Indiana."

He paused and released a slow breath. "I wish I was there to take you." I told him I knew that was a lie. "It's not." I leaned down to do the buckle on my shoe. "Camden, you hate dancing."

A small hum passed through the receiver, "Not with you."

∧∧∧∧∧∧

Camden was sitting on the tailgate of Dani's truck when we arrived. It was a sunny day, and the vivid blue of the sky surrounded him as he sat there looking out at us. Seeing him felt like taking a deep breath after being held under water for a very long time.

Tate ran out on the porch, followed by Dani, and Mom turned around and looked at me like it was my fault he was out there. I was still looking at him, but I sure hoped she was right.

I opened the door and walked over to him. He didn't kiss me. Not on the lips anyway. He took my hand in his and lifted it up. He looked me in the eyes and said, "That took forever." as he pressed a kiss into the skin of my palm. Tate wrapped her arms around me and said, "It's our senior year. This is going to be best summer of our lives."

I could feel it too, the promise of endless warmth and days by the river. Mom came over and Camden said, "Hi, Amber." She gave him a stern look and turned to me. "So, this is happening?" I tried to make my face as expressionless as possible, but I nodded and he said, "I sure hope so."

Mom looked over at Dani, who was obviously trying to hide a grin. "Well, I guess it's a step up from the sneaking around you did with her last year."

∧∧∧∧∧∧

Camden was appalled that I still hadn't learned to drive, and being openly together meant we had much less freedom at the ranch.

He took me out to the middle of nowhere and gave me very little instruction, before he left me sitting on the front of his bike, and looked at me like I should know what to do. He said, "You already know how to balance." I shook my head, "No I don't, and I'm sure the moment I lift my feet this thing is going to fall over."

He walked back over and stood in front of me, legs straddling the wheel and hands draped over mine. "Don't stand there. I don't know what I'm doing." His lips lifted playfully, "That's okay. I do." I gave him a serious look, "Listen, I've seen a lot of videos online labeled *why women live longer than men,* and this is about to be one of them."

He shook his head, "Emma, you can do this, just twist the handle and look at the horizon."

The horizon in Montana wasn't a straight line. It was bumpy and jagged. I looked out at it, and he stepped out of the way. The first time I turned the handle it wasn't fast enough, and I felt the bike wobble beneath me. Camden ran along beside me saying things like, *that's it, you've got it, give it some more,* but it didn't feel safe without him in front of me.

I released the handle and came to a stop. He ran over. "That was so good, Emma. You've nearly got it." I looked at him like I knew he was lying. "Can't you just get on here with me?"

"No, it's easier with one person, but when you get it down, I'll let you take me for a ride." He reached up and ran his thumb over my lower lip. I leaned in to kiss him. He put the helmet back on my head and I tried again. The second time was easier. I made it all the way to the end of the road.

He came running up behind me, hair blown back and shirt clinging to his chest. "I knew you could do it. Now, do you think you can turn it around on your own?" The way he was looking at me, like he believed I could, made me nod, but I ended up in the grass with one foot down and a very heavy bike leaning up against my leg.

He ran over, pulled me upright, and climbed on behind me. He wrapped his arms around mine. "It's really not that much different than riding a bike. You just have to lean into it." I told him I didn't know how to ride a bike, and he said, "Seriously?" like it was some sort of crime. He pressed his hands over mine.

"Don't worry, we'll do it together."

He got us back on the road and then put the kickstand down. "You did good." I took my helmet off. "Camden, I fell over in a field."

He shrugged, "I know, but it was your first time." My eyes rolled, "I hope it was my only time." He said, "No, we'll try again." as he leaned in and pushed the hair off the back of my neck.

He was close enough that I could feel the heat of his breath spread out over my skin as he spoke. "I like the way you look on my bike." I turned to face him, and even though the look in his eyes was very tempting, I said, "I'm not interested in playing out whatever pin up fantasy you have in mind."

He let out this breathy sort of laugh that shot straight to my core. "You're the only girl I have pinned up in my room." I couldn't tell if he was serious or not, so I said, "I had no idea you were so good at photoshop."

He told me it was more of a cut and paste job as he let his lips drag over the back of my neck. My shoulders tightened. Breath caught in my chest. His fingers grazed over the fabric of my leggings and a whimper crossed my lips.

He told me that he needed me, and that everything was better when I was with him.

∧∧∧∧∧∧

For my birthday Camden said he wanted to take me out on a real date. Tate told him she wouldn't have it and then looked at me and said, "I *will* see you later." like it was an order I had to follow. He booked a reservation at one of those places in Bozeman with exposed brick walls and industrial iron accents all over the place.

The dress I wore was light blue with thin straps and a ruffle at the bottom. When I stepped out of our room, he was looking up at me with wide appreciative eyes. He said, "You look really beautiful." in this dry raspy tone that made my core clench tight.

He looked good too, his hair was freshly washed and pushed back with some product that made it shine and come apart in pieces that fell around his eyes. He drove us into town and took my hand in his as he led me into the restaurant.

We were seated on opposite sides of the table, and the whole thing felt odd. The lighting was really dim and there were people all around us holding wine glasses and having quiet conversations. He asked if I knew what I wanted and I said, "World peace and a dog named Willow that will sit with me while I read." He looked down at the menu.

"You don't need to be nervous, Emma. It's just dinner."

"I'm not nervous, about dinner." He looked up from his menu, "Are you saying I make you nervous?" I shook my head, *no*, but it wasn't true. "I think it's just this place."

His eyes narrowed, and he looked around the room, "You don't like it?" I could tell he wanted me to like it, so I shook my head. "No, it's really nice. It's just that I don't know how to do this."

His lips ticked up at the corner and he asked me what I meant. I told him that it felt like a lot of pressure, "You know with the lights and the fancy napkins you're supposed to put in your lap."

His eyes smiled. "I can ask the waitress for paper napkins. I'm sure they have some at the bar." I nodded, "Yeah, could you?" He put his menu down. "Emma, I just wanted to do something nice for you. If you don't like it, we can leave."

I knew he didn't want to leave, and I didn't want to make him feel bad, so I said, *no*, and he said, "Would it help if I came to sit beside you?" I looked around the room, there were couples everywhere, but the ones seated at little tables like ours were all facing one another. "No, but maybe just don't stare at me while I'm reading my menu."

When the food came, he asked me if he was allowed to look at me while I ate. I spread my napkin out over my lap. "I'd rather you not." He picked up his knife. "That's too bad, I like to look at you." My cheeks flushed and I reached out to take a drink of my water.

When we left, he took me back out into the mountains. He kissed me before we'd even made it off of the trail. He held my face in his hands and said, "It's just us now. You can't feel awkward anymore, and I'm going to look at you all I want."

He took my hand in his and led me over to the water's edge. He peeled his shirt off and slid both boots off his feet. I watched as he reached down to undo his belt.

His pants dropped and I felt my eyes go wide. I didn't really want to, but I turned away. Looked out into the trees, up at the stars, anywhere but right at him.

"What's the matter, Emma?" His teasing tone made me want to turn back around. I knew that's what he wanted though, so I said, "Nothing. Just not sure what you're doing." as I studied his shadow on the ground.

He let out a breathy noise, reached out to grab my hand, ran his thumb over the back of my wrist. "Swimming, do you want to join me?" I looked back up at him.

Sexy didn't even begin to describe it.

He was delicious. Hard muscles bathed in moonlight. I wanted to kiss every inch of him, run my fingers along the crest of his hip, follow that line of muscle down and feel his thighs tighten in my hands.

He shifted his weight and said, "Emma, my eyes are up here." I looked up at him and that was not better. His eyes were hungry, *dark and intense*. He stepped in closer, and I said, "If you wanted me to look at your eyes, you shouldn't have taken your clothes off."

He nodded a breathy hum. "Good point, now are you going to come with me or not?" I looked down at his bare chest, and he said, "Before you even say it… I have towels and a blanket in my bag, and yes… It's cold."

His fingers grazed my thigh. "You packed towels and a blanket, but didn't think to grab swimsuits?" He shrugged innocently as he gathered the fabric of my dress up in his hand.

"Must have slipped my mind."

I put my hands on his waist and leaned in closer. "Fine, but you have to turn around while I get in." He shook his head. "Not a chance."

He grabbed the hem of my dress, fingers brushing against my skin. "Can I help you out of this?" I wanted him to take it off of me, but I said, "Camden, I'm serious." He lifted it up a little higher, "Me too."

He gave me an ardent look and I nodded hesitantly. His fingers raked my sides as he pulled the dress over my head. The force of the sensation pulled my eyes closed. He put a kiss right beside them, ran his fingers over my cheeks.

I asked, "You're really going to swim in your underwear?" He nodded, "Yeah, but you don't have to wear yours." A playful push against his chest and an echoing, "I'm serious." from his lips. I shook my head at him. "I know you are, but…"

He leaned down. "Here, you can wear this." He handed me his shirt and turned around to get in the water. He went under and I quickly shimmied out of my underwear and pulled his shirt on.

When he came up, he shook his head and ran his hands through his hair. There were rivulets of water running down his arms. His eyes traveled from my bare feet to my chest.

"Come here, Emma."

It was like a siren's call, *Absolutely impossible to resist.*

I walked out into the water, and he swam over and took my hand in his. We swam out to the middle and he asked me if I'd been writing anything lately. I shook my head, "No, nothing other than the story of my own life."

He gave me a contemplative look. "I'd read that."

"Oh… don't bother. It'll be complete rubbish."

He swam in closer, pushed some hair from my eyes. "Nothing you do could ever be rubbish."

I looked down at a droplet of water on his lips. "What about you? Have you been working on anything lately?" He smirked, "Coffee and tea." I shook my head, "No, I meant like your drawings." His eyes shifted away from mine. "I don't have much time for that lately, but I've made a few I like." I told him that I'd love to see them, and he nodded, "Alright."

He rolled to his back. Floating on the surface of water with ripples of moonlight in it. I said, "Do you know what you want to do with your life?" He shook his head, "No, do you?"

I rolled over onto my back. "Not a clue."

He turned to face me. "It's weird, isn't it?"

I nodded, but said, "What is?"

"Being an adult."

I laughed, "I am not an adult."

He said, "You can vote now." I gave him an incredulous look. "My mother still drives me to school." He shook his head, "Yeah, and that's ridiculous. You should have your own car."

I said, "Lots of people in the city don't have cars." His eyes rolled. "You don't live in the city." I looked up at the stars sparkling above us. "I'm city adjacent." He said, "That's irrelevant." and gave me a quick look. "Unless you're going to live in the city when you graduate?"

I shook my head, "No, definitely not." He reached out for my hand. "Will you stay with your mom?" I wrapped my fingers in his. "Actually, I'm thinking about applying to MSU."

His eyes shot to mine. "You'd be here?"

I nodded. "Yeah, do you think that would be alright?"

He turned over, eagerly pulled me in. I nuzzled into his neck, and he reached down to wrap my legs around his waist.

He stiffened, mouth dropped open, and eyes spread wide. I felt it too. Our bodies pressed together. His slick torso sliding over my bare skin.

"You took your panties off?"

I nodded hesitantly, and he said, "Sorry, I didn't know."

I felt a pang of fear. A moment of doubt. If it weren't for the fact that his fingers were digging into me like they couldn't let go, I would have thought he didn't want me.

He reached up and pushed the hair from my eyes. "Are you alright? Do you want me to let you go?" I knew I should answer him, tell him *no, absolutely not*, but the ridges in his torso were sliding over me and a deep pulse was building in my core. I managed a quick shake of my head, and he leaned in to kiss me.

Wet lips traveling over wet skin.

Needy fingertips digging into my back.

I mumbled "Camden, I want you." and he reached up and pushed his hand into my hair, pulling at the roots as he said, "I can't think when you're this close."

I pulled him in tighter, pressed my hips into him and he moaned into my mouth, "Fuck, Emma, you can't do that."

I did it again, and he reached down to hold my hips tightly in his hands. Desperation floating in his dark eyes as he said, "I'm serious, you don't know what that's doing to me."

I was pretty sure I did.

I kissed his neck and asked him if he was alright. If he wanted me to let him go. He gave me a taunting look, pressed against my thighs, and slid me down further.

I'd never felt him before. My hips instinctively tilted into him. He was hard. Pressed firmly in between my thighs. Nothing but a bit of wet fabric between us.

I tried not to react. Not to let my mouth drop open or my eyes spread wide. It was big. So much bigger than I was expecting. I tried not to say that, not to let my inexperience show. He studied my face. Looking for a reaction. Trying to decipher all the feelings I was working to suppress.

A tentative shake of his head, "No, that's not what I want, but I do want to know if it's what you want."

I let my hips rock against him. He gripped my backside, fingers digging into me as he said, "If you do that again, I won't be able to stop myself."

I pulled back, looked up at him. "Who says I want you to stop?"

His lips parted and pressed together in this move that looked like hunger. Moonlight spilled onto his cheek, and I reached up to run my fingers over his jawline. He caught them with his lips, teeth grazing up against my skin.

I said, "Please, Camden." and he said, "Yes, Emma, anything you want."

"Even if I want you?"

His eyes flared. "Do you want me to touch you, Emma?"

I looked him right in the eyes, pressed my hips into him, and bit my bottom lip. He swam us to the shore.

We got out and he pulled a towel from his bag and wrapped me up in it. He laid out a blanket and pulled me down beside him. We kissed, leaning into each other. His hands pulling at my waist.

"You should take this off."

I shook my head, and he said, "It's too cold, you can put your dress back on if you want." He pushed the towel off of my shoulders and pulled the shirt off over my head.

He leaned back, eyes roving over my body. "Do you want me to get your dress?" I looked over at it lying on the ground and he got up to go get it. He stood behind me, "Put your arms up for me, baby."

He crouched down and pulled the fabric over my hips. I thought he was going to let me go, but his hands grasped my thighs and pushed up under my dress.

He leaned in, breath hot on my skin, "Spread your legs for me, baby."

He kissed my neck, nipped at the curve of my shoulder, let his hands move up my thighs. I opened them and he dipped closer. The pulse became a hum. His fingers ran smoothly over me, small circles and repetitive swipes as he whispered, "God, yes." into my ear.

I couldn't stop my hips from moving.

He said, "You like this?" but I didn't know if he was talking to me or himself. I moaned, let my head fall back, and he pressed his lips into mine.

His hand dipped lower, fingers pressing inside. Head falling forward as he whispered, "Perfect." up against my skin.

Someone really should warn you about this.

This kind of pleasure was dangerous.

It was addictive.

The entire universe was boiled down to the points where his skin met mine. Warmth across my abdomen. Pressure on my back. Overwhelming anticipation as his lips moved lower, traveling over my collar bones and onto my chest.

My core pulled tight, eyes closed. I asked him if he had a condom and he muttered, "It's better than I thought. How can it be better than I thought?"

He kept moving. Pressing into me. Watching me.

I whimpered and his lips crashed into mine. It was the first time he'd kissed me that I couldn't take note of everything that was happening.

He was everywhere. Warmth at my back. Pressured touch on my skin. Reverberations in my chest when he said, "Next time I'm going to taste you."

A quiver then a shake. A wave of release so fierce I could barely breathe. He leaned in and kissed me. Mumbling "God you're beautiful" up against my lips.

When I'd come back to myself, I asked him what he'd done to me? His lips moved to the curve of my shoulder, he kissed and nipped at my skin.

"Have you never had an orgasm, Emma?"

I looked over at him with abject curiosity in my eyes, "Is that what that was?" Satisfaction set his jaw, "Yeah, I think so." I shook my head, *no,* and he said, "Well happy birthday then."

"Was that my birthday present because if it was that's what I want every year."

His smile widened and he leaned over to pick his pants up off the ground. He reached into his back pocket. "No, this is." He handed me a small box with a little white bow on top of it.

When I opened it, he told me he'd made it, or he'd drawn it and then had it made. It was a necklace. A golden outline of the mountains. Our mountains, the ones we saw from the ranch.

∧∧∧∧∧∧

Camden worked most mornings, so Tate and I made plans to go to the river. She and Ethan were still together, and they were like the poster children for high school relationships. I wasn't surprised to see him waiting in the water for her when we arrived. Cash was there too. He called my name as we walked up.

I waved at him and noticed the girl he was with scowl in my direction. Cash told me he thought he was going to have to go all summer without seeing me, and he said it like it was a bad thing.

Tatumn made her way over to Ethan and Cash came to sit down beside me. I asked him who his friend was, and he said, "Emma." without skipping a beat. I smiled in his direction, "You know what I mean." His brow furrowed, "Oh, that's just April." I spread my towel out on the rock, "Well are you and *just April* a thing?" He shrugged, "Sometimes."

He was looking at me, and she was looking at him, so I said, "Well, are you today?" He leaned in a bit, "I don't know. I haven't decided yet." Tatumn yelled, "Emma, come on, the water isn't even cold." I looked back at Cash, "Is she lying?"

He shook his head, "No, it's almost July, this is as warm as it's going to get."

April called Cash's name, and he looked over at me. "Come on. It's not like you have anything better to do." I disagreed with him and spread my towel out to lay down in the sunshine.

I'd told Camden I was going out with them today and he'd said he may see us later. I was in this peaceful near dream state, listening to the sounds of water rushing by and my friends talking in the distance, when he sat down beside me. I opened my eyes, and he said, "Hey." in this really casual way as he reached out and ran his fingers through the ends of my hair.

I turned toward him and lifted my hand to block the sun from my eyes.

"You came?"

"Yeah, well don't make a big deal about it. It's not like I missed you or anything."

"Naturally, I'm easily forgotten."

He gave me a stark look, "You don't actually believe that do you?" I didn't want to answer, so I turned away. He reached out and pulled my face back to his, "Emma, I couldn't forget you if I tried."

The openness in his eyes made me feel naked, *seen in a way I hadn't been before*. I looked away and asked him if he had, *tried*, and he laid down beside me, "No, I'm not one for fighting losing battles."

The shadows from the trees above moved over him. I watched with fascination as the light shimmered in and out of his eyes. He reached out and ran the back of his fingers over my cheek. "I did miss you. That's why I came." I told him I already knew that, and then Ethan asked if he was up for a game of volleyball.

The lids of his eyes fell in annoyance, "I'll play if you will."

Tatumn got out of the water and stood over me dripping wet. The puddle forming at her feet seeped into my towel. "Emma, come on. You can be on my team." I squinted as I looked up at her. "Why would you want me on your team. I'm terrible at volleyball."

Her eyes rolled as she let out a frustrated sigh, "Emma… it's our senior year. This is supposed to be the best summer of our lives and you're just laying here," she looked over at Camden, "with him."

I knew Tate was a little jealous of all the time I'd spent with Camden, but she didn't usually say anything about it, so I said, "Fine." and stood to go with her. Camden grabbed my hand, and we walked into the water together. It was cold and the rocks beneath my feet were slippery.

Tate pulled me away and Camden swam over to help Ethan with the net. Cash came over and gave me a questioning look, "Still a thing, huh?" I could tell he didn't approve. I looked over at April, "Yeah, have you made up your mind about that one yet?" He shrugged and looked at me like he wasn't bothered, or maybe he was hoping I was.

"That's easy to figure to out. What I don't understand is what a girl like you is doing with a guy like him." I looked over at Camden, he and Ethan were still setting up the net. I told Cash he was wrong, that Camden was a good guy, and his brow furrowed.

"Sure, Sweetness, whatever you think."

^^^^^^

Whenever we were leaving, I noticed a look pass between Ethan and Cash. Ethan turned to us, "Hey Pierce, you think you can get anything tonight?"

Camden's eyes darted away from mine. "I don't know, maybe. What do you want?" Ethan said, "I don't know, I'm thinking about having a party. You think you can get any pills?"

Camden's face pulled in. He shook his head, *no*. Ethan's eyes shifted toward Cash for a moment. "Oh, that's right. Your mom just got out of rehab again… maybe just a half ounce then." Camden's eyes hardened, but he nodded.

"I don't know. I'll check."

^^^^^^

He told me he didn't want me to go with him. That he would just drop me back off at the ranch. I asked him what he was doing, and he said, "Don't worry about it, Emma. It'll be fine. I'll come right back, and we'll go out together."

I could tell that he didn't like this anymore than I did, "No, I'll go with you." He shook his head, "That's not a good idea." I planted my feet and looked up at him, "Why? Is it not safe?"

He looked at me like I was being mean. I knew he was just trying to protect me, and honestly, I didn't want to go with him. I just didn't want him going alone either.

He said, *fine*, but I could tell that it really bothered him. I told him we didn't have to go, and he said, "Yeah, actually I do."

We pulled up to a cute little house on the wrong side of town. "Wait here. I'll be right back." He hopped off his bike and started walking toward the front door. I noticed the curtain pull back and a woman look out at me. He wasn't inside more than a minute before she stepped with him following behind her.

"Cora." He sounded panicked. She waved her hand in the air to brush him off, "Oh, don't be so dramatic. I just want to meet her." I watched them walking together. Their steps fell in the same rhythm. He looked up at me, just as the realization clicked, and a tsunami of shame and fear rushed through his eyes.

She walked up to me, and I looked into her grey eyes. They were just like his, only older, surrounded in lines and wrinkles. "So, you're his Emma?" she mused. I nodded and Camden looked down at her, "Leave her alone, Cora."

Her eyes swept over me, and I couldn't help but notice how frail she was. She said, "She's pretty." but it sounded like she was talking to herself. Camden rubbed the back of his neck. He told her we had to go, and she said, "He talks about you." I gave her a small smile. "Hopefully all good things?" She let out a bit of laughter. It didn't sound right though.

"Cora." Camden stepped around her and stood between us. "Oh, calm down. I'm going." She took one last look at me, and then turned toward him. She held out her arms and he looked so uncomfortable, but he leaned in and let her wrap them around his shoulders anyway.

"You got a good one there."

His lips tilted up at the corner. "I know."

^^^^^^

When he climbed into bed beside me that night, I had so many questions, but I knew he didn't want me to ask any of them. He pulled the covers back and crawled underneath.

I tried not to notice the way his eyes spread wide when he looked up at me. I knew why I was nervous, but Camden never seemed to be bothered by anything. I tilted my head up to kiss him, and he said, "You can ask. I know you want to."

I looked down and pulled the covers up over my chest. "That was your mom?" He looked so ashamed, "Yeah." I didn't know what else to say, but I really hated that he hadn't told me.

"Why didn't you tell me?"

"Because I didn't want you to know."

"Why not?"

He stared out into the darkness. "I want to say it was to protect you, and it was… I don't want you involved in any of this, but the truth is… I didn't want you to look at me like they do."

"Like who does?"

His jaw tightened, "Everyone. You're the only person I know that looks at me like I'm something worthwhile. The rest of them look at me like I've already lost. Like they're afraid of me, or disappointed in me, because in their eyes I'm just a useless loser with an addict for a mom."

"Camden, I would never look at you like that. I'm just worried."

He turned to face me, "About what?" I told him I wasn't really sure, but if he was doing what I thought he was, it seemed dangerous. "It's not really. I've done it for a while, and I'm really careful." I could tell he believed what he was saying, but I didn't. "Yeah, but what if you get caught?"

"I won't."

"I bet a lot of other people in prison have said the same thing, Camden."

The expression on his face changed so completely that I was afraid he wasn't going to say anything else. He reached up and ran his hand through his hair. "Yeah, but I won't. It always happens just like it did today. They ask and I go get it. I never have anything on me, and she's my mom. No one thinks a thing about me going to see her."

He looked over at me like he really hoped I'd say something reasonable like *oh, well in that case…* but I didn't like it, so I told him so. His jaw flexed and the lids of his eyes fell.

"I know, but she's sick, and it's the only way I know to help her."

I asked him about rehab. "She's been. It doesn't work… not for her anyway." I looked at him, carefully trying to decide what he meant by that, "She doesn't want to quit?" He looked at me like I'd said something wrong. A deep breath lifted his chest, "It's just not that simple." I told him I thought it was, at least the part he was involved in.

"No, it's not."

"Fine then, tell me."

He turned to look out the window. "I don't think you'll understand."

I knew he was right. "I'll try. I promise."

He looked over at me. I could tell he was really struggling, "Please, Camden." He looked away again, thumb rubbing over finger, chest rising with breaths that were too deep for someone who was just lying there.

"The drugs are there whether I take them or not. So, whatever I can move, I do, because if I leave it there… she uses it."

^^^^^^

After that night, I felt really protective of him. Tatumn asked me if I wanted to come out and I told her, no, I didn't think I did. "Emma, I talked to Ethan about what he said, and he swore he'd never do anything like that again."

I told her I thought it was ridiculous that Ethan felt superior to him. Her eyes shifted a bit, and I said, "You know he was the one that was going to use the drugs, right?"

Her lips pursed and she looked down at me like I really didn't understand. She sat down beside me and let out a breath so deep it sounded like a sigh.

"Oh my gosh, just say what you want to say." She looked over at me with a worried expression, "I can't. I'm too scared." I asked "Why?" She shook her head, "Because you won't want to hear it."

I shrugged, "Well, it's too late now. You've already sat down." Her eyes darted from one side of the room to the other. "I love Camden, you know I do. He's practically my brother… but his mom is a mess."

"I know. I've seen her." She looked really shocked. "He took you with him?" I told her I sort of forced him to and she said, "So you know, then?" I nodded and she said "I'm really sorry. My boyfriend is a complete idiot, but I love you, and I can't stand it when you're mad at me."

^^^^^^

Summer was nearly over, and Camden said he wanted to take me out before I left. I told him we still had weeks to go, but he said, "Still." in this offhanded way that made me wonder what he really meant.

He drove us into town and parked his bike outside of a tattoo parlor. I told him this really wasn't my thing, and he said, "I know, you're perfect already, but I'm not."

When we walked inside a girl with a flowered sundress and a full sleeve of tattoos on her arm asked us what we wanted. Camden looked down at me and said, "Can you do something like this?" as he pointed to the necklace he'd given me for my birthday. She nodded, "Sure."

We followed her back. There was a row of black leather adjustable chairs and a wall full of illustrations drawn in thick black ink. Camden pulled his shirt off and asked me where I thought it should go. I leaned back on the counter, "I'm not sure I'm the right person to make that decision."

He found my reflection in the mirror, "Yes you are."

I reached out to touch the crest of his right shoulder blade and he caught my hand in his. He held on to it and I felt a sort of fullness form in my chest.

He was looking at me in this strange way, like he was trying to communicate things he couldn't say. It made me feel sad that he kept so much of himself locked up inside, but I could tell that this meant something to him.

I asked him what made him decide to get a tattoo today, and he said, "It's for you." I told him, he didn't need to do this for me. "Yeah, but I want to."

"Why?"

"Because you'll leave soon, and I just want to keep a bit of you with me."

I looked away from him and noticed the way the girl in the flowered dress was watching us. She had this pensive look on her face. I couldn't tell if she was thinking, this is the most romantic thing I've ever seen, or these people are complete idiots.

He said, "Emma…" and I had to swallow hard before I could answer.

"Well, in that case. I think you should get my name tattooed below it, or maybe a big picture of my face all over your back." He shrugged, "Alright, if that's what you want." I shook my head, *no*. He leaned forward and rested his chest on the chair.

^^^^^^

We ended up at the trench. Camden said he didn't want to go but his phone wouldn't stop going off and Cora needed the money. I tried not to make a face or react in any sort of meaningful way, but I couldn't help but notice how different it was watching him make his rounds at the party.

I used to see him stepping in and out of groups and feel jealous of the girls surrounding him.

Now I just felt nervous, *protective, worried.*

Tatumn came rushing over with a wide smile on her face and a bottle in her hand. She said, "You will not believe what a night I'm having." I gave her a quick look, but her eyes were swimming in mirth. She said, "Everyone keeps asking about you, but I don't think we should go back over there. I think we should leave, just the two of us." I was still watching Camden with worried eyes when I said, "Where would we go?" Her eyes lit up, "Ibiza?"

I told her I didn't have my passport, and she said, "That's alright, we can swim."

I nodded, nervously watching Camden pull another bag out of his pocket. Cash came over and Tate leaned into whisper, "Do you want me to tell him to go away?" but she was too drunk to be quiet, and Cash gave me an injured look.

"No, I can do that myself."

She nodded like she already knew that, and Cash said, "There's my favorite flavor of summer sweetness." I gave him a reproachful look and his face fell. "Wait are we mad at each other, because I think I could be into this."

I shook my head, "You're insufferable." He stepped in a little closer and let the lip of his beer rub against the back of my hand. "Yeah, but you like it, right?" I told him, *no, I don't*, and he said, "Emma, we were just messing with him."

"Yeah, well it wasn't funny, and you're not my favorite person right now." He said, "I know, but you're still mine." I told him no, this isn't going to happen, and he cocked his head to the side. "What you and me? I think it might." I shook my head, "You're wrong." His lips pressed together, "Not usually."

"Cash, I'm serious, go away." He looked at me, with a quasi serious expression on his face. "Emma, I'm sorry." I pulled my sweater tighter around my waist. "You should be." His head fell back in exasperation, "I am, do you want me to grovel, because I will." I looked across the trench to where Camden was standing.

Cash followed my eyes over and asked, "Did you know?"

I gave him a brief look, "What, about his mother?"

He nodded. "No, I didn't." He said, "Well, I think if you're considering joining the family, you should probably at least know who they are."

I supposed he was right, but I still hated the way he'd exposed him. I told him that and he threw his hands up, "What can I say, I'm competitive, and I like you."

I looked back at him, "What?" His eyes filled with a very small amount of uncertainty. "I know, it's weird, but I do… and I don't want to see you get wrapped up in something that you can't get yourself out of." I told him he couldn't say things like that to me. He knew I was with Camden. He lifted his drink to his lips and swallowed.

"I do. I just don't know why."

I told him he didn't know Camden, not really, and he gave me a very serious look. "I know enough to know that you could do better."

My brows rose mockingly. "You mean like you?" He shrugged. "I'd be open to that." I told him he needed to stop flirting with me and leave me alone.

He shook his head. "Definitely not going to promise to do that, but I can try to behave myself if you'll come have a drink with me by the fire."

He led me over to where Tate and Ethan were holding court at the far edge of the trench. When I walked up Ethan asked if I needed a drink and handed me a lemonade. He had this tight look on his face and held my gaze longer than he needed to. I took the drink and opened it. He was still looking at me like he expected me to say something, but I didn't have anything to say to him.

"Tate told me you were pretty upset about earlier. I'm sorry about that." I thought *yeah, well the world's full of assholes like you*, but Tate looked over at me with a hopeful expression, and I said, "Yeah, I was, but don't worry about it. I'm over it now."

He looked back over at Tate. "That bit about his mom was really uncalled for." My eyes narrowed. He shifted his weight from one foot to the other, "Camden's not all bad, I know that, but the two of you don't make much sense and when Cash told me you didn't seem to know…"

My brows rose. He gave me a contrite look, "Anyway, it was stupid, and I'm sorry." I said something meaningless, like *yeah, well we all do stupid things*, and turned away from him to take another drink.

It was a cold night and the heat from the fire felt good on the back of my legs. I found Camden, standing in a crowd of people not too far away from where I was. He looked up at me and I gave him a little nod.

Tatumn decided the air felt too heavy and dared one of the other girls on her squad to do a backflip over the flames with her. They were both drunk enough to think it was a good idea, but Ethan insisted they do it at the edge of the circle. Tatumn gave him a pouty look and told him he was no fun.

He said, "Yeah well, when you wake up with all your hair tomorrow, you'll thank me." She picked one shoulder up in a shrug that said, *maybe, I don't know, I might not.*

Camden came over and stepped in behind me, "What's everyone on about?" I told him. The girls did their flips, *flawlessly,* and then he leaned in and whispered, "I'm ready when you are."

He wrapped his arms around my waist, and I leaned into him. I'm sure it was my imagination, but it seemed like people were watching us. I tilted my head up and he leaned down to kiss me. I told him I'd be ready as soon as I finished my drink and he said, "Okay, sure."

^^^^^^

On our way home we stopped by his mom's house again. From the outside it looked cute, *quaint,* with flower boxes in bloom under the windows and a paw print painted on the mailbox. Camden didn't knock. He just opened the door and pulled me in behind him. Inside was different. The air smelled of a burning sweetness and there were stains all over the carpet.

He called out his mom's name and someone moved in the distance. It was dim, with thick curtains and bits of fabric draped over all the lamps.

I tried not to make assumptions about the way Cora lived in this house, but it was hard not to notice the filth and piles that cluttered her space.

She came around the corner with a spatula in her hand and a cigarette dangling from her lips. Her hair was pulled up in a

214

messy knot on the top of her head and it flopped from one side to the other as she said, "Oh, I didn't know you were coming."

Camden released my hand and walked over to her. He told her he'd called. He'd left a message. She looked over toward the table with an absent expression in her eyes. "I don't know where my phone is." She said in this dreamy tone, like she was remembering something she didn't know she'd forgotten.

His head dropped and he nodded like he'd expected as much. He reached into his pocket and pulled out a wad of cash. "This should be enough to pay the electric. Do you need me to do it for you, or do you just want the cash?"

Her eyes darted in my direction, and she shrugged. "Cash is good." Camden gave her a careful look, like he was trying to determine the likelihood that she would remember this later, but he held it out and she took it and shoved it in the pocket of her robe.

She took a deep drag of her cigarette and then turned to ask him if he was hungry. "No, we can't stay." Her lips pursed. "I think you should have a bite before you go." Camden cocked his head to the side. "No, thanks, but I really need to get Emma home."

Her eyes narrowed and she turned around to walk over to the stove. She put the spatula in the pan and pushed it around a bit. Camden looked over at me and I tried to act as natural as possible. He said, "Come on, let's go." and Cora turned back around.

"Oh, I forgot to tell you... Don stopped by earlier." Camden's hand tightened around mine. His eyes shifted, and she gave him a wobbly sort of smile. "He said he'd seen you around town with the same girl a few times." The color drained from his face, "So?" She bit her cheek and nodded.

"I really think you should stay for a while."

She held the spatula out and looked over at me, "Do you mind?" I looked over at the chopped potatoes on the stove, "No, not at all." She handed me the spatula and then I heard the scratchy sound of a needle dropping onto a record.

I could hear them whispering between breaks in the music. Their voices sounded volatile. I turned the stove off, found plates in the cabinet, and put a scoop on each one of them. I walked over to the table and Camden looked up at me with a worried expression. I sat the plates down and he came over and took my hand in his, "Come on, we're leaving."

Cora came around the corner and sat down at the table. Camden leaned down and put his face right in front of hers. "I'll see you later, alright? I'll drop by tomorrow, just stay home. I'll go out if you need me to."

He spoke to her the same way I'd seen mothers talking to their children. *Slowly. Deliberately. Never breaking eye contact.* She stabbed a potato with her fork and put it in her mouth. A look I was pretty sure was a warning passed between them. Cora pulled her eyes away from his and looked over at me.

"Alright… but be careful out there."

^^^^^^

Camden didn't say goodbye before he left for work the next morning. I didn't see him that evening when he came home either. He stopped climbing in my bed at night. He barely looked at me. When it was time to go out, he'd lie and say he was too tired, or that he already had plans.

I was terrified.

Nervous about what I'd done to drive him away. Nervous about what he'd done that made him think he had to leave me.

I couldn't help thinking that it was the thought of me coming here that was really bothering him. He'd always talked about how good I was. I worried that what he meant was that I was too good to ever fit in a life like his.

Tatumn was oblivious, *happy even*, that I was spending so much more time with her. I'd woken early and watched him get out of bed and pull his pants and shirt on. He left the room without looking back. When Tatumn woke, I asked her if she wanted to go to the coffee shop.

I don't know what I expected. He'd been avoiding me for days, but when we walked in and he quickly turned away, a stark emptiness filled my chest.

Tate had been babbling about the senior sleepover. Her mom was still on the fence. Ethan *needed* her to go. I didn't care at all. I didn't care about anything but figuring out why he wouldn't speak to me. Or look at me. Or touch me.

Camden was in the back of the café. He had a tray in his hands, and he was talking to a group of middle-aged men. I regretted coming here. April walked up to the counter. "Hey Tate, you want your usual?" She nodded and April pulled a blueberry muffin out of the case. I looked up at the chalkboard menu hanging above her head, and then down at the perfect rows of pastry in the case.

April asked, "Did you want something?" and I looked over at Camden again. I ordered a mocha latte and a chocolate croissant and then we went to sit down.

Tate asked me if I would go with her to the sleepover. I nodded and said something like, *sure, I'll go*. April rang a bell and Camden's head snapped forward. I watched him make eye contact with our lattes and then he made his excuses and left the men he was talking to. He went to the counter, picked up a small thin piece of paper, and turned to look at us.

The way his face changed in that moment was excruciating. It was like he had cast a forbidden curse with his irises alone. I felt my insides twist up and then he loaded up his tray and came over.

"Hey." he said in a quiet voice that let me know he didn't really want to talk to me. I gave him an equally unenthusiastic reply. The tray fell to his side, and he ran his fingers through his hair.

His discomfort was nearly palpable.

Mine was overwhelming.

I wanted to yell at him. Shake him until he snapped out of it and told me what I'd done wrong. I looked away, and Tatumn asked, "What time do you get off today?" I picked up my latte and took a sip.

"Late. Well, I close anyway."

The coffee shop closed at two in the afternoon. He didn't get off late. "You should come out tonight. We're going to the arcade. The boys have some sort of tournament going." She was doing all the talking. He was just waiting for the moment when he could walk away.

He asked me if I was going, and I let my gaze drop and watched his finger rub a continuous circle over his thumb. I looked over at Tate. Her smile filled with pity, and she said, "Yeah, she'll be there."

Camden kicked the toe of his boot into the ground. "Maybe. I might come."

I didn't believe him. I knew he just wasn't ready to say no yet. When he turned and left Tatumn asked, "What was that all about?" I picked my cup up and took a drink. "What was what all about?" She looked at me like I knew. I didn't though. Not really.

"That. You guys. What's going on?"

I wished I could tell her. "I don't know. He's been distant." She tore off a piece of her muffin, "He's always distant." I fiddled with the zipper of my hoodie. "No, he's not, not with me anyway."

It was true, and it wasn't. I knew him, but it was mostly because I could hear the things he didn't say as well as the ones he did. "Well, he is with me. I've never seen him be like that with you though. Are you guys fighting?" We weren't. It would almost be better if we were.

"No. Not really."

She let her eyes go somewhere else. I let mine find him. He was looking at me with an expression that almost made it look like he missed me. Like he wanted to come back over here and say more, but then April rang the bell again and he turned away.

"Have you two slept together?" Tate asked like she was inquiring about what my favorite color was, or how much honey I liked on my oats. It was strange the way she said things like that so easily.

"No." I answered, trying not to sound too affected.

"That's odd." She said, and it was. I knew it was.

I looked over just in time to see April wad a receipt up and throw it at Camden's head. He turned to her with a smile on his face and I asked, "Has he slept with her?"

Tate's eyes filled with apprehension, like she knew what she was about to say would hurt me. "Oh yeah. Several times."

A thin layer of ice coated my veins. I looked over at them standing behind the counter together. A bombardment of unwelcome images flooded my psyche. Her on the counter. His apron pushed up. Her legs spread wide. I felt the color drain from my face and Tate looked over, "I don't think he has recently though."

She tore off a piece of her muffin and a blueberry rolled onto her plate. "Have you done it with anyone else? I looked down at my croissant, "No." Her lips pursed, "Me either."

"Seriously?"

She laughed and leaned in. "I know, Ethan's very patient, but he's been hinting at it a lot more lately."

"Is there some reason why you haven't?" I asked.

She shrugged and leaned back in her chair. "I don't know. I used to think I wanted it to be special, or something like that. I would picture it happening in our normal lives. You know like in his truck, or up against a dirt wall at the trench, or in Finn's basement and it sort of gave me the creeps." I took a small bite of my croissant.

"Now though, we've just waited so long. I'm just scared now."

"Of what?" She shook her head, "Well, what if I'm not any good at it? What if I made him wait all this time and then I'm absolute rubbish in bed? It would be humiliating."

"I don't think that's likely, Tate."

I looked over at Camden, and she said, "Anyway, I'm going to do it at the sleepover."

He was still talking to April. I said, "No trucks or basements, but tents surrounded by strangers is fine?"

She laughed, a twinkle of a noise that filled the entire café. "Yeah, I know, but at least we'll get to sleep together after. I can't imagine doing something like that and then just going home and climbing in my bed alone."

^^^^^^

We'd been at the arcade for a long time, but I wasn't expecting him to come at all. He walked in and sat down beside me. I refused to look over at him, but it was useless because he didn't look at me anyway. He just sat there. Smelling like he did. Talking to the guys about the game they were playing.

It was clear he wasn't here to see me, but when I tried to stand, he put his hand down on my thigh. It was warm, rough, and heavy. I looked over at him, but he was still looking at the screen. Ignoring me. I looked over at the door, and he said, "Don't go." like he actually wanted me to stay.

It was too weird, this *I can't stand to look at you, but I don't want you to go* thing he was doing. I reached down, lifted his hand from my leg, and dropped it on his own lap. His eyes darted in my direction, and I stood up to go outside.

221

As the sounds of the others faded, I realized I was hoping he would follow me out. I thought about turning back around. Going back inside. Demanding that he talk to me, because what was I doing purposely walking away from the only thing I actually wanted?

Every time the door opened my chest tightened with anticipation. I looked back several times, but it was never him, so I stopped looking.

When he came out, he asked, "Why'd you run off like that?"

I didn't know how to answer him. How to tell him that his indifference stung worse than spite. That it hurt to be so close to him when he felt so far away. He ran his fingers through his hair, and I said, "Why'd you come out here?"

"Because I wanted to see you."

"It doesn't seem like you want to see me."

He stepped in closer and put his thumb beneath my chin. My eyes closed as he lifted my lips towards his.

"Emma, look at me."

I couldn't see him, but I knew exactly what he looked like. His hand dropped and my chin followed it down.

"I don't know what I'm doing." he admitted.

I didn't either.

∧∧∧∧∧∧

The room was dark. I heard him come in and pretended to be asleep. He walked over to me. I could hear the sound of his hands rubbing over the fabric of his jeans as he dropped them to his sides. I felt the weight of him pull against my covers.

My eyes opened.

He kissed me.

"I did want to see you." he said as he pulled away.

^^^^^^

I went back to the coffee shop the next morning, but this time I went alone. When I walked in his eyes tightened, and I turned away. I wanted to give off an air of indifference. As if it was mere coincidence that I'd shown up in the one place I knew he'd be.

He walked over to the register. I ordered a mocha latte with a chocolate croissant and took a seat at a table in the back.

I positioned myself where I could glance up at him without him knowing and pulled out my book. Each time a new group of people came in I took the opportunity to look over at him. He was better at talking with the customers than I would have thought. He didn't smile, but he didn't sneer either.

I read several chapters. My mocha latte was cold, and my croissant was nothing but a few golden flakes on the plate in front of me. I didn't know what I had hoped to accomplish with coming here, but whatever it was. I hadn't done it.

I closed my book and shoved it in my bag. The place was emptier now. Just me, Camden and April, and that same group of middle-aged men I'd seen him speaking with the other day.

I thought about standing to clean off my table, but the thought of leaving without ever having caught his attention seemed so sad that I went to the bathroom instead.

When I came out, my table had been cleared. There was a fresh latte decorated with whipped cream and shavings of chocolate on it. I looked around, wondering who would have chosen to take the only dirty table in the place. There was no one there though, and he said, "It's yours. I made it for you."

I turned around and he was standing there looking lost, like a puppy that had been left behind when his family went out for a walk. "Did you?" I asked because I didn't know what else to say. He nodded. "Yeah, I'm off in a bit. I didn't want you to leave yet."

I didn't know what to do with that, but my eyes automatically shot to the counter where April stood. "Alright. Thanks." I took a seat and pulled my book back out. I watched as he slowly turned his head toward the counter, and then looked back down at me.

"You don't think…"

I placed my finger in the spine of the book and looked up at him. He didn't finish his question, but he didn't need to. We both knew what he was asking, and the answer was, *yes*.

"No." I said, but I could tell he didn't believe me.

He did leave though.

I picked up the latte and took a drink, warm, creamy sweetness coated my tongue. He made several rounds around the café, filling little porcelain ramekins with small rectangular sugar packets and talking with any customers that came in.

I read several more chapters. My drink wasn't gone, but I was done with it. I looked at my phone and then over at the door.

He put the towel he was using to wash off the counters down and began walking my way. I leaned down, pretending not to see him and shoved my book in my bag. When I sat up his hand was held out to me.

"Come with me." He said, like I didn't have a choice. *I didn't.* Not when it came to him, but for some reason I didn't want him to know that. I stood and looked him in the eyes. It was a mistake, they were tumultuous, filled with cloudy divots and insecurities.

He led me to a door in the corner and pulled me inside a dark room. He dropped my hand, and I could hear his sliding up against the wall. The light turned on. It was still dim, but now I knew where we were. It was a utility closet, a big yellow bucket filled with dirty mop water and shelves lined with stacks of paper towels.

He rubbed the back of his neck, "I don't know what I'm doing. I definitely shouldn't be doing this." I told him it looked like he was locking me in a utility closet and asked him if I should be worried. He shook his head in this absent sort of way, "There's not a lock on the door."

I didn't think that was really the point but decided to let it drop. "Well, then I guess that means I can go." I said hoping he was going to beg me to stay. He did. He told me he didn't want me to go, and he sounded broken when he said, "I don't ever want you to go."

"You don't want me to stay either."

"I do too." He ran his hand through his hair. "Why do you do that?"

"Do what?" I asked because I really didn't know.

"Make assumptions, about what you think I want." He was looking at me like he was the one who should be upset. "I'm not telling you what you want. I'm telling you how I feel." He shoved his hand in the pocket of his apron. "I don't mean to make you feel that way. It's not what I want anyway."

"I don't know if that's true. I feel like you've made it very clear how you feel lately."

"I haven't though."

The smell of the room faded, and I caught a bit of his scent, it was mixed with fresh coffee grounds and the sharp acidic tang of the cleaner he'd been using.

He reached up to scratch his head. I could tell he was thinking. Trying to figure out what to say to me, so I just asked, "Then how do you feel?" It was risky. Camden wasn't always good with his words, and I knew that.

He looked up at me, "Scared."

It was more honesty than I was expecting. I braced myself for the worst. This was where he told me it wasn't me. It was him. That MSU was a bad idea. That I was too good a girl to fit into a life like his.

"About what?"

"Mostly you. It's just not a good time, Emma." I didn't know what that was supposed to mean, but I knew he was telling me that we couldn't be together, at least not right now.

I bit at the flesh beneath my bottom lip to divert some of the pain in my chest, "Not a good time?" I didn't know what that was supposed to mean, but I knew he was telling me that we couldn't be together, at least not right now.

I bit at the flesh beneath my bottom lip to divert some of the pain in my chest, "Not a good time?" I said as the words echoed in my mind. His head fell, "I can't explain, but I promise you it's not April."

"Yeah, sure whatever you say, Camden."

I took a step toward the door and his hand shot out to block me. He pulled me in, took my hair in his hand, and kissed me. I wanted to be strong, *to resist him*, but I was weak and he was irresistible. When he pulled away, he said, "I don't care about April. I haven't been with anyone else. It's not about that."

I could tell by the way he'd said it, that he was being honest. "Then what is it about?" He looked away from me, "You." I had no idea what he meant, but I knew it hurt.

I pulled away from him and he seemed to realize that he'd said the wrong thing. "No, Emma, that's not what I meant. I'm trying to protect you. To do the right thing so you don't get hurt."

"Well, it's not working."

"Yeah, I know, but it's the best I've got."

There was a knock at the door. April's voice floated through. "Camden, Don and the guys are ready to go. They asked for you."

"Don?"

He nodded.

"Wait, what are you trying to protect me from?"

His eyes went distant, and I got a sinking feeling in my gut. This didn't have anything to do with me. Something was actually wrong. I immediately thought of his mother, and said, "You know you can tell me anything."

He looked down at me, but when our eyes met his darted away, "Not this."

I wanted to say, *sure you can, tell me, maybe I can help*, but I knew it wasn't true. I nodded. He backed away and looked over at the door.

It was risky, but I said, "It's your mom, isn't it?"

Shame closed his eyes, "Yeah." I asked him what was going on. "Nothing really, but I do need to be careful."

I said, "Yeah, I agree." and he said, "Emma, I'm not doing that anymore." I asked him when he'd stopped, and he wrapped his hand around mine, pushed his thumb into my palm. "As soon as I realized you could get hurt."

April knocked again, "Camden?"

He looked away from me. "Yeah, I'll be right out."

^^^^^^

There was a charity event in downtown Bozeman and the moms were going. Tatumn had already left with Ethan, but Camden and I were staying in. The sun was shining down on us through the large open windows in the living room, and I was thinking about all the things I hoped he'd do to me while everyone else was gone.

He said, "You look really cute when you're thinking." His hips shifted beneath me, and my hand fell to his chest. He gave me a teasing look and I pushed against him, "You don't mean that?"

"Yes, I do. I love watching you think. Your eyes are really expressive. If I watch them close enough it's almost like I can see the thoughts passing through your head." I ran my hands over his shoulders. "Oh really?" He shrugged into them, "More or less."

"Well then tell me what I'm thinking right now."

His eyes appraised mine, "You're nervous, but I'm not sure why. It seems like you don't always trust me, or you don't know what I think of you, and you want me, but you don't want me to know that. At least not all the time."

"Do I want you to know right now?"

His eyes narrowed in on mine, "I don't know. I think so." I pressed my hips into his. He reached out and tucked a strand of hair behind my ear. He said, "I've missed you." and I told him that was his fault.

"Yeah, I know, but it's still true."

"Is everything okay now?" I asked. He pressed his hands into my hips, "Right now? Yeah." I leaned forward. "What about tomorrow?" He shrugged. "I guess we'll just have to see."

He wrapped his hand around the back of my neck to pull me closer. He kissed me, slowly, softly opening my mouth with his. He ran his hand down my spine, and I pressed my hips into his. He said, "Emma…" in a tone so desperate it clenched my core tight.

He said, "I've never wanted anything like I want you."

I told him he could have me, *all of me that he wanted*, because I'd always been his. His hands fell to my thighs and pushed up under my skirt.

"Say always again."

I did.

"You know I love you, right." I didn't. I shook my head.

"I do. I have. Always."

^^^^^^

Senior sleepover was a big deal. At least it was for Tatumn. For me it just signified the end of summer. It was just one less night I got to spend with Camden, and one night closer to the many nights that would have to pass before I saw him again.

Tatumn had picked out matching pajamas for us. So, I was wandering the woods with a Nerf gun in hand and a pair of very tiny shorts on. Everyone was spread out. There were tents tucked into every nook of the forest. Tate and some other girls brought streamers and string lights with paper lanterns hung on them.

There was a fire ring, and all the lucky ones, *the ones who had managed to get out already*, were sitting around it or wandering in whatever direction they pleased.

"Watch out, Sweetness… Tate's over there." Cash whispered.

I saw her but she was alone, so I looked up. Ethan's gun was pointed at Cash, but he wasn't even looking at me. I shot him and a frustrated noise escaped his lips when he felt the sting of the bullet.

Tate looked up at him and Cash shot her. She was disappointed, but when she walked by, she said, "Peyton and Logan are the only ones left. You've got this." I nodded, even though I didn't care a bit about winning and followed Cash further into the woods.

He shot both of them before they even knew we were coming, turned around and wrapped me up in his arms. He smelled different than Camden, like Irish Spring soap and expensive cologne. He swung me around, "I knew you'd be my good luck charm." I knew he was just excited, but I didn't like him all over me. I tried to pull away and Camden said, "You won."

Cash put me down and pulled his shoulders back. "Damn straight we did. Emma's a stone-cold killer." Camden looked at him with a bored expression on his face. "No, she's not. I bet she didn't even want to play."

I knew he'd caught me at a bad moment. Tangled up in the arms of another guy, but I could tell he wasn't going to make a thing about it. He was dressed in all black, hair still a little damp from his shower. He walked over and wrapped his arms around my waist.

"I didn't know you were coming." His eyes shot to Cash, "I did."

He leaned in to kiss me, and then he took my hand in his and led me over to the fire. Tatumn was sitting in Ethan's lap, talking loudly, and letting her eyes shift from side to side. I could tell she was nervous, but Ethan didn't seem to realize.

Camden pulled me down into his lap. "How long do we have to stay out here?" I turned to look at him, "You just got here." He kissed the crest of my shoulder blade and gave me a suggestive look. "That doesn't mean I'm not ready to leave." He ran his hand over my thigh and told me he liked my shorts.

Tatumn stood up and gave me a significant look. I followed her over to the cooler in the back of Cash's truck. She said, "I didn't know he was coming." I told her I didn't either and asked her if she was nervous. She shook her head, but said, "Yeah, a little. Is it that easy to tell?" I told her I could tell, but I didn't think Ethan knew. She nodded, "Will you stay out until I find the courage to leave with him?"

I didn't really want to stay. I wanted to go to my own tent with Camden, but the insecure look in Tatumn's eyes forced the *yes* from my lips. "Okay, good. I can do this. It's just Ethan." She said more to herself than me.

We walked back over to the campfire and Camden pulled me back down into his lap. People got louder as the night went on. Several of the girls started dancing and Cash joined them. The song from *Dirty Dancing* came on and Tatumn did the lift with Ethan. They left when the song was over.

Camden tapped my hip. We climbed into my tent. He sat down beside me and pulled off his backpack. Handed me several tea lights with a switch on the bottom that I turned on and spread out around us.

He reached back in and pulled out my book. I gave him a playful look, "Are you planning on catching up on some reading tonight?" He put it down on the ground and looked up at me. "No, but I thought you might want it." I did, but not right now.

I leaned over and pulled at the collar of his shirt. He kissed me. His lips soft and pliant against mine. A rushing sensation in my chest. A quickening in my core.

His lips were my favorite place to be. Mine parted and he pushed me back onto the pillow. His lips trailed down my neck, over my collar bones, onto my chest and torso.

Somewhere between being lost in the way his hand wrapped around my ribs and wanting him closer than he already was. I realized this was the only night we'd ever been together like this.

Just the two of us.

Shrouded in candlelight reflecting off the tent. The sounds of the forest protecting us from the others. No one to walk in or interrupt. We had hours. I was breathless at the thought of what we could do with them.

He kissed down my belly, pulling at the waistband of my shorts. I looked down at him, hungry eyes devouring my skin. How ever long it was, it wasn't going to be long enough.

He pushed my shorts aside and gave me a hungry glance. I pushed my hips up and he leaned in. Licked me. Sensation so intense it stole my breath from my chest. Tucked it low in my belly. He did it again and I moaned.

He reached up, ran his fingers over my lips. "You have to be quiet, baby." He licked me again. I couldn't do that. My hips wiggled under his tongue. Moans tore out over my lips.

He smiled up against me, pulled back and said, "I'll have to stop if you can't be quiet." I shot him a desperate look and he said, "I don't want to, but those sounds belong to me. I can't have you sharing them with everyone else."

I wrapped my hands in his hair. Pulled him up beside me. We kissed and I tasted myself on his lips. He reached down and touched me. Muffled my moans with his kiss.

This was the happiest I'd ever been. He was so close. I didn't ever want to let him to go. The thought of being away from him hurt. My body stiffened and he pulled back. Dark, hungry eyes with a question in them. "What is it, Emma? Have I done something wrong?" I gave him a hasty no, and he leaned back in, pushed my shirt up and pressed a kiss to my belly.

I whimpered and he said, "If you don't tell me, I'll stop."

It was a threat, but for some reason it made my back arch. He pulled at the waistband of my shorts. Tugging them down just enough to kiss the curve of my hip.

For a moment he was all there was. His lips, fingers, breath on my skin. He nipped at the soft skin of my belly, hand dragging up my thigh, looking up at me, "You don't think I'll do it?"

I wasn't thinking at all. Until he sat up and took his hands off me. I said, "No, what are you doing?" He gave me a concerned look, "Tell me what's bothering you."

I said, "Nothing. Nothing's bothering me."

He looked at me skeptically and pulled his sketch pad out. I panicked. "I just realized that tonight is our only night. That tomorrow I have to leave."

He nodded, "I know. Do you want to stop?"

I didn't. Not at all, but the way he said it gave me an uneasy feeling. I shook my head, and he said, "It's alright if you do."

I nodded, pulled my shirt back down. He picked up his pencil and asked me if he could draw me. I wanted to ask how he could let me go so easily. I wanted to hear him say he couldn't.

I nodded. "Sure, how do you want me?" His face pulled in, contemplative look in his eyes. "How can I have you?" he asked.

"I don't know, is this drawing French or American?"

He couldn't suppress his smile. I could tell he was considering it, but he said, "That's not what I meant. I meant how would you be most comfortable. It takes a while."

"What if I'm most comfortable with all my clothes off?"

He looked at me like he didn't believe I'd do it, but he said, "I won't object."

I turned onto my stomach and pushed the strap of my shirt down. "Are you really going to do this?" I looked back at him, "Are you really going to let me?" His pupils dilated. "I don't know if I'll be able to make it through it without touching you."

^^^^^^

After everything, when my head was nuzzled into the curve of his arm, my cheek lying flat on his chest. He told me he didn't want me to leave, and I said, "I don't want to go another year without you." He kissed the top of my head. "I know, me either, but it's just one more year and then we'll be together. Always."

13

Now

Emma

Tatumn's Bachelorette party was planned slowly over years of growing up together. It started with a few comments, young girls lying in our room, feet propped up on the wall in front of us. Tatumn thumbing through the pages of a fashion magazine and telling me that she thought the wedding and reception seemed like they were for everyone else, but the bachelorette party was actually for the bride.

She put the magazine down on her chest and looked over at me. "For my bachelorette party I want penises everywhere, *confetti, balloons, headbands*, and I definitely want a stripper." I nodded, "Because, when are you going to have another opportunity to justify that?"

She gave me an approving look, "Exactly."

When she found out about Ethan's contract and he signed on the new house, she said, "I was wrong, it can't be just a party. I'm leaving, and that means that I need some serious alone time with my girls."

Alissa helped me arrange it all and we'd spent all day being escorted in and out of dimly lit rooms with soft moody music playing in the background. We'd had lotions and oils rubbed into all of our muscles. Hot rocks had been laid on our backs under a Vichy shower treatment, and our faces were all steamed, exfoliated, and moisturized.

Tatumn is sitting in the center of the relaxation room, sipping a mojito out of a penis shaped straw, and talking about what a genius I am for planning it all. The other girls all agree, and Tatumn looks over at me.

"The only problem is that two days isn't long enough." Something about the tenor of her voice is off, and even though all the other girls just laugh and say things like, *I could stay longer*, or *I know, my masseuse was so good I almost proposed*, I look over at her.

Her eyes shift from one side of the room to the other, "Maybe I should just cancel the wedding and use the funds to book a permanent room here."

The rest of the girls say, *yeah*, and *do it*, but I can hear the hint of truth in what she's said. I give her a questioning look and her lips settle into a sad smile. Dani says, "You can't cancel the wedding. It'll break Agatha's heart."

My mom looks over at her. "What about Ethan's?" Dani shrugs. "Oh, he'll be alright. He isn't nearly as attached to his tux as Agatha is to her dress. She'll never forgive you if she doesn't get to walk down the aisle in it." Tatumn says, "Oh my God, I know." but her eyes dart to the side, and I feel like something might actually be bothering her.

Jessica says, "Well no matter what you do, I'm keeping my dress." and all the other girls agree.

We have dinner in town at one of those restaurants with white tablecloths and meticulously laid out place settings. We order too much wine and not nearly enough food.

Everyone is talking loudly and leaning into one another. Dani jokingly asks Tatumn if she needs any pointers for her wedding night and April says, "No, what we really need to know is, have you guys done it with his uniform on?"

Tatumn lifts her glass. "Not yet, we're saving that for the honeymoon." Jess says, "I'd make him wear it all the time." and the other girls say things like *right*, and *definitely*.

We're all staying together tonight, and even though I was relieved to pack an overnight bag and leave the ranch this morning. I can't help but think about him as we walk into Tatumn's suite.

There's a row of mattresses on the floor, covered in pillows and fluffy down comforters, a side bar cluttered with bowls of candy and popcorn, and individual gift bags on the table.

Tatumn rushes over to pick hers up. It's a pajama set, soft white cotton with the words, *Women belong* on top, written across the chest. She squeals and the rest of us open ours.

Mine say, *Good girls have all the fun*, while Jess's say, *Looking for a sweet country boy*, and April's say, *I'll be your cowgirl*. Cynthia walks out of the bathroom hiding her face behind her hands and we all laugh at the delicate swirly print that reads, *Daddy issues made me do it*.

I open a bottle of white and pour for everyone. Tatumn chooses the movie, and I cuddle in between her and Dani and watch as Baby gets out of the car.

Dani leans over and tells me this is really great, that I've done well, and Tatumn seems really happy. I look over at Tate, but she is completely enthralled with the movie, so she doesn't notice. I tell Dani, thanks, and say, "Tate deserves all the happiness in the world."

She takes a drink. "Yeah, she does, but so do you." A tingle of discomfort crawls across the skin of my back and I have to readjust my shoulders on the pillow behind me. Dani asks, "How has it been at the ranch?" and I tell her it's been fine.

"Well, that's good to hear. I know how much he's missed you."

I feel like I should make an excuse to get up, just to avoid the rest of this conversation, but I just look over at her and she says, "You're the only thing he ever talks about. Every time he called, I could almost count down the seconds until he said, *and how's Emma*, and then we'd spend the rest of the time talking about you." A large lump forms in my throat.

She gives me a careful look, "You know there's no shame in second chances."

I nod and turn away.

^^^^^^

The next day starts with breakfast on the rooftop, followed by a long leisurely swim in the heated pool. We have appointments at the spa for hair and nails, and when we're all done there, we get a coffee and walk through Lindley Park.

We come back to the hotel to get ready, and the girls and I present Tatumn with her bachelorette outfit. It's an exact replica of her high school cheer uniform except for instead of *Eagles* it says, *Bride,* and all of ours say *Bridesmaid.*

I'm the only girl that wasn't on the squad, and this was the only part of the party that really gave me pause. Jessica was the one that convinced me, she said "You'll just feel left out, and Tatumn will love it." Tatumn does love it, so do all the other girls, so I just suck it up and put mine on.

We leave the hotel and make our way down Main Street. I feel absolutely ridiculous, but the other girls own it. We stop in several bars, and even though I have everything covered, all the shots we order get paid for.

There are phone numbers left on napkins and several requests to join us at our next stop. Tatumn decides that she likes all the attention and she and April take turns doing body shots off of Cynthia's back, chest, and thighs in front of a very invested audience.

Alissa sends me a text that says, *we may have a problem.*

I reply with a question mark, and she says, *Gabriel has the flu.*

I went back and forth on whether or not to actually get a stripper, and Tatumn doesn't know about it, but the other girls do. I pull Jess aside and tell her what Alissa said, "Oh, well maybe we can get one of these guys to strip for her." I have no doubt that we could do it, but it seems like a really bad idea.

April slams her shot glass down on the bar and looks over at us. "I know someone who would." She pulls her phone out and swipes her finger across the screen and then I hear her say, "We need a favor."

^^^^^^^

Tatumn didn't want to leave but we told her she didn't have a choice, and she wouldn't regret it anyway. We're all back in her suite, drinking wine and eating handfuls of candy and day old popcorn.

We've been there maybe fifteen minutes when there's a knock at the door and someone says, "Open up, there's been a noise complaint."

I look over at April and she giddily grabs onto Cynthia's arm. Tatumn looks over at me, eyes wide and mouth dropped open, "You didn't?" My brows raise in this *I don't know, maybe I did* sort of way. Jess opens the door and Cash says, "I hear there are some very naughty girls in here."

He's dressed like a police officer, and he reaches into his back pocket and pulls out a pair of cuffs. He looks back over his shoulder, "Come on boys. I think I'm going to need some backup." Gabe and Josh walk in behind him wearing black pants and white t-shirts that are pulled tight over their muscular chests.

Tatumn says, "No way." and then Ethan walks in and turns the music up.

Cash walks over to me and leans in close. "I heard you needed some assistance." I shake my head, *no*, and he says, "Don't worry, I won't be too gentle."

I push against his chest, and he turns away and goes over to stand in front of Cynthia. He rips his shirt off and she falls back on the bed. Gabe and Josh both undo their belts while standing in front of Jess and April, and Ethan walks over to Tatumn.

It's a lot of *oh my*, and *did you see that*. The guys turn around and swivel their hips and Jess grabs hold of April's arm. Cash is committed and Cynthia is practically drooling as he pulls his belt off and unzips his pants.

Tatumn and Ethan seem to be in their own world. Making a lot of eye contact and unspoken promises. I catch Cash's gaze, and he winks, "Come on over here, Sweetness. There's plenty of me to go around."

Cynthia's eyes dart to mine and she waves me over. I don't go. I slip out the door thankful that no one follows me.

The lounge downstairs is dimly lit and quiet. There's low music playing in the background and groups of men in button down shirts sitting around drinking whiskey in club chairs. He hasn't turned around, but I know it's him. He's sitting alone, talking to Alan at the bar. I go over and take a seat, and he turns to face me.

"What are you doing here?" I ask.

His eyes travel down to my chest, and he gives me a distracted, "I came to get my bike." I nod and ask Alan for a glass of red. Camden picks up his own drink. "Where are the rest of the girls?"

I can tell by the way he's asked that he already knows. "Upstairs." His eyes narrow, "Why aren't you up there with them?" Alan hands me my wine. "Because it's like a *Magic Mike* movie up there right now."

He runs his finger along the edge of his glass. "And you're not into that sort of thing?" I shrug. "Too good a girl?" It stings, but I shake my head, "No, but they were all sort of coupled up and I felt like an intruder."

His brow wrinkles in thought. "So, it was more of a numbers thing than a true moral superiority?" I take a drink of my wine, "I'm really not that good a girl, Camden." His eyes pinch in, and he looks like he is thinking a whole lot more than he's going to say.

His head dips, "Sure, you are."

I ask him if he's staying here tonight and his eyes dart to mine, "No, are you?" I think about going back up there. Walking into the aftermath, *pheromones and alcohol permeating the air. A tight sexual tension that no one will be able to sever. Me trying to find a quiet spot to slink away while everyone else crowds around each other, making crude comments and laughing loudly.*

"No, I'll probably get an Uber home." He leans in, rests his elbows on his knees. "I can take you." I think about getting on his bike with him. Wrapping my arms around his waist and feeling the cool wind blow my hair back.

"I don't know, maybe."

He looks down again. "So, are you going to explain the outfit, or should I just continue to make up scenarios in my head?" I look down at my pleated skirt. "It's for Tatumn." He nods, this slow seductive move that makes my skin tingle.

"Well maybe it was."

I feel my cheeks flush and take another drink of wine. I ask him what he means by that, and he leans back and looks at me. "You didn't want to wear that, did you? I shake my head, "This? Are you kidding? Everyone who's anyone is wearing this right now." His eyes tighten and he nods, "Well, anyway… it looks good on you."

A sultry glance passes between us.

I look down at the glass in his hand, "How much did you have to drink with the guys today?" He shrugs, "Probably too much, but I'm not drunk, if that's what you mean."

He looks over toward the stage and asks me if I want to dance. I shake my head. "No, do you?" He shrugs again, "Not really." I look down at my glass, run my finger along the stem.

"Then why did you ask?"

He's quiet for a moment, gaze cast down and focused on the spot right between my knees. His grip tightens around the glass in his hand, and he looks up, "Because it's really hard not touching you when you're this close."

I laugh, "It's just an outfit, Camden." His eyes travel over my legs, *hips, chest.*

"It's not just the outfit, Emma."

I pick up my wine and narrow my eyes at him. "I don't know if I *should* get on your bike with you?" He leans in closer, "I think you should."

He smells like warmth dipped in whisky and the sweetness of his breath is hard to turn away from. I take another drink, and he puts his glass down on the bar. "I'm ready when you are." The heat of his breath on my cheek pulls my shoulder up. I nod and tell Alan to put my wine on the room.

Camden stands up and holds his hand out to me. I narrow my eyes at it because I know this isn't a good idea, but then he says, "Come here, Emma." and lifts his chin in this way that makes me want to follow him. I put my hand in his.

We've barely made it out of the building before he turns around and presses my back into the wall.

A whole lot of *no, this can't be happening,* goes to battle with the very loud and resounding, *yes,* that runs through me.

He reaches up to tuck some loose strands of hair behind my ear and I say, "Camden what are you doing?" but my voice sounds too sensual to be convincing and he steps in closer.

"Isn't it obvious?"

His eyes travel all over my face and I can tell he's struggling with something. They settle on my lips. I think he's going to kiss me. He leans in close, and I am very tempted to close the distance between us. I don't though. He hesitates, and I press my back firmly against the wall.

"What is it?"

He runs his thumb over my bottom lip and looks up at me.

"I didn't come back for the wedding. I'm here for you."

He says it like a confession, and it's like getting an early Christmas present that's wrapped up in cellophane and duct tape. You know you want it, but it seems impossible to get to.

"Yeah, but you're still leaving." He gives me a heated look. "Maybe you should ask me what my plans are before you make up my mind for me."

The tips of his fingers travel up my thigh and stop at the hem of my skirt, *muscles flex, core tightens, breath catches*. He looks at me like he knows, and I say, "Well, what are they?"

He grabs hold of the edge of my skirt and presses into me.

He says, "I don't know. You tell me." and it's probably the wine… but I kiss him.

On the Outside of Everything

^^^^^^

Camden

I don't care about my bike. I came here to see her and even though I know she just stumbled into that bar, it felt like I'd summoned her. Like my wanting it to happen made it so, and now she's kissing me.

I pull away. "Come on, let's go home." She gives me a puzzled look and I can't help but look down at her lips again, *dark pink, slightly swollen, wet.*

They're so tempting that I have a hard time turning away from her to walk over to my bike. I put the helmet on her head. She asks where mine is, and I tell her I only have one now.

She wraps her arms around my waist, and we take off. I can feel her pressed up against me and it's difficult to keep the bike on the road. We make it to the ranch. I pull the bike to a stop and turn around to face her. She takes off her helmet and I wrap my hand in her hair and pull her closer.

I kiss her for a long time, because she lets me. I tell her I've missed her, and she says, "You shouldn't have left." I nod and press my lips into her neck, "I'm sorry, I won't do it again."

She pulls at the fabric of my shirt. "But you live in New York." I press my hands up under her skirt. "No, I don't." She pulls back and looks at me. "I live here now. If you'll have me."

She looks hesitant, like she doesn't trust herself enough to believe me. I push her hair off of her shoulder and lean down to press my lips into her skin.

She tastes delicious, but I miss the warmth of her thighs. I reach back down and wish I could still feel her hair falling through my fingers. There's not enough of me. I need more hands, *fingers, lips, tongues*. She says, "I don't understand." I kiss all along her collar bones and up onto her neck.

"It's not difficult. I never should have left you, and I don't want to do it again."

Her lips part and I lean in to kiss them. She scoots forward and I turn around and pull her onto my lap. She says, *I want you*, and *I've missed you*, and *don't leave*.

I dig my fingers into her sides and tell her I want her too, and I won't leave, not if she wants me to stay. She says, "I do." as we struggle to get our clothes off and get closer to one another. I ask, "Here?" and she says, "Everywhere."

I try to tell myself to hold on, but she feels so good. Her hips rock up against mine and I drag my lips over her chest. I tell her I love her, and she says, "Still?" I say, "Yes, *still, forever, always*."

^^^^^^

Emma

He sleeps in my bed, and I hold his hand up against my heart. He tells me he's sorry, and I say, "Enough."

His hands travel all over my body and we find each other several times throughout the night. I wake with his mouth on me and reach down to wrap my hands in his hair.

He mumbles something about lost time, and says, "I don't think I'll ever be able to stop." I tell him he can't survive on me alone, and the way he looks at me like he thinks he can, makes my core clench tight.

My hair spreads out on the pillow behind me as he peppers my skin with kisses and tells me I'm *perfect, lovely, delicious*. We fall in and out of sleep. He wraps himself around me and I climb on top of him.

When he's inside me he says, "I'll never get enough. I'm never going to be able to stop touching you." I tell him I know, "pleasure like this seems impossible." He says, "It's more than pleasure. You can't be summed up in one word."

I tell him I've missed him, and he tells me his life has been full of mistakes, but he only regrets one of them. I ask which one and he says, *the one where I lost you*. I want to stay here, *cloaked in darkness with him*, but the sunlight starts peeking through the window and my phone pings with a message from Tate.

When I pick it up, I half expect it to say, *I told you so*, but it doesn't. It says, *I'm here, where are you at*. I realize that today is the day we have to decorate the ranch. Everyone is coming. Tatumn is apparently already here.

I push Camden's hand off of me. "Get up. You have to get out of here." His brow furrows and he reaches up to rub the sleep out of his eyes. "I'm serious Camden, you have to leave."

"Are you actually kicking me out of your bed right now?"

I nod enthusiastically, "Yes. Now go, before someone sees you."

He looks incredulous and I get up and throw his pants at him, "Get dressed." He reaches up to run his hand through his hair. "No, I don't want to. Come back to bed."

I walk over to my closet, pull on a pair of shorts and tug a shirt over my head. He says, "Emma, what's happening?" I tell him Tate's downstairs and everyone else will be here soon. He gives me a puzzled look, "and you don't want them to see us together?"

I tell him, *no, obviously.*

He pushes the covers back, sunshine pours over his chest and abs. "It doesn't seem very obvious to me."

I have a very small moment of indecision, where I imagine crawling back in bed with him, but then I hear Tate's footsteps on the stairs and say, "Camden, get up. You have to get out of here."

I can tell he doesn't like this, but I cannot even begin to process the mess it would make if Tate walked in and saw him in my bed.

With a small knock, Tate says, "Emma, I need you, my head hurts."

I look over at the door and then back at Camden. He jumps up out of bed and starts shoving his legs into his pants. I say, "Tate?" like I don't know it's her, and I try to sound sleepy while I do it. Camden pulls his shirt on, and then I grab his arm and shove him in my closet.

Tate opens the door, and I turn around and pull at the hem of my shirt. She looks worse than she sounds. Her eyes are droopy, and her skin is dull. She says, "Help." in this really small voice, and I take her hand to lead her out of my room. I leave the door open, so she won't hear him walk out, and take her downstairs to start a pot of coffee.

She sits at the bar with her head resting on the cool granite, and I get her a glass of water and tell her to drink it.

She tells me Alissa called and woke her up and that they should be here soon with all the chairs and flowers.

She sits up to take a drink, "Why did we plan it like this?" I pour her a cup of coffee and tell her, she's lucky she doesn't have to walk down the aisle today. She nods. "I wouldn't do it. I would just cancel, or at the very least postpone it all."

I'm just about to ask her what she means by that when Camden walks downstairs. She looks up at him. He says, *hey*, and she grumbles something under her breath. I turn around and pour myself a cup of coffee and he steps up behind me.

His fingers graze my arm as he reaches to get a cup and everything in me tightens.

I look over at Tatumn. She's staring down at her coffee with a glazed expression on her face, and even though I'm worried about her, I'm glad she didn't see.

He steps to the side and presses his thigh into mine and I push him away with my hip.

Tate puts her head back down on the counter, "Did he take you home last night?" Thinking about last night makes my throat go dry. Camden's lips tick up. His eyes dart to mine. A flush of heat runs through me, and I have to fight to keep my voice neutral as I say, "Yeah, he was at the bar. I was going to Uber, but he was already coming here. So yeah… I just rode out with him."

He puts his cup down and picks up the coffee pot. Tate looks up at me and it feels like she knows. She says, "Well, that worked out nicely." I nod and look away from her, "Yeah, I guess."

He pours himself a cup and looks at me over the edge as he takes a drink. His thoughts are very clearly written out in the grey of his irises, and even though my traitorous core tightens, I shake my head. His brows rise in a way that says, *alright, but it's your loss.*

It is. I know it is. If anyone finds out about us, he won't be the one that looks like a fool.

I will.

He left me. I'm the one that is supposed to be strong enough to resist him.

^^^^^^

Camden

Emma walks off to get the door. I watch her go with some remorse and then everyone walks in at once. Alissa points everyone in one direction or another and I go outside to help the guys unload the chairs.

Alissa walks out with Emma trailing behind her and even though I watch her walk all the way up the hill, she doesn't look over at me. Her avoidance stings worse today than it did before. Before I knew why she was avoiding me. Today it feels different, like she's ashamed of me, *specifically*, and there are plenty of reasons why she should be.

It's just that she never was before.

Alissa tells us where to put everything and Emma walks behind us making small seemingly insignificant changes and avoiding my gaze. I don't like the way she looks everywhere else just to keep her eyes from landing on mine.

I know one night isn't enough to really change things, but I had hoped she'd at least be able to look at me.

It's very hard not to turn around and touch her. I know she wants me to pretend like nothing happened, and I'm not a terrible liar, but I don't like pretending. I spent so much of my life having to hide, lying to one person to protect another. Constantly finding myself in impossible situations, *drugs, money, love.* It was all tied up together. Every time I solved one problem, there was another one waiting.

I was living so many different lives it was hard to keep up with. Emma was the only thing that made sense, and it used to feel like my love was a poison running through her veins. More toxic than the shit my mother used to put in her arm.

It's not like that now though, and I don't like feeling like I can't touch her. I don't like having to pretend I don't want her. I'd rather her yell, *tell me off, kick me completely out of her life if that's what she needs,* but I want her to be able to look at me when she does it. It's not like her, looking away, being so concerned about what everyone else thinks.

Emma is the exception to the rule. She dives in where others shy away. It makes me nervous. It makes her feel too unpredictable. She was never so easily swayed.

I know there's a lot going on, *Tatumn's wedding, her leaving, me coming back.* It has to be a lot. I want to believe that's all it is. *Overwhelming.* Too much to process in one day, but it feels like maybe it's more. Like maybe I waited too long, and she'll never come back to me. Like I sequestered myself to the darkness. Made the possibility of us seem so far-fetched that it's only allowed to exist as a secret.

Her avoidance only makes me want her more. I find it impossible not to touch her. I graze her leg with my own as I walk by, or run my fingers over the back of her hand as she passes me.

She pulls away and acts like nothing's happened, but I can feel the tension building between us, see the effort it takes for her to keep looking away.

When the chairs are all set up, Ethan says, "Hey man, come help me get the altar." Emma is talking to Cash. Her cheeks are flushed with laughter, and I want to go over there just to find out what they're talking about. I nod, and Ethan says, "How's that going anyway?" I look back over my shoulder, and she quickly looks away. "I'm not sure."

He says, "It's not easy coming back." I nod, "It's not easy staying away either." He shrugs, "I know. I left right after you did." I look back over at him. "She was pregnant." His expression is stark, and I know this isn't something he actually wants to talk about, so I look away. "That must have been tough."

"It was worse than tough, and I thought I'd never get her back."

I nod and he says, "You get that side, and I'll get the other." We pick up the altar and start walking back up the hill. Cash has his hand on Emma's shoulder and the ease and familiarity that he touches her with sends a flash of jealousy through me like I've never felt before. I clear my throat.

"Well, it looks like it worked out." He shrugs. "I don't know if I'd say that." I give him a skeptical look. "You know you're the groom, right?"

His smile tightens, worry floats through his eyes. "I sure hope so."

We make it to the top of the hill and set the altar down in front of the aisle. Emma and Cash turn and start walking toward the house. He says, thanks, and I say, "Are you scared she won't show up?"

He gets a serious look on his face. "The thought has crossed my mind. I did leave her. So, it would only be fair."

I look over and see the door closing behind Emma. "I don't think love works like that." He looks at the closed door. "Yeah, but trust is a really hard thing to get back."

I nod and tell him I know, "but I still have to try." We start walking down the hill together and he says, "Yeah, me too."

^^^^^^

Emma

The ranch looks more like a resort than a home now. The stairwells are covered in light pink peonies and eucalyptus sprigs. There are cocktail tables set out on the porch and string lights hanging over the island in the kitchen.

Dani hands me a box of napkins with Tate and Ethan's name on them and asks me to go put them in the storage room.

I walk down the hall, past the washer and dryer, and step inside. There are boxes all over the floor and even though I'm already exhausted, I decide I need to at least try to clear a path for tomorrow. I bend over to put the box down and Camden asks, "Where should I put this one?"

I look around the room. "Just leave it there, I'll find a place for it." I hear a soft thud as he puts the box down, and then he steps inside and closes the door behind him. I turn around, "What are you doing?"

He looks at me like he can't quite figure me out, steps over the boxes between us, and wraps his arm around my waist.

He pulls me in close. Kisses me. "Emma, I don't like this." I ask him what he means. "You've barely looked at me today. I don't know how you're doing it, but it's driving me mad."

I tell him, I can't look at him. "Why not?" He pushes the hair off of my neck and leans down to kiss the patch of skin he's exposed. I say, "Camden." and he says, "I know."

His hands press into my sides, and my head falls back. He pulls me in tighter, and I want to give into him, but I say, "We can't. Someone will find us."

He lifts the hem of my shirt and runs his hand over my back. "I don't care. I can't stay away from you anymore." He leans down and kisses my neck.

Everything in me feels tight. *Too tight.* I want him, but I can still hear them all out there. Walking around and debating trivial things like if the wine should be served in the kitchen or outside on the patio.

I tell him, *no, we can't, not here,* and he says, "What happened to everywhere?" I pull back and look at him. I know what I said, but surely, he realizes that last night and today are two entirely different things. It seems like something I shouldn't have to say, but I tell him, "We lost everywhere when you left."

His eyes pull in and an unmistakable sliver of pain runs through them. I hate hurting him, but it's the truth so I don't take it back. He nods. "I thought that might be it, but Emma, you can't keep avoiding me."

I don't like feeling the way I do. It's confusing, wanting him so bad and needing him to stay away. He puts his thumb under my chin and raises my face to his. "Just talk to me."

I pull my lower lip in with my teeth and chew on it while I try to think. He looks anxious, *stiff shoulders, tight jaw, eyes pulled in at the corners*. I don't really know what to say, there's so much it seems overwhelming. *Impossible*. I look up at him and his eyes run over my face like they're the lead detectives on a murder case.

"I'm not avoiding you."

His brow furrows. "You haven't spoken to me. You won't look at me. You make an excuse to leave the room every time I walk in."

"Yeah, because you won't stop touching me."

He looks at me like he really doesn't understand. "I licked your pussy for an hour and a half last night." I shrug, "Exactly, I'm not avoiding you." He says, "That's not what I mean, and you know it." I tell him maybe not, but it's the truth.

"The truth? I don't think that has anything to do with the truth."

He looks down at me like he's waiting, and I think about all the time I spent waiting for him. Years. Wondering where he was. If he was okay, *alive, hurt, alone*. Wondering what I'd done to drive him away from me. Why I was part of what he needed to escape from. My chest felt like a cavern, *empty, cold, lifeless*.

I think about asking him, making him give me an itemized list of all the reasons he left, *stayed away, ignored my messages*. It's too late for that though, so I say, "You said always, and I believed you. You told me you'd be here, and then you left me like I meant nothing. You didn't even say goodbye, and everyone out there knows how badly you hurt me. They were all here when you left, and I don't know how you handled it… but I was a mess."

His eyes close tight. "Yeah, I was a mess too, but that was a long time ago Emma, and I've already told you I'm not going to leave again." He looks lost, so I reach out and take his hand in mine. "I know, but you said something like that before." His hand gets heavier. I trace over his knuckles with my thumb.

I don't really know what I'm doing. I want to believe him, but I say, "and they don't know that anyway." He looks up. "I'll go tell them right now." I shake my head, "No, don't." He asks why, and I say, "because this is Tatumn's wedding."

He gets this determined look on his face. "Yeah, it is… and Ethan left her while she was pregnant. They were all here. They all know that, and have any of them turned away?"

"It's not the same for me, Camden." He asks why and I tell him I'm not the same as Tatumn. He nods, bites his lower lip in this way that makes me want to know what he's trying not to say, "… and I'm not the same as Ethan."

I hate the defeated look in his eyes, but it's true so I just say, "We just need to give it a little time." He reaches out to tuck a strand of hair behind my ear. "How much time?" I shrug. "I don't know, you were gone for years, so maybe at least give me the week."

"A week, as in this week, you'll tell them after the wedding?"

My shoulders pull up and he says, "I'm not going to keep pretending. I've done too much of that already. I want you, *all of you*, and if that's not what you want then you just need to tell me, and I'll go."

A small volt of electricity pulls my face tight.

His arm tightens around my waist. "I don't want to, that's not what I'm saying, but I told you. I came here for you. If you don't want me, I'll leave."

An avalanche of disappointment and validation falls on me. "That's so much easier to believe."

He gives me a questioning look.

"That you'll leave."

He nods slowly. I can tell I've upset him. "I'm sorry, but this is all I can offer right now. I need some time." He runs the back of his hand over my cheek, "How much time?" I lean into him, "I don't know."

He bends down and places a soft kiss at the corner of my lips. "That's not good enough. I can't be this close and this far away. I can't pretend I don't want you forever."

I tell him it won't be forever. He presses his lips into my neck, drags them over my jawline, and stops at my ear. Everything in me tingles and tightens with anticipation. He says, "It's okay, it's only us in here." I nod and wrap my arms around his shoulders. He threads his hand in my hair and pulls.

It's just enough pain to make everything else disappear. Their voices fade and all I hear is his breath and the sound of fabric sliding over skin. He lifts me up and I wrap my legs around his waist.

His lips move over mine. I feel him getting hard and rock my hips over him. He reaches down and moves my shorts out of the way.

My back presses into the wall, and I say, "We can't." His fingers press inside. "Tell me to stop and I will." My head falls back, and I hear the light scratching noise of my hair as it travels over the wall behind me.

It's hard to speak but I manage a breathy, "No, don't."

He presses in deeper, "I always knew you were a good girl."

He reaches down and unzips his pants. I look over at the door, "We really don't have long." He lifts me up and says, "It never is long enough." as he pushes into me.

It's fast and rough, but I like the way his fingers dig into my back like he needs me. I have to bury my face in the curve of his neck to muffle the moans and whimpers that refuse to stay inside my throat. He says, "I'm not going to be able to do it." I want to ask him what he means, but every time he pushes into me my thoughts go blank. He says, "I can't stay away from you. I love you, *I never stopped loving you. I'll never stop loving you.*"

He takes my hand in his and presses it into the wall above me. He looks me in the eyes and says, "Leave it." as he drags his fingers down my arm and over the side of my body. I come completely undone, every time he pushes into me, I think, *yes, this, you.* His breath comes in quick powerful bursts up against my cheek and he says, "Tell me you love me. Tell me you're mine."

I want to, and all I can think is *you, you, you,* but the words get stuck behind a knot in my throat. He says my name like it's a prayer, like he worships me, *wants me, needs me.* I try to tell him *I love him, that I'm his, I always have been,* but there's a quiet knock at the door and then Tate says, "Emma, are you in there?"

I push Camden away and reach down to straighten my shorts. Camden backs up and turns around to face the shelves behind him. I hear the sound of his zipper closing and then Tate pushes the door open.

My heart is beating too quickly, and I know my breathing is off. I'm scared to speak, knowing that my voice is likely to come out in forced intervals, but Tate looks over at me and I say, "Yeah, what is it?" as naturally as possible.

Her eyes narrow as they shift between my face and the back of his head. I start walking toward her and she says, "Oh, nothing really." I nod and step over a pile of boxes. She looks at me very carefully and says, "Your mom's looking for you." as she reaches up and runs her fingers through my hair to fix it.

I can tell by the look in her eyes that she doesn't approve, or at the very least she doesn't understand. I feel guilty for upsetting her and mouth the words, *I'm so sorry*. She shakes her head in this slow sad way, and then my mom steps in behind her.

She looks over at Camden and then back at me. I see her eyes shift from suspicion to comprehension and then she says, "I was just looking for you, what are you doing in here?" I feel the heat in my cheeks, but I choose to ignore it. I tell her we were just arranging things for tomorrow. She looks back over at Camden, and then she looks at Tate.

I let my head drop, but I can feel the waves of disappointment as they waft off her.

"Yeah, it's a real mess in here."

I look up at her, and I know she's not talking about the boxes. I say something stupid, like *yeah, it is, but we're still working on it*. Her eyes narrow.

"Well, don't spend too much time on it. Sometimes you just have to know when to call it quits." I notice Camden's shoulders pull back. Mom shakes her head like she's trying to clear it, "Well, I just wanted to say, bye. I'll see you at the dinner later, right?"

^^^^^^

Camden

When we get to the restaurant Cash is outside waiting for her. I turn off the bike and she takes the helmet off and hands it to me. I grab ahold of her fingertips as she's pulling away and she looks over at him and says, "Camden, don't."

I watch as she walks away. The moment she reaches him, Cash wraps his arms around her and stares back at me. I don't like him, but there's a very short moment where I see how much easier her life would be if she did. She pulls away from him and he reaches down and takes her hand in his.

I can tell it makes her uncomfortable. She gives me a brief glance over her shoulder before she walks away. I get off my bike and walk inside. I tell the hostess I'm here for the Martin – Ellis party and she leads me to a private dining room in the back of the restaurant.

There's a band playing soft jazz in the corner and all the tables are covered in thick white cloth. A man in a black vest and bowtie offers me a drink and I order a scotch and soda. Dani sees me standing in the doorway and waves me over. Amber is standing right next to her. She looks up and quickly turns away.

I know she knows, and I've known Amber long enough to know that she won't want to talk about it. Neither do I, but

Emma was so upset when she left that I don't feel like I have a choice.

The room is full of people, but I can't help but notice the way she's still standing next to him. His eyes are on her, but hers are cast out over the crowd. Searching the room. Refusing to land in any one spot but repeatedly passing over the back of Tatumn's head.

The waiter returns with my drink, and I walk over to Dani. She pulls me in beside her and tells me I look nice. I tell her the same and she introduces me to a few people. I nod and shake their hands, and they all start talking amongst themselves again.

Amber won't look at me, but her glass is almost empty. I ask if I can get her another and she gives me a dismissive, "No. I'm good." It's obvious that what she wants is for me to go away, but she's squeezing the stem of her glass so tight that her knuckles blanch. I say, "Are you sure about that?" She looks over at Dani, pulls her shoulders back and stands up a little taller.

A young lady with a black cummerbund and dark red hair piled high on her head passes by. I lift my glass and nod towards Amber's. I watch as the girl weaves her way over to the bar and picks up a bottle of red. My eyes drift over to Emma and Amber says, "I'll bet New York is nice this time of year."

I nod, "Yeah, it is." The girl returns. Amber holds her glass out and forces a smile. Dani looks over at us with a nervous expression. I wonder if she knows too, but then Amber steps in closer, hiding her face behind the edge of my shoulder, and I realize she doesn't… and Amber doesn't want her to either.

"You've lived there a while now." I nod in agreement, and she says, "I hear you have someone waiting on you to get back."

It takes me a moment to realize, but then I ask, "Do you mean, Gabby?" Her eyes sharpen, "Is that her name?" I lift my glass and take a drink. "Gabby's just a friend. There's no one waiting for me in New York." She raises an indifferent shoulder and looks over at the band.

"But you are going back."

It's more of a statement than a question, and what she wants is for me to confirm it.

Tatumn walks over toward Emma. Emma's face tightens and her lips press in. Our eyes meet and then hers dart to her mother. Tatumn says something that makes her face fall, and I have to force myself to stay put.

Frustration needles my chest as Amber's hand falls to her side and Emma looks back over at me. I can hear her silent plea over the sounds of the stand-up bass, the piano, and all the voices surrounding me.

It's clear that what she wants is for me to walk away. To pretend like nothing happened and hope it will all just wash over and get lost in the current of Tatumn's wedding, but I did that once, and now I'm not even allowed to stand next to her at a party.

"Actually, I just graduated, and I don't plan to return to New York."

Amber's chest rises and Emma's eyes pull in. I smile at her reassuringly and Amber asks, "Where will you go then?" I turn to look at her. Her eyes are tight with concern. I tell her I plan to stay here for now, and Dani says, "Are you serious?"

Several people look our way. "I am." Amber looks over at her daughter, "Does she know that?" I nod and she takes a large gulp of wine, "What kind of business are you in now?"

I lift my glass to my lips to cover the taste of bitterness with whisky. I tell her what she wants to know. That I'm not and haven't been in that kind of business since I left here. She nods and looks over at Emma.

"You just had to come back."

I look over at her, *tight shoulders, wide eyes, finger tapping relentlessly against her glass.* I know she doesn't want to hear it, but I tell her the only truth I know.

"I love her, Amber."

^^^^^^

Emma

As soon as Cash pulls me in the restaurant, he says, "What the hell did you do? Tatumn told me not to leave your side." I cannot tell him what happened, so I just say, "Nothing, I don't know what you're talking about."

He gives me a disappointed look, "Sure, Emma, whatever you say." I tell him he really doesn't want to know, and I need a drink not a lecture.

The hostess leads us back to the party and he says, "If it's that bad. I definitely want to know." I roll my eyes and walk into the room, but he reaches out and takes my hand in his.

"Sorry sweetness… strict instructions."

I look around to find Tate. She looks perfect, *blonde waves, sophisticated navy dress, and a smile that radiates.* "As in I'm not allowed to talk to her?"

He shakes his head, "Not right now."

He finds a waiter and orders a glass of wine for me and a whisky soda for himself. Camden walks in the room and I see Dani wave him over. My eyes drift to my mother, who's standing right next to her, and I say, "I'll take one of those too, but you can hold the soda and make it a double." Cash's eyes shoot to mine and the waiter asks, "and you still want the wine?" I nod, "Definitely."

I finish the whisky in one drink. "Sweetness, what have you done?" I tell him I want to talk to Tate, and he shakes his head. "I'm not sure that's a good idea."

He looks worried, which is a strange look for him, but I ignore it and look around the room to find Tate again. She and Ethan are standing in a group with Gabe, Josh, and a few other guys I don't recognize. April and Jess walk up to join them and Tate smiles, but her eyes look too tight.

I take a step toward her, but Cash reaches out and takes a hold of my wrist. I give him a stern look, "Cash, you have two choices right now, and one of them involves me attempting to get away from you in heels after swallowing a double whisky."

He shrugs. "Sounds entertaining, what's the other?"

My eyes narrow, "You don't think I'll do it?"

He lets go of my wrist and takes a sip of his whisky. "No, I know you won't."

Camden is standing next to my mother now. Her face is tight, and her eyes are all wrong. Cash follows my gaze. "I figured it had something to do with Pierce." My cheeks flame with anger and embarrassment. "What did he do?" I say, "It wasn't him. It was us, and I don't want to talk about it."

He looks back over at them, "Your mom doesn't look very happy."

Something about the perfection of this room, *the flickering candlelight, soft jazz, vases full of white roses and blue hydrangeas spread out on the tables,* makes me feel even worse than I did earlier.

"No, she doesn't."

Tatumn walks up but she doesn't look at me. She tells Cash she put us at the back table together, and then asks if we got a drink. Cash lifts his glass, and I say, "Yeah, can we talk?" Her eyes shift from side to side, "Anyway, I've still got a few people to get to, but you two have fun."

She walks off and I feel everything in me fall, *crash, crumble.* Cash says, "Emma, did you stab somebody? Tell her she looked fat in her dress? Screw her fiancé?"

I sneer at him, "Very funny." He nods like he's proud of himself. "I know, but you might as well tell me because at this point it can't be worse that what I'm imagining." I tell him I can't, and he says, "Why, because you don't want anyone to know?" with his voice dripping in sarcasm.

"Yes, exactly. I don't want anyone to know." He takes another drink of his whisky. "Well, it seems like people do." I feel my cheeks flame and he gives me a serious look.

"Just tell me. I promise I won't judge."

I don't want to do it, but I know Cash, and he isn't going to let it go. I tell him I was… *caught in a compromising position.* His eyes pull in, "With Pierce?" I bite my lower lip, and he asks, "When?" I take a really large drink. "Earlier, at the ranch." He looks over at my mother, "How?" I tell him. His gaze shifts toward Camden.

He takes another drink, *jaw tight and shoulders stiff.*

"Well props to him, but what were you thinking?"

The tone of his voice is dismissive, but I can't tell if he's disappointed or angry. "What's that supposed to mean?" He gives me an irritated look, "Come on, Emma, you're a smart girl." I take a drink of my wine, "It wasn't planned." He raises a curt brow.

"Well then, shouldn't be anything to worry about."

He lifts his glass to his lips and finishes it in one drink. I don't know what his problem is, but between the snide looks my mother is giving Camden, and the fact that my best friend won't even talk to me. I don't feel like I have the capacity to deal with it.

When the waiter comes back, he orders us another round. Dani comes over to tell us that it's time to be seated, but before she goes, she says, "Can you believe he's staying?"

Cash's eyes narrow and I give a meek, "No, not really." We both take our seats, and he barely talks to me all through dinner. When they clear our plates, and he's finished his fourth whisky soda, he turns to me and says, "I don't get it. He left and I've been here the whole time."

My skin goes uncomfortably tight, "Sorry?" He lets out a harsh breath. "You know. I know you do." I shake my head, "I really don't." He looks me right in the eyes, "Emma, I love you." I think I know what he means, but he can't mean that, so I say, "I know. I love you too. You're one of my best friends." His chest shakes with this dull sort of laughter.

"I don't want to be your friend. I'm in love with you."

I feel like I'm walking through a minefield. Like every step I take causes a new explosion. Dani stands up to make a speech and I use it as an excuse to look away from him.

I can feel him watching me when she turns to Tate and Ethan, and says, *"Most of us are lucky if we find real love once in our lives, and somehow you two have managed to find each other twice."*

Cash scoffs and waves the waiter over to order another drink. I know I should say something. That's how this goes. He says, *I'm in love with you,* and I say… something. Anything. But what?

I picture myself saying, *I love you, just not like that* and then watching his perpetually bright eyes fade into darkness. Or maybe begging, saying something like, *Cash, please don't do this, don't ruin what we have, because what we have is good. It always has been,* but then I realize maybe it hasn't. Not for him, and then I'm panicking because am I really that self-absorbed? So much so that I didn't even notice he was in love with me.

The waiter puts his drink on the table. He picks it up and drinks the whole thing in one gulp. I know he deserves better than this.

He's right. Camden left and he's been here the whole time.

If I could choose him I would, because I do love him. Just not in the way he needs me to. I don't mean to do it, but I look over at Camden. He's staring at me like he knows something's wrong. I don't want him to come over here, so I force a smile, but Cash sees and says, "That man could stomp on you, and you would still come crawling back."

I don't think I've ever seen Cash upset before, but right now his body is practically vibrating with anger. I turn to him,

"It's not like that." He leans back in his chair, *lips twisted, angry eyes boring into mine.* "It is. It always has been."

I don't know what else to do so I just say, "Cash, please." He puts his empty glass down on the table and looks up at me. I can see the exact moment when he decides I'm not worth the fight.

I never have been.

He pushes his chair back and stands up, "You know what, I'm done. I'm going home." I get up to follow him. He waves me off with a sloppy hand and a sad, "Don't bother." I tell him he can't go, that he's too drunk to drive and he says, "Please." in this really scornful tone.

He walks out of the room, and I follow him down the hall and out into the parking lot. I know he knows I'm here, but he has no plans to stop and talk to me. "Cash, wait. I'll come with you." He turns around and for someone that never shows any real emotion there is an awful lot of pain and disappointment in his eyes.

"You want to come home with me?"

I hear the layers of insinuation in his question, and I know what he's really asking. I hesitate and rejection tightens his jaw.

"No, you want to go home with him. Don't you?"

I can tell I've hurt him, *actually, really* hurt him. My heart falls down from my chest and opens up into my abdomen. A heavy rotten feeling settles in my gut. I look up at him, but I'm scared to speak. There's nothing I can say to fix this. No way to convince him I don't want exactly what he says I do.

Out here there's more room for his anger to spread so I don't feel it pressing down on me quite so hard. His shoulders roll back, and he shivers with distaste.

"Don't worry about it, Emma, I'm used to going home without you."

I walk up and grab his arm. He looks down at my hand like it's a branding iron. Searing, burning, pain passes through his eyes. I tell him to give me his keys. "If you want them, you can get them yourself."

I know what he's doing, but I really am worried about him driving off like this. He's too angry, *drunk, rejected.* I reach down and pat his pockets. He says, "There in that one." I reach in and take them out.

He looks down at me. The sadness in his eyes takes on the slightest tinge of satisfaction, "I think that's the first time you've ever touched me there." I pull my hand back, "Cash, don't." His eyes pull tight. "Oh yeah, I forgot. You only want things you shouldn't."

I don't know what it is. Maybe it's lingering embarrassment from the way my mother looked at me when she walked out of the room earlier. Or perhaps it's the unspoken admonishment that Tatumn gave me. Or the way that I was relegated to the back corner, allowed to, or even expected to sit with Cash while having to avoid Camden all together. Perhaps it's the way everyone around me looks at him. Like he's ruined. *Guilty. Damaged. Dangerous.* Or maybe it's just the current of anger, disapproval, and resentment running though his voice, but I say, "Well, at least I want things."

His brow furrows, "What's that supposed to mean?" I tell him he has had everything handed to him, that he's never made a real choice in his life. He steps in closer, "Well, I'm making one now."

"Oh really, what choice is that?"

"You."

Disbelief pulls my face in, "The last time I saw you, you were half naked and gyrating seductively for Cynthia." He cuts me off with a glare, "I did that for you." My eyes go wide. "How can that be possible?"

His head rolls back in exasperation. "Everything I do is for you." I take a step back, "I don't understand. I thought we were friends, and you never said anything."

He reaches up, frustratedly grabbing at his own hair. "I did too. You just never listened." The pain in his voice makes my knees catch. "Cash, I have heard everything you've ever said to me. I just didn't realize you were serious." He bites his lower lip in frustration, "Of course I'm serious, why would I bother saying it if I weren't?"

"I don't know, but you talk to everyone like that. You're always joking, and you never made a move." He steps in closer. "I have made hundreds of moves. You just never see them."

I think back to all the times he told me I looked pretty, came over to sit with me and Agatha when Tate went out, took my car to the shop, danced with me, bought me drinks, took me to lunch, dinner, the movies.

"I see them. I just see them happening with everyone else too."

He puts his thumb under my chin and lifts my face to his. "That's because I can never get your attention."

I don't know what I'm thinking, but I say, "Well you have it right now."

His eyes dart over my shoulder and then he leans down and kisses me. At first, I don't know what to do. His hands are tangling in my hair and his lips are moving over mine in such desperation that I don't feel like I can pull away, but then something happens and I'm kissing him back.

I feel the moment of surprise pass through him. His hands press into me, pulling me closer. His lips soften against mine. I feel the sting of tears in my eyes because I love him. I do. There have been moments. When he's sitting on the couch with me at the ranch or holding my hand as we walk through the park that I have thought about this.

Wondered what it would be like to kiss him again, to hold him close and listen as he says things like *I love you*, or *I want you, only you*, but it never seemed right. It still doesn't seem right, and as much as he doesn't want to hear it, and I don't want to say it. It's nothing he's done, or could, or will ever do.

He's perfect, *funny, loyal, kind,* an amazing kisser and probably very attentive in bed, *good job, nice family, cute smile.* There's only one thing wrong with him, and it's completely beyond his control.

Or mine.

Love is a funny thing, infinite in nature and variations, but it's also fickle and very particular. I push away from him and bring my hand up to cover my lips.

I tell him I really didn't know, and I never meant to hurt him.

His eyes close and he swallows hard, "I'm so sorry, Emma."

His voice sounds pained. He opens his eyes and looks back over my shoulder. I turn around and Camden is standing in the middle of the parking lot. Watching us. His face stricken with pain and confusion.

Cash turns to walk away from me, and I know I should just let him go, but instead I start walking off after him.

"I can't believe you did that."

He turns around with a sullen expression, "Did what?"

"You saw him there." His shoulders stiffen, "Yeah, I did." I reach up to wipe beneath my eyes and he says, "I thought you liked men who fought dirty."

Camden starts walking over to us and I look up at Cash, "This isn't like you." He nods in Camden's direction.

"Nah, I figured I'd try taking a page from his book."

Camden walks up behind me and puts his hand on the small of my back. "Is everything alright over here?" His voice is tight, there's a tremor in his hand.

Cash's eyes narrow in his direction and he lets out this ugly sounding huff of air, "Oh, is that your plan, leave her, and then waltz back in here like you're the hero."

Camden looks down at me and I expect to see anger, or distrust, but he just looks worried. He says, "I'm nobody's hero." and Cash says, "Well, at least we can agree on that."

Camden runs his hand over my back, and I say, "We're fine, just a misunderstanding." Cash scoffs, "Yeah, a misunderstanding." Camden's eyes tighten and he looks up at Cash, "Are you alright man?" Cash shakes his head. "No, not really. Not since you came back."

Camden runs his hand through his hair and looks down at me, "Do you want me to go?"

I know what I should say. I should tell him no, *not now, not ever*, but Cash's jaw tightens, and he says, "Come on man, don't you want to hit me?"

I look up at Camden, "No, please don't." He shrugs, and it comes off as indifference, but I can see the way his jaw tightens and feel the increased pressure in his fingertips as they press into my back. He does this little nod. It looks practiced, *measured*, like he's had to do it before.

"No, why would I do that?"

Cash's eyes narrow, "I know what you're doing."

"Really, you want to let me in on it?"

The night air feels heavy. I can hear voices in the distance, some of our party leaving the restaurant. They don't seem to notice us, but I know if this goes any further they will. I say, "Guys, please." but Cash's hands tighten at his sides. I step in between them and say, "Don't do this." but they don't seem to hear me.

Camden presses his hand against my hip and scoots me to the side. He says, "Go on man, I can see you itching to do it." Cash says, "You're trash. You've always been trash." Camden's eyes harden, "That's not news to me."

Cash shakes his head and looks over at me, "This is the man you want?" I start to answer, but Camden looks down at him and says, "Leave her out of it."

Cash nods approvingly. "This is a good look for you. I can tell she's really eating it up." Camden steps in closer, and even though he and Cash are roughly the same size, he seems much larger right now.

"I said leave her out of it."

Cash clenches his jaw, biting down on the anger that's trying to get out. "Why? What are you going to do about it?"

"I'm not going to do anything, you are."

He shakes his head, "You'd like that wouldn't you?" Camden shrugs, "Not particularly, but it's going to happen." Cash says, "I can't stand you man. It's sick the way you manipulate her. You're a completely different person when she's not around and she may buy this act you've got going on, but I know you won't be able to keep it up."

I notice Camden's hands twitch at his side. "I'm not manipulating anyone, but you're right. I am a completely different person when she's around."

Cash seems to accept what he's said. The tension leaves my shoulders, but then his fists ball up and he says, "You know what, fine." more to himself than anyone else.

He hits him and blood comes pouring out of Camden's nose. I step in, but Camden's hand shoots out to keep me back and Cash hits him again. I say, *stop, don't do this*, but he can't hear me. Camden just stands there and after Cash hits him for the third time, he says "You feel better now?"

Cash reaches down to wipe the back of his hand on his pants. "You're the worst man." Camden shrugs and Cash looks over at me, "He's not who you think he is." He turns around to walk off and when I reach out to grab his arm, Camden wraps his hand around my wrist.

I look back at him, *busted lip, bruised eye, blood running down his chin.* Cash doesn't have any wounds, but his chest is heaving and there's a strange distance in his eyes. Camden's hand tightens on my wrist, and I turn back around. I don't want to say it, but… "I can't leave him like this."

I watch as a wave of acceptance passes through Camden's eyes. I know what this looks like. He kissed me. Camden watched it happen, but that's not what this is and all I can do is hope he knows that.

I see his eyes dart toward Cash. Mine do the same. I'm surprised to see his face held tight in anticipation. Obviously hoping Camden is going to try and stop me. I don't actually want him to do it, but I realize I'm hoping for that too.

Camden releases my wrist and reaches up to wipe the back of his hand across his chin. Blood smears from his lips to his ear and he takes a step back. Away from me.

"Yeah, you should probably take him home."

His voice is too calm. Alarm bells go off inside my head. Cash yanks his arm away. "Nah, you can go with him. I know you want to." I do, but his voice is too tight, *angry, spiteful,* for me to walk away.

I feel like I'm standing at the edge of a cliff, certain I'm going to fall. There's nothing I can say to make this better. No way to soothe one without hurting the other.

I just stand there feeling helpless and wishing I had known. That I had paid more attention, *seen the clues, had time to warn him*… well actually I'm not sure who I would have warned.

I didn't know Cash cared, and the way Camden looked when he saw me kissing him.

I think he already knew.

14

Camden

The morning after Emma left, I went to see my mom. Cora was never in a good place so I never felt like I could leave her for long. When I showed up, she was passed out with a needle in her arm. It wasn't the first time I'd found her this way, but it was the first time it really bothered me.

I couldn't help but think of Emma. The way she looked at me last night. Her deep blue eyes so full of trust and acceptance. The way she looked at me made me feel like a stranger in my own skin.

I could only ever see myself the way she saw me when I was actually looking at her. When it was over, and I had to pull the image up in my mind it never made any sense.

Not when this is what I came from.

I knelt down and put my hand beneath Cora's nose just to make sure she was breathing and then I went to the kitchen. I did the dishes and took out all the trash. I pulled the vacuum out and let it bump up against her leg a couple of times, but she didn't budge. I went outside and pulled the mower from the garage.

Her lawn was small, and she didn't have many plants to water, but she still couldn't seem to take care of them. When I finished, I went back inside, and she was awake. Sitting up on the couch with a dazed look in her eyes. The needle was gone. I didn't ask about it.

"You know you don't have to keep doing this." She said when I stepped in front of her. "Someone does." I tried not to notice the way the lids of her eyes dropped in shame. Cora was like a little girl. She didn't mean to do the things she did. She was constantly in survival mode, running from something no one else could see.

"So, are you back in?" she asked.

I looked down at her hand, shaking around the cigarette she was holding. "No. I already told you I'm out." She lifted the cigarette to her mouth. "She's gone though." I'd never told her Emma was the reason I'd stopped, but she said it like she knew.

"For now."

Cora took a deep drag off of her cigarette and looked up at me. "She's coming back?" I thought about what she'd said, about applying to MSU. If she came it wouldn't be just for summer anymore. She'd be here all the time. I didn't want her around any of this.

"Yeah, she is."

"When was the last time you ate something?" I asked as I watched Cora's hand shake in her lap. She waved me off. "That girl means something to you." It was a question and a statement. One I had no plans of discussing with Cora. "I'll make you a sandwich. You still like PB&J?"

She pushed herself up off the couch. "You're always fussing over me. I can make my own sandwich." I watched as she made her way into the kitchen. She wasn't steady on her feet. Nothing about Cora was ever steady, but she looked worse now than she had before. I felt bad for not coming by sooner.

She pulled open the refrigerator and took out a package wrapped in thick white butcher's paper. She looked over at me, "I need to get rid of this." Her voice was shaky, *desperate and frail.*

I hated telling her no. I knew I was the only person in this town that had anything to do with her, and I wished I could help her, but not like this. Not anymore.

I shrugged. "Don't know what that has to do with me."

"It's just this. I can find someone else after." She looked up at me, her cheeks were gaunt and there were permanent shadows under her eyes. "Is that the stuff you put in your arm?" I don't know why I said it. Mostly just to make sure she knew that I knew she was using again, and I wasn't okay with it.

She pursed her lips and gave me a look that said she didn't want to talk about it. She never wanted to talk about it. "You were supposed to be making a sandwich, not pulling whatever that is out of your fridge."

She let her gaze drop. "I don't need a sandwich. I need you to take this." She held the package up and looked at me like I was the one with the problem.

"No." I took a seat on the couch and watched as she made her way back over to me.

"I could make it worth your while."

"I doubt that."

She took the seat beside me and picked the pack of cigarettes up off the table. Her hand was so shaky she could barely keep a hold of them.

"You really like that girl, don't you?"

Her eyes shot to mine and I looked away. I didn't feel right talking about Emma with her when she was like this. She lit her cigarette. "I bet a plane ticket to Chicago is pretty expensive."

I looked back over at her, sitting there with her shoulders slumped, barely able to hold her own head up. "I have a job, Cora." She looked over at me with pity in her eyes. "At the coffee shop? How long does it take you to make a thousand dollars there?"

She wasn't wrong. I didn't make much at the coffee shop. I had some money saved, but not enough to go see Emma.

"These guys I'm working with now. They have real money. This drop alone will get you ten grand. You decide to stay in, and I've got a guy in Chicago that could use some help. You could pay that girl's way through college by the end of the year."

I looked over at her. She confused the look of revulsion on my face for one of interest. "Chicago? That's convenient."

Her eyes shifted away from mine. "When did you decide to make a contact in Chicago?" She lifted the cigarette to her mouth and took a drag.

When she looked back over at me, I said, "Emma is not a bargaining chip, Cora." She blew out a big cloud of smoke.

"I know that."

"Really, because it doesn't sound like you do. It sounds like you're trying to use her to get what you want." She leaned forward and tapped a bit of ash into the tray. "It's not as simple as all that, Camden."

"No, I know. It never is."

Her leg started bouncing. "It would be so easy." I shook my head, "For who?" She looked at me through narrowed eyes, "For all of us." I told her it wouldn't be easy for me, or Emma, and she said, "Emma wouldn't know a thing about it, and it would be easy for you."

"No, Cora. It would be easy for you."

She took another drag of her cigarette and told me I was looking at this all wrong. It was an opportunity, one that we didn't even have to fabricate.

"It'd be seamless, Camden. You'd book a flight to go see your girl. I'd get my guy to leave you a package at a coffee shop, just like we'll do here, and then you bring it back to me. I'm talking real money. You'd be set for a long time."

I asked her if she was actually asking me to do this. If she really thought it was a good idea for me to move drugs through an airport and across state lines.

"Do you know how much trouble I'd get in if I got caught?"

"That's just it, Camden. I've thought about it. You won't get caught. You're too smart for that. I'd do all the work. You'd just take your girl to go get coffee. No one would suspect a thing."

"Then what do I do with it? Shove it up my ass? I have to fly home, Cora."

"God no. This is an organization. They've got guys in TSA. You'd just walk on the plane, just like everyone else."

"This is ridiculous. It's too dangerous and no matter how seamless you think it'll be. We will get caught." She said, "Camden, you know I wouldn't ask you to do something if I didn't feel like it was a sure thing. This isn't just me. You would do the pickup, but I would arrange the rest."

"What are you talking about? What do you mean it's not just you? You make it sound like you're working with the mafia."

The air in the room changed, *turned from charged to electric.* Her silence spoke volumes. "Are you working with the mafia? Are you in trouble?" Her shoulders pulled back, "I need to get rid of this."

Her hand tightened around the package, the paper crackling beneath the weight of her fist. "It's not the mafia. I don't even know what that means, but these guys do want their money, and I can't deliver this. The heat is on me hard. I can't even buy groceries without being tailed."

"Yeah, I know. Don is at the coffee shop every day. I haven't had anything on me in weeks and he's still coming. You know he asked me to roll over on you?"

She looked over at me, *her eyes widened, pupils dilated, shoulders tensed.* It felt like an insult. Like she trusted me even less than I trusted her. "Relax. I didn't say anything, but what you're doing now is worse. It's going to get you pinned." She leaned back, folded her hands over her waist.

"Pinned is better than purged."

"Is it really like that? How much trouble are you in?"

Her head fell back on the pillow in defeat. "What were you thinking?" She gave me a nasty look, "You know what Camden, I don't need a lecture. I already know I messed up."

I thought about all the times I'd heard her say that before. How she'd sworn it wouldn't happen again and how it always did.

She let out a long hopeless sigh, "I've tried to find someone else, but no one in this town will talk to me."

I looked down at the package sitting on the table. "If I take that, can you get out?"

She opened her eyes and looked up at the ceiling. "No, probably not, but it would buy me some time. They'll still want me to get the next one. They were pretty clear about that."

"The next one? The one in Chicago."

"Yeah, the one in Chicago."

"I'm not promising to do that." She leaned forward and picked the cigarettes back up, "No, I know."

"I'll take the one you've got though."

∧∧∧∧∧∧

The package felt like a block of lead on my back. Cora had everything set up so I wouldn't have to have it long, but my next shift wasn't until the morning, and I had to drive home and then back to work with it on me.

It was a simple enough set up. Put it in a bag of coffee. Sell it to the person that said the magic words.

April and I were both working. She was handling the pastry case. I offered to fill the whole bean coffee bags. It was just like normal. I opened the bag and slipped the package in and then I sat it beneath the dispenser and pulled the handle. I watched as the dark beans surrounded it and then placed it on the shelf next to the others.

It was about ten thirty when she showed up. Her hair was in one of those messy buns and she had on a pair of Birkenstocks. She looked just like every other woman that had come in this morning.

I was working the register today. April gave me a look when I offered, but I just said, "It's good to switch it up sometimes."

The woman looked over the menu and then she ordered an iced chai latte. I rang her up. She pulled a bag of our coffee out of her purse, "You know I bought this to try, but I just really don't like it. I prefer the Sumatra blend. Is there any way I could exchange it?"

She didn't look nervous at all. I felt a bead of sweat form on the back of my neck.

"Sure. Yeah, let me grab that for you."

I turned around and pulled the bag from the shelf. Her smile widened. April put her chai latte up on the counter. She picked it up and took a drink. I reached out and took the bag she'd left on the counter and put it beneath the register. She put the bag I'd given her in her purse, and then she left.

∧∧∧∧∧∧

When I got off work I went to Cora's. She was awake, standing at the kitchen sink doing dishes. It was stranger than coming in to her passed out with a needle in her arm. She

286

didn't hear me come in. She had headphones on. I listened as she hummed along tunelessly to the music in her ear.

She picked up a plate and swung her hips as she scrubbed the food off of it. When she caught sight of me, she cursed and asked me if I was trying to kill her. I said, "No, but I thought you might want this."

I threw the bag at her. She caught it, and then put it down and picked up a towel to dry off her hands. "Is it all there?" I didn't know. I didn't want to count it, but it looked like a lot of money.

"I don't know. That's your job."

She took the bag and poured it out on the table. Stacks of hundred-dollar bills fell out. The look of relief that crossed her face was so profound that I felt it too. She picked up one of the stacks and handed it to me.

"You did good kid."

^^^^^^

The drop was so seamless that I agreed to do it again. Cora and I had a good thing. She seemed happier, *less worried and lost in her own head.* The money was good too. I had made forty thousand dollars in three months. More than I made at the coffee shop in a year.

Emma and I had been texting a lot. She was safe and happy, hundreds of miles away from me. I didn't even think of the danger of what Cora and I were doing until I saw her name flash across my screen. I missed her. I didn't want her here though, at least not right now.

The coffee shop drops were easy. It really didn't feel dangerous, but I knew Emma would think otherwise. I wasn't going to tell her, not unless she asked. Luckily for me senior year was busy. Emma was occupied with college applications and volunteer work.

She applied to MSU. I knew she'd get in. The screen shot of her application submission form made me feel a little queasy, but I'd replied with, *congratulations*, and *I can't wait to see what you look like in the snow.* She said *it really wasn't worth waiting for*, and I said, *I'll be the judge of that next year.*

Cora promised me that she could get out if I went to Chicago. I knew the only way I would ever be done was if she was too. Emma had a dance coming up. She was going solo, or really, she was going with a group of girls that were all going solo. She seemed excited about it, but I knew she was doing it for me.

My fingers shook as I typed out the message, *let me take you to prom.* She replied almost immediately, *oh my God, are you serious?* I had to think about it, and she sent back a question mark, with an unhappy emoji. I told myself it was for her, for us.

I am.

Yes.

^^^^^^

Emma

Camden Pierce was taking me to prom. It was like I'd dreamed it. I told him to come see me, *several times over text*, but

I never thought he actually would. Mom wasn't thrilled about it. She thought I should go with a boy from here. She thought Camden was too old to go to prom with me, but I didn't care what anyone thought. Camden Pierce in a suit, on the dance floor with his arms wrapped around me, was all I cared about.

His flight was early. I took seventh period off to come to the airport to pick him up.

When I pulled into O'Hare, he was waiting on the curb for me. He had a backpack and a small suitcase with him. I jumped out of the car and ran over. He wrapped his arms around me and told me he missed me. I said, "Naturally." and he said, "Oh really, should I go back in there and head home?" I shook my head, *no*, and he leaned down and kissed me.

On the drive back to my house we listened to a playlist I'd made of all the songs he'd sent me over the last couple of years. His hand rested on my thigh the whole time.

He was staying with us, sleeping in Eli's room. Mom had insisted. She'd tried to play it off as a show of support, but I knew she just didn't like the idea of him having his own hotel room on prom night.

My dress was ivory, with a plunging neckline, and swaths of lace running down the center. I went to a salon to get my hair done. It was in a loose low bun with lots of tendrils hanging out. Camden got ready in Eli's room. He and Mom were in the kitchen when I came down.

The way his face changed when I walked in the room made me feel a little anxious about my mother being there. He said, "You look really beautiful, Emma." in this dry shaky sort of tone, and I told him he looked nice too. He turned around and picked a large bouquet of flowers up off the countertop.

Peonies with just a hint of pink in their petals. "I didn't think you'd want a corsage."

He had this shy look on his face. I could tell he was nervous and a little uncertain. I took the bouquet from him and leaned down to shove my nose in it. A light soft fragrance filled my head. "They're perfect. Peonies have always been my favorite."

Mom was still standing there watching us. I knew that somewhere in the periphery of my mind, but it didn't feel that way. It felt like it was just the two of us.

I honestly didn't care about prom. Before Camden asked me, I had planned to go with Grace. She and Anthony had broken up and she was off men for a while. I cared about this though. Being here with him. The dress, the suit, and the party were all just bonuses.

Mom took at least a hundred photos of us standing in the yard in front of the big tree where the swing hung. She sent a few of them to Dani.

When the limo pulled up her phone rang, and she waved us off. "You didn't have to get a limo. We could have just taken my car." He took my hand in his and pulled me forward.

"It's not a big deal, Emma. I wanted to."

We climbed in the back seat and somehow it seemed even longer on the inside. Camden leaned over and kissed me. "You really do look beautiful. I'm glad I get to take you."

When we got to the prom, Grace and Lanie ran over. Grace said, "So, you're the illusive man Emma's always going on about." Lanie looked at him. "You know we thought she'd made you up just to get out of dating the rancid boys we go to school with."

He tightened his hand around mine and nodded.

They kept talking, saying things like, *well for her sake I'm glad you're here, but I just lost ten dollars to Jerimiah because you actually showed up.* Grace told him she never doubted he would come, but she had fully doubted his existence all the way through tenth grade.

They were talking a lot. I could tell that Camden found it amusing by the way he kept looking over at me. Camden was cool in any situation, but when Lanie looked him up and down and said, "I think I get it now." I felt my cheeks flush and told them to *please stop talking.*

The thumping beat of the music changed to a slow hum, and he said, "Come on, Emma, let's go out there." He held me close and told me he liked my friends. "Really, because I don't like them very much right now."

He told me it was cute, knowing that I'd talked about him for years. He turned me around and caught me in his arms again. "No, it's not. It's embarrassing."

He shook his head. "No, it's cute. I like it."

I decided to let it drop and leaned into him. We danced to several more songs. He looked light and happy under the colorful lights. Every time I looked back at him, his eyes were waiting for mine. I wanted to take these moments and bottle them up, so that anytime I wanted I could take a sip and remember him exactly how he was right now.

After a while, the straps of my heels were digging into my feet, and I needed a break. He led me to the punch table and poured me a glass, and then we went to wait in line for our photos. He kept his hand on my back, letting his fingers make soft passes over my skin as we waited to step up in front of the gold streamers and pink balloons.

When it was our turn, he wrapped his arms all the way around my waist and pulled me tight up against him. I could smell him, a bit of salt from the sweat he'd worked up on the dance floor, and a bit of whatever it was that made him him.

The camera pointed at us and the flash went off. His fingers brushed over my low back as I moved away. I looked back at him, and he reached out and took my hand in his. He led me over to a dark corner and we tucked ourselves behind a cardboard cutout of the New York City skyline.

He kissed me.

His lips moved mine, fingers tangled in my hair. The music was loud. I could feel a pounding in my chest. He pulled back and I asked him if he was ready to go.

He gave me a doubtful look, "Are you? Don't you want to find your friends again?" I looked up into his eyes, there was barely a sliver of grey surrounding his pupils.

"No, I just want to be with you."

We made our way across the dance floor, and I gave Lanie and Grace a hug before we left. Camden took his phone out and called the limo. I pulled my arms across my chest and rubbed my hands over them. He shrugged out of his jacket and laid it over my shoulders. "Thanks." I said as he tucked a tendril of hair behind my ear.

The limo pulled up and Camden told the driver to take us to the Hotel Azure on the riverwalk. I asked him if we had a room there, and he said, "Yeah, I figured we might need it."

The room was nice, but what was nicer was the way Camden took me in his arms as soon as we entered it.

Our lips met and his hands swept up the sides of my body. I pushed his suit jacket off. He pulled the straps of my dress down. I couldn't get enough of the way his hands were pressing into me as he moved us closer to the bed.

His eyes swept all over my face. I let mine settle on the curve of his bottom lip. He kissed all the softest parts of me and told me I was perfect, *that I was everything, the only thing that mattered.* It was exquisite. The way his bare skin felt up against mine.

His hands were everywhere. His mouth wasn't far behind. My hands were in his hair, *on his back, grasping at his sides* as he pressed into me. I came loudly and the look on his face was like nothing I'd ever seen before. I leaned up, struggling to capture every delicious catch in his breath as he finished.

We laid there for a long time. Our skin sticky and warm up against each other's. His fingers trailed lazily over my back. My hand rested on his hip.

He was looking at me very intently, the air in the room felt heavy with unspoken promises. "So, this is why you wanted to take me to prom?" His lips picked up at the corner. "No, I don't need an excuse to want to do that to you."

I told him I liked the room, and he said, "We have it all night."

^^^^^^

Camden

Before I was here with her this seemed like a good idea. Well not a good idea, but a manageable one. Now the two of us were on the train headed for the city and I was absolutely panicking about having her with me.

Emma was like a full moon on a dark night. She'd always been the light in my life. I was terrified I was going to extinguish it.

Cora's guy was in the city. Emma and I had a full day planned. We were going to walk along the river and go to the top of the Sears tower. I was going to take her for coffee, and she wasn't even going to realize I had anything on me when we left.

I was though.

I was going to have to look at her perfect face, *those deep blue eyes, and that soft trusting smile.* It made me feel rancid, knowing I was going to betray her trust. She was sitting so close and even though I hadn't done anything yet, I could feel her getting further away.

A more disturbing thought had never crossed my mind. I took out my phone and sent Cora a text. *Not going to happen.* She texted back almost immediately.

Emma was sitting next to me licking an ice cream cone. Her lips were covered in chocolate. *What do you mean?* She held the cone out to me, and I leaned over and licked it. The innocence in her eyes hurt me.

I mean what I said.

There was a screeching noise as the train pulled into another stop.

You can't mean what you said.

I looked down at Emma and touched my lower lip, "You've got something." She got this mischievous look on her face and leaned into me.

I licked the chocolate off of her lips and she made a small noise on mine. My phone pinged again. Emma pulled away and I leaned over and took a bite of her ice cream. She turned her lips down to feign a pout. I looked at my phone. She did too. I felt a bit of panic at the thought of her seeing it.

I'll take care of it.

^^^^^^

Emma

Camden seemed a bit off. I tried to tell myself it was just the chaos of the city. That he was a mountain man. His soul was just more comfortable beneath the stars than the streetlights. Still, I couldn't quite shake the feeling that he was worried or upset about something.

He was sitting next to me, and his phone kept pinging. I shouldn't have done it, but the worried look in his eyes as he read over the text made me look down at his phone. I saw Cora's name and quickly looked away. His body stiffened beside mine, and I felt a heavy weight settle in my gut.

Everything about Camden's mother made me scared for him. She was volatile, *reckless, and seemingly unconcerned for his safety*. I knew I couldn't just ask, but there was obviously something wrong.

We left the train station and walked across the bridge. I pulled him down beside me and we sat on a cold metal bench together. I asked him what he thought of the city, and he said, "It's alright. A little crowded." I nodded. "Yeah, but I actually think the people are the only thing that makes it tolerable." His eyes shifted to mine.

I could tell he was still uncomfortable. He said, "You like the crowds?" I told him, no, not really but I can't imagine how desolate and empty all these streets would feel without them here.

He looked at me like he was trying to figure something out and then he asked me if I'd miss it here. I shook my head, "No." He looked away, "Are you sure?" I started to wonder if what was bothering him was the thought of me moving to Montana.

"I am... are you?"

He looked over at me with a furrowed brow, "About what?" I felt like maybe I was wrong. Maybe he wasn't thinking about me at all. "Nothing, never mind." He reached over and took my hand in his. His thumb drew small circles on my palm.

"Did you get in?"

I looked over at him and felt my heart sink in my chest. "Yeah, but I got into CU too."

He looked away again. "You're going with Tate?" I wasn't planning to, but the hope I'd seen in his eyes before he'd turned away hurt enough to make me wish I was.

"I don't know. I guess I haven't decided." I looked down at my lap. "Are you planning to go to college?" He gave me a doubtful look. "No, I don't think so."

I wrapped my hands around the curve of the bench. "You're smart. You should consider it." He looked down at the pavement. "Yeah, well that's just not something I can really think about right now." His hand rubbed over his thigh. He looked up at me and said, "I've never been to Colorado. There are mountains there too."

It was just a string of words, *like any other string of words*, but the way he'd said them sounded like he was saying something else entirely. I asked him what he meant by that. "I don't know. It's probably a nice place to live."

I knew it wasn't what he was saying, but it sort of sounded like it was. "A nice place for me... or for you?" His eyes narrowed and shifted. "I mean it. Would you move there?" He pulled his shoulders back.

"Maybe, if it wasn't for Cora I might."

"You don't want to leave her?" He shook his head. "No, it's not a want. She just needs someone, and I'm all she's got."

"So then if I move to Montana, you'll be there?"

"Of course. Where else would I go, Emma?" His head dropped and I turned away. Neither of us said anything for a while.

I watched as the people in front of us went about their days. There was a mother and child walking a small dog, he stopped to smell a spot on the pavement and the little boy leaned down to pet his head. A man on his phone nearly ran into him, but the mother pulled him out of the way. I don't think the man noticed at all.

Camden was staring out at the building in front of us and I felt like this whole thing had been a mistake. I also felt a little bewildered because I'm pretty sure coming to the city was his idea. I told him we could just grab a coffee and then head back into town.

His eyes widened, "No coffee, but I'm ready to go when you are."

^^^^^^

Camden

I knew it was a mistake to leave before we'd actually gone anywhere, but my relief compounded with every mile we put between us and the city.

By the time we'd made it back I nearly felt like myself again. Emma asked me if I wanted to go back to her place or find something else to do.

I told her I wanted her to show me all her favorite places in town and we ended up on a large hill at a park near her house. She told me this is where her mother used to take her sledding, now it's where she, Grace, and Lanie sat and talked on their way home from school.

I told her I liked it, it was a nice spot, and she said, "Yeah, and it's even better now."

We walked around, she let me push her on the swings and then I kissed her beneath the branches of a large oak tree. I could tell by the way her eyes kept cutting to mine that she was still suspicious of me. I tried talking about anything I could think of, just so long as it didn't involve Montana, or Cora, or me.

Emma told me she actually wanted a coffee, that she was looking forward to that part of our day. "Sure, let's go get one." The shop was small and busy. Emma ordered a mocha latte, and I got an americano. We took them outside and walked along the river. Emma pulled me into a few of her favorite stores and I bought her everything she said she liked.

When we got back to her house, she sat the bags down on the foot of her bed. "You must be doing really well at the coffee shop."

I could hear the implication in her voice, but I tried to ignore it. "Yeah, I guess I am." She turned around and looked at me suspiciously.

I knew she was waiting for me to tell her something, but nothing I had to say would do either of us any good. I asked her if her mom was going to be home soon. She looked at the clock beside her bed.

"Maybe, sometimes she stays late."

I didn't know what else to do, so I walked across the room and kissed her. She wrapped her arms around me, and I pressed in closer, running my fingers over her back and tugging at her hair. She crawled on her bed. I said, "Are you sure?"

She looked back at me, "I'm always sure when it comes to you."

^^^^^^

Emma

Camden seemed really hesitant, but I knew it wasn't because he was afraid to touch me. I reached out and pulled him in closer.

He laid down beside me and stroked the skin of my cheek, jaw, and neckline. He said, "I like touching you." I told him I liked it too.

My mom came home and yelled up the stairs at us. He pulled away and I said, "Camden." His eyes were wide, cheeks flushed, and lips wet. "You know you can tell me."

He scooted to the edge of the bed and sat with his back to me. "I really don't think I can." I scooted in behind him and put my hand on his shoulder.

"I already know."

He turned around and I saw the resolve in his eyes crumble. "No, you don't."

I felt this strange current of fear and apprehension run through me. I told him I saw the text, "I know you're worried about your mom."

He ran his hand through his hair, "Yeah, well that's true."

He stood up and walked over to the door. It felt like my legs were stuck to the bed. Like even though I knew, and I was right here in front of him, there was nothing I could do to keep him from walking away.

^^^^^^

Camden

It was our last night together and she was too far away from me. I left Eli's room and went to hers. I climbed into her bed and pulled her tight up against me.

She opened her eyes.

I kissed her.

She didn't ask, but I said, "You know if I had a choice I wouldn't do it." Her eyes pulled tight at the corners.

"I hate that you think you don't have a choice."

^^^^^^

Cora hadn't texted again. Emma and I made breakfast. Waffles with chocolate chips and whipped cream for her. Eggs and coffee for me.

She drove me to the airport, and we kissed goodbye standing on the sidewalk with a whole city full of strangers surrounding us and a traffic cop telling her she needed to move her car.

Once I was inside, I took out my phone and texted Cora. *At the airport.* I looked down at my screen, waiting for her reply. *Great, have a good flight.*

I read it and reread it, but there didn't seem to be any hidden meaning. I stepped into the security line, pulling my suitcase behind me. When it was my turn, I scanned my ID and ticket and waited for the man to let me through.

He looked up at me, asked me to remove my hat and repeated my name back to me. I gave him a nod and he waved me on. I took off my shoes and belt and placed them in a bin. I pushed my suitcase behind them along the conveyor belt and then stepped in line to get scanned.

When I stepped out, one of the security agents pulled me to the side and asked me to raise my hands in the air as he patted me down.

He looked back up at me and then he asked which bag was mine. I pointed at the black suitcase sitting in the bin at the end of the line. He went over and grabbed it. He pulled me behind a screen and asked me to take a seat.

I did.

He unzipped my bags and rummaged through my things. It didn't take him long, and I didn't know what he was looking for, but I was thrilled he wasn't going to find it.

I slept the entire way home. When I landed, I went straight to Cora's.

She was up, waiting for me in her living room. "Did you get it?" She asked like she actually expected me to have it. "No. I texted you. You knew I wasn't going to get it." She looked over at the door and asked me if I'd made it through security alright.

I told her I'd been searched. She went outside and unhooked my suitcase from my bike. She rolled it inside, opened it up, and tore through it the same way the security agent had.

A heaviness I wasn't sure I could carry settled in my limbs. She pulled out a black shirt. It looked just like mine. She untucked the corners and pulled out a package I had never seen before.

I told Emma I didn't have a choice, but up until this moment I didn't realize how true that was. Cora pulled the outside wrapper off and a whole lot of smaller packages filled with pills and powders fell out onto the table.

Cora started talking. Already setting up the drops in her mind. I watched as she paced the room, ecstatic about her apparent success. I pushed my hands into my pockets and tried to remember even one time when she'd done right by me.

I started to put my things back in my bag and she asked me if I was leaving. I pulled the zipper closed and looked at her. There was no remorse in her eyes. She didn't even seem to realize the way the things she did affected me.

"Yeah, I'm going."

She looked at me like she didn't understand, "But you'll come back?"

I wasn't sure I would. I turned to walk out the door.

"Camden, I didn't have a choice. These guys don't take no for an answer."

I heard Emma's words echo in my mind. "Actually, you did. I didn't though." She looked up at me with wide cautious eyes. "I never have had a choice. You make them all and I just have to figure out how to make it work." She reached her hand out toward me, and I took a step back.

"I still need your help. I can't move this on my own."

She sounded desperate, *pressured speech layered with fear and disbelief.*

I turned back around to look at her. She was so thin and pale. Her hair and skin were dry, and she had chronic dark circles under her eyes. "Camden, don't do this." I felt for her, just like I always had, but I couldn't do this anymore.

I walked over and wrapped my arms around her bony shoulders. She reached out and wrapped hers around my waist. When I pulled back, I told her she did need help, but not the kind I could give her.

∧∧∧∧∧∧

A week later Cora showed up at the coffee shop. It was strange seeing her out, and I asked her what she was doing there. She said she came to apologize. That she knew she'd messed up. I told her not to worry about it and made her a chai latte.

She took a table in the back and when Don got there, he looked between us several times. The suspicion in his eyes made me doubt her all over again.

I watched as she sat there alone, drinking her latte, and pulling the gazes of those around her. When she was finished, she took her cup to the bin and went into the ladies' room.

She gave me a hug on her way out and told me that she had everything under control. That I didn't need to worry about her anymore.

I knew there was only one way for her to get everything under control, and it didn't make me feel better, or worry less.

∧∧∧∧∧∧

The next day, I went to check on her. She was lying on the floor with her head beside the speaker. For a moment I thought, *she's fine, just listening to music*, but she was too still.

I knelt down and put my hand beneath her nose. She wasn't breathing. The ambulance took her away. I waited in the lobby. The doctor came out and said things like *overdose* and *laced with fentanyl*.

He told me there were some men there that wanted to talk to me. That there were other cases like hers, but not all of them had been so lucky.

His words sounded muffled. The sounds of the people shuffling around behind me were louder than they should have been. He put his pen in his coat pocket and looked at me with thinly veiled revulsion.

"It'll only take a minute."

I told him, *no, I had to go*.

∧∧∧∧∧∧

That night Don showed up at Dan's house. He put me in handcuffs and took me away. When we pulled up to the station he said, "Listen kid, we've got footage of you accepting a package at Chicago O'Hare, years of speculation about the things you and your mother do, and a dead girl in a house on the outskirts of town."

I didn't say anything.

He reached out and turned the car off. "It was an overdose. The same stuff your mother had in her system."

305

He turned around and looked at me through the partition, "It doesn't have to be this way, Camden. You just need to tell me the truth."

I knew he meant tell him it was Cora, that she had done this, but she was in the hospital, and I was still trying to convince myself she hadn't.

I thought of all the chances I'd had to walk away before now. All the times I could have told her no.

He said, "Son, this isn't the time to be brave or noble."

I didn't feel brave, and I wasn't noble.

I didn't say a word.

They led me though the station and I followed aimlessly behind. They took my hand and pressed my fingers into a wet ink pad. They took my picture and led me into a brightly lit room where they told me to take off all my clothes and threw a beige jumpsuit at me.

They barked orders in rapid succession. I held my arms out at my sides. When they were done, and I was dressed again, they led me to a cell. It wasn't until the door slid closed in front of me that I thought to wonder what I was in for.

^^^^^^

All I could see was her face. The brightness of her smile and innocence in her eyes. I could hear her saying things like, *this isn't your fault*, and *you were just trying to help*. I wanted her with me, but I was glad she wasn't here.

I didn't understand how she could be so sure of me when I wasn't even sure of myself. I knew she wouldn't walk away from me. Not even now.

Leaving her would be the best and the worst thing I'd ever done.

^^^^^^

Emma

Tate's voice didn't sound right. I knew something was wrong. She told me that Camden had been arrested and Cora was in the hospital for an overdose. They weren't sure if she was going to make it, and they didn't know what he was in for.

There was a news story, about a girl from Bozeman who had died of an overdose. I asked Tate if she'd seen it. "Yeah, Mom is getting a lawyer, and she looks scared, Emma. I don't know what's going to happen."

There were only three weeks left before graduation. I had high A's in all my classes and my teachers agreed to let me take my finals early. I called Mom from the highway to tell her I was going to skip the ceremony. She was furious, "No, you can't go."

"Mom, I already am."

Her breath shook, "I will not let you throw away your future for that boy."

I knew she was upset, so I tried not to sigh into the receiver. I told her I wasn't throwing away anything, that I already took my finals, and it was done.

"Emma, you're graduating with honors. You have family coming in. What am I supposed to tell your grandparents?"

I felt a twinge of guilt at the thought of Grandpa's wrinkled face. "I don't know, Mom. I just know I have to go. Things are really bad. Tate's freaking out and she shouldn't have to do this alone." She said, "She shouldn't have to do it at all. It's his fault." I told her she was wrong, that he didn't do anything wrong.

"Emma, he's in jail. He did something wrong."

"You're only saying that because you don't like him. You never have."

She let out a strong huff of air. "That's not true. I love Camden. He's Dani's family and she's mine, but Emma… you've been trying to save that boy since the day you met him, and it can't be done."

"I can't just leave him."

She sighed, releasing this long breath of defeat into the receiver. "Emma, I know you don't want to hear this, but we all have to suffer the consequences of the choices we make."

I wiped a tear from my eye. "What about the consequences of the choices that are made for us?"

There was a moment of silence, "You are not responsible for him."

"I love him, Mom."

"I know, but sometimes love just isn't enough."

^^^^^^

When I arrived, Tate was the only one home. Dani was meeting with the lawyer, and no one had heard from Camden.

She cried when she told me about the girl. No one knew her. She didn't go to school with them, but she looked so young, and Tate said, "He couldn't have done this."

Camden's room was across the hall. It was much darker than Tatumn's. He had a big bed with one of those fluffy duvets on it. His walls were covered in art, most of it his. It was strange, seeing my own face peer back at me from so many different angles.

I slept in his bed. Dani woke me up early. "Come on, I have coffee and doughnuts." We went into the kitchen, and she handed me a cup full of coffee and cream and a plate with a chocolate doughnut on it.

I could tell she was nervous. I was too. I just didn't realize it wasn't about him until she said, "Your mom is not happy." I nodded, "I know." She told me she appreciated that I'd come, but that I really shouldn't be here.

"There's nothing you can do anyway."

I hated hearing her say that. I didn't even know what was really going on and it felt like she'd already given up. "There has to be something we can do."

She gave me a pitying look and shook her head, "There's not. They have footage of him accepting a package from someone at the airport in Chicago. The lawyer doesn't seem hopeful."

I felt several things at once and tried to keep the shock off of my face. *Chicago? This was all happening because he'd come to see me.* I looked down. Away from her. Watched her thumb trace over the edge of her cup.

"He won't see anyone. I don't know if that would be different for you, but he won't see us."

I asked her if she'd seen Cora. "Yeah, she's not very with it, but I've seen her." I took a bite of my doughnut and Dani said, "He's lucky to have you, but you know your mom is right. You can't save him, and if you don't walk away now… he'll just take you down with him."

^^^^^^

Tate went to school, and I went to the station. I told them my name and they led me through a series of locked doors. I sat down in a hard plastic chair and waited a long time for him to come.

Eventually the guard came over and told me I had to go. I asked him if Camden knew it was me waiting. He nodded, "Probably." I asked him to make sure. "I can't do that, sweetheart. It's time to go."

"Can I leave him a note?"

He looked at me like I was annoying him, but he said, "I guess so." I asked him for a pen and paper, and he reached into his pocket and handed them over. I wrote, *tell me it isn't true*, and then handed it to the guard.

"Can I wait here?"

He looked at me with pity in his eyes, "Okay, but if he doesn't answer, you've got to go." He took the note to Camden. When he came back, he handed me the paper. All it said was, *It's not.*

^^^^^^

Cora was awake when I got there. She looked a little surprised to see me. I didn't know how much time I had so I just said, "You know he's in jail?" She looked away and fiddled with the wrinkles in her blanket, "Yeah."

I asked if she knew what for and she said, "I have a pretty good idea."

"It's really serious, Cora." She gave me a placating look, "I know."

I sat down at the edge of her bed and asked her if she was feeling better. She looked surprised, "Truthfully?" I nodded. "I feel awful inside and out."

I said, "I tried to go see him, but he wouldn't talk to me."

She turned toward me and the tube in her nose pulled against the skin of her face. "He's just scared, honey." I bit at the skin beneath my bottom lip. "I know that, but I wish he didn't think he had to do everything alone."

She nodded. "That's my fault." I didn't argue. "He's been taking care of me his whole life." My hand fell into my lap. "I know. He loves you." Her face took on a pained expression, "I wish love didn't have to hurt so much."

I asked her what she meant. "Camden's the only good thing I've ever done, and now my mistakes have ruined his life too. I love him, it's just that I've never been able to get out of my own way long enough to do it right."

I said, "I don't think there is a wrong way to love someone." She looked over at me through sad grey eyes. "I hope you get to keep thinking that." A tear fell onto her cheek, and she reached up to wipe it away.

Don walked in, "Is this a good time?" Cora looked over at him. "It's as good a time as any." He reached into his pocket and pulled out a recorder. "You said you wanted to see me. I assume that's because you're ready to make a statement."

She looked down at her lap. "I am, but I want to know that he'll be released after I tell you." Don eyes darted toward me. "I guess that depends on what you have to say."

She told him that Camden didn't do anything wrong, and he said, "We have footage of him accepting a package at the O'Hare airport." She looked up at him.

"That's not possible. He didn't know anything about that, and you can't accept something you don't know exists."

Don took a wider stance. "The camera shows it happening." Cora looked out the window and then she turned around to face him.

"No, the camera shows the package being placed in his bag. I know... because I'm the one that arranged it that way. Camden didn't know, and when he found out what I'd done he told me I needed help and walked away. That girl that everyone keeps talking about. I sold her the drugs. He didn't have anything to do with this."

∧∧∧∧∧∧

Camden was released. He didn't come home, but I left anyway.

∧∧∧∧∧∧

Dani and Tate came to my graduation. Mom was still mad at me for leaving, but the way she looked at me as I climbed down those stairs with the diploma in my hand let me know I was going to be forgiven.

After the ceremony there was a party. Grandpa gave me an envelope with a hundred dollars in it. I kissed his cheek, and he gave me a tight hug and told me how proud he was of me.

Tate and I escaped to my room. She nervously paced around the edge and when I asked her what was wrong, she said, "I'm pregnant."

I asked her if anyone else knew. "No, I'm going to tell Ethan when we get back."

"Are you still moving to Colorado?"

"No, but I'm pretty sure he will."

I told her she didn't know that, that Ethan loved her. Her eyes pulled in and she bit at her bottom lip. "Yeah, but he has a scholarship and it's not like we've ever talked about the future… beyond college anyway."

She sat down beside me on my bed, and I took her hand in mine. She said, "Camden called Mom. He told her he wasn't coming home for a while."

I tried to imagine Montana without him in it, but it was too painful to think about. She looked over at me, "Will you still come to Montana, even if he's not there?"

I could tell by the look in her eyes that she needed me to say yes. I nodded. "Of course I will. You're not going to get rid of me that easily."

"I really want you there."

I squeezed my hand around hers, "Don't worry. I'll be right there with you."

We all drove back to the ranch together. Tate graduated the next weekend. I held out hope that Camden would show up for her. He didn't though. It was weird being there without him.

I could see him everywhere, even though he wasn't there to see.

15

Emma

The ranch is empty when I get back and the silver platters and flowers lining the stairwells mock me. Make me feel like a fool for believing in a love I knew was destined to fail.

He was always going to run. That's what he does. I don't understand how this thing between us can feel so real, so permanent and essential when we're together, and then the moment something threatens to tear us apart, it's over.

I should have listened to that niggling feeling in my gut that said he was dangerous. I shouldn't have left that hotel room or walked into that bar, because now instead of muddled memories and whispers of a man I used to love.

I have the smell of him on my skin, *pillow, sheets*. I know exactly how his voice sounds, and how it feels when he says my name like he needs me. I can't seem to stop thinking about the way he said, *I'll never stop loving you*, because if that's true then where is he?

At least this time I was expecting it. He told me himself, *if you don't want me, I'll leave*, and I believed him. At least the last part. I knew he would leave. I also knew it wouldn't have anything to do with whether or not I wanted him, because I do. I want him so badly it feels visceral.

I am nothing but a beating heart.

A gaping hole.

Breathless lungs, and a mind that won't stop.

This is why I didn't want anyone to know. It was embarrassing enough being caught with him in the storage room, but I'd do that a hundred times over before having to face Tate, or Cash, or my mom even once.

I don't want to tell them the truth. That I'm still not enough. That he left, and I don't even know why. Okay, well maybe I do. The look he gave me when I left with Cash was pretty easy to read.

It was pleading, *begging me to stay, to choose him*, but he didn't say anything. He just let me walk away, and Cash was in no shape to drive himself home.

I knew when I climbed in his truck that I had made the wrong decision. Walked away from the wrong man. I couldn't tell Cash that though. I knew I had already hurt him, and it just seemed easier to feel my own pain than to add to his.

He was different in the car, anger turned to quiet indifference as he seethed in the seat beside me. When we pulled up in his driveway, he turned to me, and I had never seen a man look so broken. He said, *you know what, I'm not even mad at him. He's doing exactly what I would do, but you should know better.*

Here's the thing though. I do.

I know better, and when he's not standing in front of me it's easy to deny him. I did it with Cash, I said, *it's not what you think,* and he scowled and told me it was exactly what he thought because he thought I loved him, even though he'd hurt me, and he'd proven to be disloyal and corrupt.

I couldn't tell him I didn't love him, because I do. *Still, forever, always,* and not superficially or even consciously. The love I have for him is deep. It lives in the darkest parts of me. The parts that no one else can see. The parts I try to deny or don't even know exist. It's just there, thrumming through me like the blood in my veins.

Endlessly.

Perpetually.

Part of me.

I walk from room to room hoping to find him and knowing I won't. Telling myself not to hope and still closing one door and moving on to the next. Looking for something I know I won't find.

I am rubble.

There are ancient ruins with better internal structure than I have right now.

His stuff is still here. His bag is open on the floor, clothing piled neatly within it. I walk over to the chair and run my fingers over the pair of pants laid across the back.

When I was younger, and more naive, all the things he left behind gave me hope. Made me feel like he wasn't really gone. That he was coming back. *For me.* I would see a shirt of his in the laundry and think, *he can't be gone, not really, not forever.* Now I know that for him it's all the same. Everything in his life is replaceable. Nothing is sacred or essential. Not his shirts, pants, drawings, and definitely not me.

I go over to sit on his bed and a tear rolls down my cheek. I reach up to wipe it off and another one follows. I lay my head down on his pillow. Memories I wish I didn't have float through my mind.

I feel empty. *Hollow. Lifeless.*

Not scared though. Last time I was. Terrified actually. I didn't know how to be without him. I survived on hope alone, hope that he was okay, *alive, happy, thriving,* but also wrecked. The way I was. Now I know I'll be alright. It'll be a rough morning. Telling everyone. Answering the same question, *the one I don't have an answer to,* over and over again.

I learned last time, the more you say the less people want to talk to you about it. I'll probably just come out with it. *Yes, he left. He's gone and I don't know where. No, I don't think he's coming back. I'm more surprised he showed up than that he left. Yes, I'm fine. I'm good. Don't worry about me.*

^^^^^^

Camden

His truck is out front, and when I see it, I don't know what to think. Is he here? Is she with him? Are they together? Have I waited too long? Come on too strong? Scared her away?

I run inside, searching every room, hoping like hell I don't walk in on them together. See something I can't unsee, but I find her, alone. In my bed. Covers pulled up to her chin, long dark hair cascading out around her, lashes resting peacefully on her cheeks.

It hits me all at once. Like a wave crashing over me, heavy and wet, *shocking and wonderful,* salt and brine seeping into every cell of my body.

This is what I regret.

Not getting to see this. Every day. Not knowing what it is she dreams of. Never getting to hear the first thing she says when she wakes up. Or tuck her in beside me just before I drift off to a place so mercilessly honest that I lose myself in the truth of her. The only truth I actually know.

I love her. Endlessly.

Without limits or expectations, and up until this moment I have been too proud or too foolish to realize what that actually means. I know I love her, and worse I know she loves me.

Up until now I didn't have a grasp on what a gift that was, but love is like power, there's great responsibility in it. I have let her down. Failed her in the worst way, because while I should have been willing to walk on hot coals, swallow swords, fight gators with my bare hands to keep her... I just left.

I just walked away from the only good thing I'd ever known because I thought I was too broken, *damaged, ruined* to ever deserve her.

I let everyone else in my life choose my choices. I told myself there was no helping it. People will think what they will, and you can't change where you came from. My own mother used me. Abandoned me. Left me to strangers, made me watch her destroy our family, her body, our future. She had a choice, and years of life experience to help her make it, but she never chose me.

No one ever chose me.

Except her.

If she needs time, I'll give it to her. If she doesn't want to tell anyone about us, so be it. I will wait in the shadows. I don't deserve her. I never have and never will. It's not possible to be deserving of a love like hers. A love that's just there. Understanding, and acceptance, and reverie always dancing in her eyes.

She knows who I am. Where I came from, and still.

I want to let her sleep, but her cheeks are blotchy, and I know she thinks I left. I hate that I know that. Not like I'm worried that she might think I left.

I know she thinks I left because I did, and I told her I would. Why did I say that? I knew it wasn't true. I knew that even if she didn't want me, I wouldn't leave her again. She said she believed me. That it was easy to believe that I would leave again, and now she thinks I have.

I reach up and run my hand over her hair. Her eyes open and the shock in them is quickly replaced with disbelief, "Camden?" I nod and bend down beside the bed so that I can look her in the eyes. She sits up, bits of dark hair sticking to her face. "Is this real. Are you really here?"

I tell her *yes, it is,* and *I am,* and she nods, "Yeah, I guess so. You never look this bad in my dreams."

I run my fingers over her lips. "You dream about me?"

She looks embarrassed, like she's been caught out, but she says, "Yeah, I always have."

A very selfish vein of relief uncoils within me. I want to ask her what her dreams look like, hear her tell me the way I look in her head. I want to hear her say things like, *you're always very close*, or *in my dreams we never stop touching*, but I realize that's not likely to be the truth. That I left her, abandoned her, promised her always and then gave her never.

How can I be what she dreams of? She is perfection embodied. I am damaged beyond repair. I force a smile, "Mostly nightmares?" She shakes her head, "No, they're always good, but sometimes they hurt when I wake up."

I take her face in my hands and press my lips to her cheek. She relaxes into me, and I tell her I dream about her too. That in my dreams I can always see her hair, that I'm constantly chasing her, trying to catch up, but never quite getting there.

That my favorite dream is recurring, her sitting on the couch, sunlight pouring over her face, a small but content smile on her lips. She looks at me, and I know whatever it is she's about to say is meaningful. That she knows the secrets of the universe. I listen. Holding my breath, waiting on her to tell me how to live. How to make my life worthwhile. Be someone I'm not ashamed of, but she never says anything.

She just sits there smiling in the sunlight.

When I pull away there's a spot of blood from where my brow keeps breaking open on her forehead. I reach up to wipe it off and she says, "I think you might need to go to the hospital." I shake my head, *no*, and take her hand in mine. "I do need to sew it up though."

Her face wrinkles as she stands. I look back at her wondering how I can love her completely, with my whole heart, and then somehow love her even more.

I pull her into the bathroom where I have fishing line and a needle soaking in betadine. She sees it and says, "You're serious?" I tell her, I am, this isn't the first time I've had my face bashed in, and I don't like emergency rooms.

I pick up the needle and align the skin. Emma sits on the counter, knees and thighs poking out of the dress she has on. I push the needle through, and she gags.

I tell her she doesn't have to watch, and she says, "No, it's okay. I can handle it." I can tell she's just trying to be brave. That she would much rather not see this, but she doesn't leave.

I pull the needle through and then tie a knot, the same way I used to tie my hook on when I was younger. I hold out the line and ask her if she can cut it for me. She picks up the scissors and then I tie another loop.

"Where did you learn how to do this?" I tell her fishing and bar fights. Her eyes go wide, "Bar fights, as in multiple?" I shrug and look at her in the mirror.

She looks expectant so I say, "I had some anger issues to work through when I first moved to New York." I hold out the line. She cuts it. "Should I be worried?" I shake my head, "No, oddly enough, a fight is what brought me back to you."

She looks intrigued. I finish tying off the last knot and tell her that I had to call Dani for bail money, and she came to see me with a list of demands. Emma cuts the line and asks, "What were they?" I list them off, volunteer work, a weekly phone call, and therapy. She nods. I lean over to splash some cold water on my face to wash the rest of the blood off.

"Is that how you became an old wise man?"

"I'm not old, and I don't know if I'll ever be wise."

She watches me put the towel down and picks it back up to dip it in the running water. "You looked pretty wise tonight." She reaches up and carefully wipes at the spots I've missed. I look at myself in the mirror. "Is it the black eye or the severed brow that does it for you?"

Her eyes roll and she pulls me over in front of her. "You didn't hit him back." Her legs open and I step in between them. "I know but what does that matter? I was still foolish enough to deserve a punch in the face."

"You did not deserve that. No one does."

She has that look on her face, *understanding, acceptance, reverie.*

This is the time when I want to look her in the eyes. Tell her she's right, *see the world the way she does*, but the truth is, some of us do deserve it. Her lips press together in a disapproving pout. "Camden, I know what you're thinking and you're wrong."

I lean into her, and cup the back of her head in my hand. "I'm not."

Her shoulders fall and she releases a sorrowful breath. "You've always thought the worst of yourself, and I hate it when you talk like that. Do you really think that's how the world works? That we only get what we deserve? That some of us are worthy and some of us aren't, because if that's true... then what did I do?"

She gives me a look so stark and lifeless that a shiver runs through me. I can hear the intensity in her voice. The way she has disguised a real question, something she's dying to know, as a punch line. I brush the hair away from her eyes, "You didn't deserve it."

She gives me a determined look. "Didn't I though. I mean it happened. I'm obviously not enough. Not deserving of love. I give mine too freely and for that I get nothing in return. Everyone I love leaves me, you did, my dad did, Tate is."

I wrap my arms around her. "I didn't leave you. I left for you, there's a difference."

"Does it really matter if there's a difference if the end result is the same?"

I think about it and decide it does matter.

"Emma, I don't expect you to understand but I had to leave, and I know you don't want to hear it, but it was for you. I grew up here. I knew these people. They already thought the worst of me and my mom, and when everything happened. When I was arrested, lying in that cell. I knew there was no coming back from that. Either me, or my mom, was going to jail. She was convicted of manslaughter, and you were coming here. For college. You had a good life, a life you'd worked hard for, and I could not be the man that ruined that for you."

She looks up at me with understanding and remorse. "I know you think what you did was noble." I interrupt her. "No, that's not what I mean. It was cowardly. I know that, but it was also the best solution to an impossible problem. I wanted to stay, or actually I wanted to take you with me, because I never wanted to come back here, but I couldn't do that. My choices had always been made for me, but you still had yours."

"Except for the one you took away from me."

I nod, feeling at a loss. Knowing she's right and wondering what, if anything, there is to say to help her understand. Her hands fall to her lap, and she says, "I thought you left." quietly, like she doesn't want to say it at all.

A wave of shame. A knot to swallow around.

"I know. I'm sorry about that, but no. I'm here and I'm not going anywhere."

Her eyes crinkle, "Even when you're feeling noble?"

I nod and think about falling to my knees, begging her to believe me.

"No, especially not then."

^^^^^^

Emma

He takes off all his clothes and I follow him into the shower. The water's warm and he presses into me when he reaches up to get the shampoo. He squeezes it on my head and massages my scalp. Leaning into me. Saying things like, *do you have any idea how many fantasies you're making come true right now*, and *I'm so jealous of those bubbles.*

I feel like I have to be gentle with him, careful not to press my lips too hard into his. Worried that I'll hurt him more, make him bleed again, but he isn't gentle at all. He presses his lips into the back of my neck, grabs at my hips, pushes inside.

We have ice cream while sitting cross legged on the kitchen floor. He steals bites off of my spoon and feeds me from his. He asks me lots of questions, about school, *writing, living with Tatumn.* He says, "Do you think you want kids?" I tell him I know I do, but not for a while.

I ask him about New York, *living on his own, his art.* He tells me the worst thing about living in the city is all the people, but that's the best part too. "There's really no way to do it wrong, no way to be an outsider while you're living in the city."

I steal a spoon full of his ice cream. "I bet I could figure out a way." He watches my lips as they wrap around it. "Not a chance. You fit in everywhere you go."

I feel truly affronted, "Are you calling me basic?"

He laughs around a bite and leans in to kiss me. His lips are cool and sweet. I lean into him, and he puts his bowl down on the ground. He pushes me back and runs his hand over the top of my thighs.

"Not at all."

The third time he takes my clothes off, they stay off. We stand together on the patio, cool breeze hitting my skin, and his warmth wrapped all around me. He says, "I'd forgotten how beautiful it is. The stars never come out in the city."

I look up at the dark sparkling sky, "Is that what you missed most?" His hand runs over my arm.

"No."

The wind starts blowing and I turn around to tuck more of myself into him. He says, "You know it's you right. That it's always been you."

A raindrop hits my skin, and then another. He leans over me, pulling me in close, protecting me. I shake my head, *no*, and he lifts my chin with his thumb. "Tell me that's not true."

"I'm just not sure if I believe in always anymore."

His eyes cloud over. "Well, I'll have to see if I can change that."

The sky opens up and he leans down to kiss me. He says, *always*, and I feel it lingering on my lips. He wraps his hand in my hair and pulls my head back. His lips travel down, over my jawline, *neck, chest*. His hands circle my waist. He lifts me up and carries me over to the couch. The rain washes down my face, and he runs his hands over my slick torso.

He promises me forever and I tell him I don't need it. I just want what we have right now.

He touches me, wet fingers sliding over me. Making my hips tilt. He says, "I do. I need it. I don't want to live one more day without you."

I let out a noise, somewhere between a whimper and a moan and he lifts me up, wraps his arm around my back and says, "Say it. Tell me." I don't know what he's asking for, but the words *always, you, forever* fall from my lips.

^^^^^^

Dani knocks before she opens the door. I reach my arm out and run it over the empty spot beside me. I can still feel his warmth on the sheets and see the hollow spot where his head was resting on the pillow.

I sit up to look for him and Dani says, "Emma, are you up?" I look at the clock. We slept in, or actually we barely slept, but it's still eleven thirty and I should have been up hours ago.

I throw the covers back and sit up in bed feeling frantic and confused, "Yeah." She pops her head in, and I turn to look at her. "Oh, sorry beautiful, didn't mean to wake you. Just wondering if you've seen Tate. She wasn't at the hotel this morning and she's not here either." I pick up my phone and open the messages app, Tate hasn't texted in two days.

I tell Dani this and she walks over to the window, a raindrop hits it, and she says, "Not the best day for an outside wedding, but I guess that won't matter if there's no bride." She sounds worried, but also certain, like she might actually believe that Tate plans to leave Ethan at the altar.

I jump out of bed and go to the closet, swing the door open and there he is, *naked*, standing in front of my sweaters. I pull the door in and give him a *what the hell do you think you're doing* look. He brings his finger up to his lips, shushing me even though I haven't said a word.

Dani's still standing at the window, looking out at the dark clouds hanging over the mountains. She says, "Do you think she's seemed off the last few days?"

I think about the way she refused to look at me last night, and the first thought that comes to mind is that this is my fault. That's she's gone missing on her wedding day because I'm here and she doesn't want to see me, but then I remember the way her eyes shifted every time someone brought up Ethan, or the wedding, and I think I know what's wrong.

Dani gives me a worried look and I have to decide whether to tell her the truth. That I think Tate might have run. That she has been off for days, and she might not have been kidding, or it might have been more than just prewedding jitters that made her say she was going to cancel the wedding so many times.

"I don't know, do you?"

Her face wrinkles in thought and then she nods, "Yeah. I think she has been, and I'm a little worried that she ran." I open the closet door again, and this time I can't see anything but his toes poking out from the corner. I grab jeans, a shirt, and a jacket. Dani asks what I'm doing, and I tell her I'm going to look for her.

She nods in this slow appraising way and then she asks me if I'm alright.

I give her a quick perfunctory, *yeah,* and she says, "It's okay if you're not." I bend down to grab a pair of shoes and then push the door closed again. I'm not sure what she thinks is the matter, so I do my best to give her a reassuring look and she says, "His bike isn't out there either."

I realize she thinks he left, and the careful way she's said it tells me that she thinks that would upset me. Which also means that she's talked to my mother, and I've become a salacious piece of gossip.

I am not about to talk to Dani about my sex life, so I go along with it. "Well, he was drinking last night, maybe he took an Uber home from the party, or maybe he's just gone out for breakfast?"

Her eyes pull in and she reaches up to rub my back. "I don't think so, we planned to meet here this morning. I have coffee and doughnuts for everyone downstairs."

She looks over at me with a remorseful expression. "I'm so sorry, Emma. I should have known better. I did, I just wanted to believe…"

I know exactly what she's about to say, that she wanted to believe he'd changed. That he'd learned to face his problems instead of run from them, and since hiding in my closet doesn't really count as either, and I know he can hear every word we say. I just tell her she didn't do anything wrong. That if he said he'd meet her here, then I'm sure he's here, somewhere. "Probably just went for a walk or something."

^^^^^^

Tatumn is sitting on Long Rock looking out over the water when I find her. There are still storm clouds overhead, and the grass is wet and sticky.

Tatumn looks up like she was expecting me and says, "I was just about to leave." I feel a bit apprehensive, wondering if that's true or if she's only said it because I'm here. If she really doesn't want to talk to me.

My whole stomach fills with hesitant dread, but I push it aside and climb up to sit down beside her.

"Where were you going to go?" I say as lightly as I can manage.

She looks over at me with an uncertain expression on her face, "Ibiza?"

Her beautiful blue eyes are shining brighter than ever, but only because the whites are red from crying. I scoot in closer. "Tate, what's going on, because if this is about me, I can explain." Her whole face wrinkles, "Why would this be about you?"

I think, *oh, I don't know because you walked in on me in a state of preorgasmic bliss, with your cousin… the one that left me, broke my heart, the one you told me I needed to ignore that I definitely didn't…* but I say, "You couldn't even look at me."

Her head tilts back and a strand of her long blonde hair sticks to her neck. I reach up to release it and she says, "Yeah, because I don't have any sort of poker face, and I knew if I looked over at you everyone in the room was going to know exactly what I was thinking."

"Oh… so you're not mad at me then?" She shakes her head and wraps her hands around the edge of the rock. "Why would I, of all people, be mad at you?"

The preorgasmic state she found me in runs through my head again. She shakes hers, "I know better than anyone what it's like to love someone you shouldn't. Ethan left me when I was pregnant, with his child, and I'm about to marry him."

She says it like she needs me to hear, but also like she's talking to herself. I can hear the threads of panic in her voice and see the raw fear in her eyes, "Or there's always Ibiza?"

She pulls her hands into her lap, restless fingers poking into thumbs. "I don't know what I'm doing. Why I agreed to this?"

I reach over and say, "Tate…" but she pulls away and buries her face in her hands.

"I know, but Emma I don't think I can do it."

"Alright, then don't."

She gives me a scrutinizing look. The breeze picks up bits of her hair and floats them around her face. "Really?" I shrug, "Sure, why not?" She laughs and reaches up to wipe beneath her eyes. "Will you come with me?" I lean back on my hands and the rough edges of the rock press into my palm.

"To Ibiza?"

She nods and pulls her hands into the sleeves of her shirt.

"I assume we're leaving everything else behind?"

She looks back out at the water, "I don't think there's any other way." I pretend to consider it. "It is a pretty long flight, Agatha probably wouldn't even like it." Her head drops and she pulls her knees into her chest.

"I can't leave Agatha."

I know that already.

"Okay, we'll switch her from OJ to Sangria and you can bead her hair."

"Please, she'll barely let me brush it." I lean forward and shrug in this *well, I don't know what to tell you sort of way*, "Pretty sure the beads are going to be a requirement. We'll all have to get them." She pulls her lip in and bites down.

"I can't take her."

"Not if you can't get those beads in her hair, you can't."

"No, I mean I can't take her. I can't go." I know exactly what she means but I say, "To Seattle?" Her eyes go distant, "I don't know what to do." I nod, "Yeah, I know what you mean."

Her brow furrows, "You have to decide whether or not to leave the love of your life today too."

A knot forms in my throat, but I swallow it down. "No. She's already made up her mind. She's moving, Seattle… Ibiza, either way she's not going to be here."

She leans over and lays her head on my shoulder. "I know. Everything feels so real now. With him here… every night. Everyone keeps asking me about Seattle. They all act like I should be ecstatic. *I'm going to be the wife of a pro football player, live in the city, finally get out of here…* but I don't think I want to go. I don't want to live there. I don't want Agatha to grow up in a posh private school. I don't want to make new friends or have to figure out a new grocery store. I like Rosiners, they have really fresh produce, and Agatha loves their mac and cheese. What if city people don't eat mac and cheese?"

I shake my head, "Well, that may be a deal breaker. I hope Ethan checked the box next to the mac and cheese clause on his contract."

She sniffles and pushes her hair back, "I'm serious."

I know she is.

A cold droplet of water hits my arm, and I look up at the sky.

"What is it you're afraid of?"

She closes her eyes tight and whispers, "What if I get pregnant?"

The decent thing to do is lie to her.

To lift my hand up and rub it gently across her back as I say things like, *Ethan loves you, you're getting married and everything is going to be fine, better than fine, good,* but then she says, "What if he leaves again? What if he says, *I'm just not ready to be a dad,* like he did last time, and then I'm stuck. Alone in a city I don't even know, with a child that he was supposed to love enough to stay for but didn't."

I shake my head because I don't know. I would love to do the right thing, to tell her that this is all nonsense, just normal wedding jitters. That she can trust him, and he won't leave her, but the truth is… he might.

He did it once already.

She looks up at the sky, "I mean this is a bad omen, right? Rain on your wedding day." I look up at the dark nebulous clouds above us, "That depends."

She asks, "On what?" I tell her that in some cultures it's a good omen. "Rain signifies the last tears the bride will ever cry because she's going to be so happy in her marriage." She looks at me skeptically.

I throw my hands up, "I know, but I'm not making it up. Other cultures believe that rain on your wedding day will wash everything bad that's ever happened away, so you get a clean slate for your new life."

She reaches up to wipe her tears on the sleeve of her shirt. "How do you know all this weird stuff." I shrug. "You know me and my boring books." She still looks sad, so I tell her in Hindu culture it means that your marriage will last.

She nods, looks down at the river flowing below us. "I like that."

I take her hand in mine. "Do you love him?" There's no hesitation in her nod.

"Do you want to be his wife? See him every day, hear his thoughts… even if they're on things you don't really understand, pick up his socks by the bedside, know exactly what his morning breath smells like, make him dinner in the evening, take long walks together, have him beside you… at parent teacher conferences, holidays, in your bed, shower, kitchen. Do you want to dream beside him? Grow old with him? Tell him you love him, every day, and let Agatha grow up with him too?"

She squeezes my hand tight. "I do. Of course I do. I just…"

I squeeze back. "Your mom said there's no shame in second chances, but I'm not sure I agree with her. I think they're full of shame and that's why they are so hard to give, and I understand why you don't trust him. If you don't want to marry him, I'll go home right now and tell everyone there to leave, but what if that's the problem? What if trust, the second time around doesn't feel like the first. What if it feels scary, and leaves you vulnerable, because it's not unconsciously given. It's a choice you make, and that makes it feel like you could make the wrong one."

"But what if I'm right?

"Yeah, what if you are? What if everything you're scared of comes true? Will you be better off here wondering what might have happened? Is it really better to know that he won't be there because you chose it? Instead of just trusting yourself enough to let him love you, to love him back, and know that bad things do happen, but good ones do too."

^^^^^^

Camden

I don't know how to tell her that Dani knew I was in her closet. She waited for me to come down. I told her I'd just gotten back from a walk, and she said, "If you hurt her again, I will feel personally responsible, and she may not chase you down, but I will."

I nod and she hands me a cup of coffee. She says, "I'm sure you heard… but Tatumn's missing." I look over at the clock above the oven, it's only noon. I shrug, "The ceremony's not for six hours."

She gives me a look and I think about what Ethan said. About the thought of her not coming crossing his mind, and how it would only be fair if she didn't show up.

Her phone rings and I pull on my jacket and walk out the door. Cash's truck is still in the driveway, but Tatumn's is parked at the bottom of the hill. I walk over to it, even though I can tell it's empty, and look in the windows.

There's a bag on the back seat, a pair of heels in the front, and a few old French fries scattered around on the floorboard.

The fact that it's parked here and not up by the house tells me two things. She ran, but not very far.

I turn and start walking down the hill, toward the river, and Cash and Ethan pull in and jump out of their car. Ethan calls out my name and I turn around.

He looks over at Cash and says, "Dude, you are such an asshole." Cash gets a contrite look on his face, "Shit man… I didn't mean to do all that."

I shrug, "Yeah you did, but it's alright."

Ethan grabs both of Cash's arms and pins them behind his back. He says, "Go ahead, man make him bleed." I step up to him, like I'm thinking about it, and Cash says, "Man, don't. I'm in the wedding and you heard Alissa." I pull my fist back and he squints. My hand drops and Ethan says, "Come on man. He deserves it."

I nod. "Yeah, I did too."

Ethan releases him and I turn around to walk off. He says, "Are you looking for Tatumn?" I can hear the concern in his voice, and I want to say, *no, she's already inside getting ready*, but I just nod, and he jogs up beside me. "Then I'm going with you."

We find the girls sitting on a rock, looking out over the river. It's obvious that Tatumn has been crying, her eyes are swollen and her cheeks are red, but she's not crying now. She looks over at us, "No, you can't be here. It's bad luck for you to see me on our wedding day."

Ethan steps up. "Is it… our wedding day?"

Tatumn stands and hops down off the rock. She walks over to him. "Are your feet cold, Ellis?"

He takes her in his arms. "No, mine are nice and warm, but yours seem to be a little chilly." Her face falls and I hear her say, "It's not you..." as I'm walking off.

I climb up to sit down beside Emma and she looks over at Cash. I don't like all the confused emotions that are floating around in her eyes, but I say, "You should go talk to him."

She gives me a questioning look and I nod. "Really. I'll be alright."

^^^^^^

Emma

The first thing Cash says when I walk up is, "On a scale from marshmallows in your chocolate to nuclear disaster, how badly did I fuck this up?"

My head tilts to the side and his face tightens. I can tell how nervous he is to be here. Talking to me, and he should be, because he acted like an arrogant fiend.

"I don't know. I guess that depends on what you say next."

His face softens, and he looks at me through hopeful eyes. "I'm sorry, Emma. I had no right." I nod and fiddle with the hem of my shirt. He says, "I just... lost it. I mean the guy does not deserve you, but I'm not sure I do either. I just thought we..."

His voice trails off, but I want to know what he was going to say, "We what?"

His eyes crinkle at the edges and his lips pick up. "We have something. Don't we?"

I nod, because we do, it just isn't what he thinks it is. I look over at Camden, who is admirably looking away, but he seems to feel my gaze and turns his head to the side. Our eyes meet and my chest fills with a mix of desire and shame.

When I was younger, I thought I understood love because I could feel it, thrumming through me like a life force. Fueling my optimistic desires, making me feel like nothing could go wrong.

Then when he left, *didn't call, didn't come home*, I thought I understood love because without it I felt empty, and for a while that seemed like the lesson. Like I had been too young and naive to understand that you had to rely on yourself first. That I had to love him the way I did, in order to fall out of love with him, and in love with myself.

I did that. Slowly, but while I was doing that, I fell in love so many times, with so many different people, things, ideas. I realized that love is one word for a multitude of emotions. That when we say I love you, it doesn't always mean the same thing.

I love Cash. I know I do, but not like he wants me to. Not like he deserves, because when I look at him, I feel affection, but no longing.

He clears his throat. "You know what you don't need to answer that." I look back over at him and say, "Cash..." His eyes pull in and I can tell I've hurt him. Again.

"You've never looked at me like that before."

Guilt moves into all my open spaces, but he says, "Emma stop. I'm not about to watch you torture yourself for this, and I can't be messing all this up anyway." He waves toward his face, "We have pictures later." I laugh and he says, "There's the sweetness I was looking for."

I nod and he reaches out to take my hand. I look over at Tatumn and she gives me a little nod. We all walk over and climb back on the rock.

Ethan pulls Tatumn into his lap and Camden looks over at me. Cash reaches into his pocket and pulls out a joint. Ethan says, "What are you doing man?" Cash lights it, "Just loosening things up."

Ethan looks nervous but Tate says, "Yeah, I'll take that."

When it's my turn, I shake my head and try to wave it away, but Tatumn says, "Oh no you don't. We have a deal, and today's my wedding day so you can't tell me no."

I reach out and take it, but I say, "Really, this is where you're pulling the bride card." She laughs, "I have not pulled it nearly enough. You know how I hate sharing you, and you've been making googly eyes at him all week."

I look over at Camden and Cash laughs and says, "Googly." In this slow deliberate way, drawing out all the syllables… and then we're all laughing.

^^^^^^

Nothing has ever felt as good as this does right now. Somehow, I'm in the river. Well actually I know how, I jumped in, we all did, and it is cold and somehow wetter and softer than it usually is. My skin feels slick and the rocks beneath my feet feel impossibly smooth.

I am floating on my back, contemplating the vastness of the universe when Camden swims over and gives me the most devastating smile. I reach out to touch my own lips and he says, "I wish I could kiss them." I tell him he can, and he says, "Here?" I nod and he leans in and oh my god, his lips. Wet and slick. Soft and warm.

Tatumn says, "Does anyone else think that rock looks like a penis?" Cash says, "Are you serious? I thought that's why you called it Long Rock?"

Ethan lets out this adorable bit of laughter. I look over at the rock. It's long and thin with a slight outcropping at the top. I nod and tell Tatumn I think she's right, "It does look like a penis." Cash says, "Yeah, a big hard one."

Something delicious flickers in Camden's eyes. I give him a, *what is it,* sort of look and he pulls his bottom lip in and bites it. Ethan says, "I always loved watching you lay out on it." Tatumn says, "Is that why you liked coming here so much?" Ethan shrugs and Tatumn flips to her belly and swims over to him.

Camden is still watching me. I feel his fingertips caress my side. I look over at him and the look he gives me makes me forget where I am. I say, "What?" and he shakes his head at me. I become two hundred and thirty percent more curious and reach down to run my fingers over the top of his hand.

His breath catches, "Don't do that."

I pull my eyes in and say, "Tell me."

He looks down at my chest. "I can't stop thinking about…"

Cash says, "I really like it when they jump off." Ethan nods, "Yeah, that's nice too." Tatumn's face scrunches, "We look like jizz, don't we?" The boys share a glance.

I feel Camden's gaze and look back over at him, "Is that true?" He does this sort of pouty thing with his lips. They push out and up and he shrugs in this really cool way, "I don't know. I never really thought about it."

Cash turns to him. "You don't have to lie to make friends, Pierce."

I laugh and Camden says, "I'm not trying to make any friends." Tatumn points her finger in the air, "No… but you are trying to make out with her some more." I feel my cheeks warm, and Camden leans in close and whispers, "That's not all I'm trying to do."

Ethan says, "It looks like it's about to start raining again." just as the sky opens up and we all skitter out of the water, grab our clothes, and start running toward the ranch.

We run inside without thinking and Dani says, "You found her." Just as my mother says, "What the hell happened to you all?"

We are standing in the kitchen, dripping wet, with our underwear clinging greedily to our skin. Everyone is looking at everyone else and we are all thinking the same thing. Or maybe we are? I don't know, but I am thinking about strawberry pop tarts.

Alissa walks in the room with her phone pressed to her ear. She looks over at us and says, "Never mind, we found her."

Tatumn looks over at me and says, "I'm so thirsty." I feel all the moisture in my mouth evaporate and say, "I really want a strawberry pop tart." Ethan's eyes widen and he says, "You have strawberry pop tarts?" in this desperate sort of way. I nod and walk past my mother to open the pantry.

Alissa stops in front of Tatumn and slowly peruses her. "You look like a deranged swamp rat." Tatumn burst out in laugher and Alissa says, "I'm serious. Your eyes are red. Your hair is matted and what is all over your feet?" Cash takes the box of pop tarts from my hands and pulls out a package.

Alissa says, "No… no pop tarts. You all need to go get in the shower." She looks down at her watch. "We don't have time for this, and I will be expecting a very large tip when we're through here, but I have worked too hard to see this all go to pot."

Ethan looks at Cash and he looks over at me. Their faces split into contagious grins and Tatumn bends over in laughter.

Ethan reaches in to grab a package of pop tarts just as Alissa reaches out to take them from Cash. She says, "Really?" and he smiles abashedly and hands it to Tatumn. She says, "I'm marrying the sweetest man in the world." I look over at the shiny package in her hand, "You're going to share those right?" She opens it up and holds one out for me.

The first bite is the best, sweet, buttery goodness coats my tongue and even though my mother and Dani are herding us like cattle to the master suite I say, "It's the best thing I've ever tasted." Tatumn looks over at me, and I don't think she looks like a swamp rat at all. I think she looks like a mermaid, wavy hair, and dewy skin, both sort of sparkling in the sunlight.

I tell her this and she says, "Maybe I am a mermaid, because I feel like I'm drying out."

I take another bite. "Didn't you plan for this sort of thing? Isn't there a vat of cucumber water waiting for you in there?" She shakes her head. "I don't want cucumber water. I want lemonade, a really tall glass of lemonade with lots of ice in it."

I shrug. "Well, it's your wedding, you're the bride, can't you just tell someone to get it for you."

She gives me a serious look, "Do you think I can?"

I turn around to look at Dani, "She's thirsty. Can you bring her some -" Tatumn says, "Lemonade, I want lemonade." Dani laughs. "Sure, yeah I'll get that for you." Tatumn's eyes light up and Dani says, "Get in the shower. The stylist will be here any minute."

Tatumn nods, like Dani has said just the right thing and we step in the shower together. She takes one nozzle, and I take the other. When Dani and Mom leave the room she says, "I can't wait to eat that pop tart." and we both dissolve in a fit of laughter.

∧∧∧∧∧∧

The ceremony takes place at sunset. The clouds have cleared and there's an actual rainbow over their heads. Tatumn looks glorious. Dewy fresh skin, white chiffon cascading down her bodice and spreading out in disordered waves around her feet... but all I see is him.

Sitting in the front row, right next to Dani. He's the only person in the room not looking at her. He's looking at me, and every time my eyes dart in his direction he gives me this sort of half smile. *Crooked grin. Smirk.* I keep turning back around, refocusing on what's important.

Tatumn, getting married, right now.

I can't help but notice the way Ethan's watching her, one side of his lips pulled up. His eyes full of wonder and joy. Looking at her like she is his sun. The giver of life. Mother of his child, *future children, pets*. The woman he wants to see, *do, feel* everything with. She looks up at him and I don't see any apprehension in her eyes.

She looks happy, *settled, sure*.

∧∧∧∧∧∧

Camden

I can't take my eyes off of her. The way she looks as she studies them. *Like their joy fills her heart up.*

There's no one else like her.

∧∧∧∧∧∧

Emma

After the ceremony we get whisked away for pictures. Alissa hands us a glass of champagne and says, "Don't down it until after you're through here."

Cash scoffs at her and says, "Please Alissa… everyone knows champagne is for sipping."

She walks off and he says, "She acts like we're a group of heathens." I shrug, "Well, what are you going to do? You can't win them all."

He takes a sip of his drink and gives me a heavy look. "No… I guess you can't." He sounds sad, too sad for champagne.

I look over at Cynthia, who hasn't taken her eyes off of him since the moment she saw him today, "but you win most of them."

He smiles, this cocky sort of grin.

"Yeah, I guess that's true."

^^^^^^

Camden

I grab a scotch and soda and find a spot to stand on the porch. There are people everywhere. People that I either don't know or don't like me.

I stand looking out over the valley. Letting my eyes rest on the mountains. Waiting for her to come back and wondering if I'll even get to talk to her when she does.

Don walks up and leans his belly on the rail. He comments on the view, and I say, "Yeah, it's nice." He puts his glass down in front of him and looks over at me.

"I thought you said I shouldn't expect any trouble."

I feel my jaw tighten, but I say, "Well, I didn't do this to myself."

He nods, "That Alexander boy get you?"

I shrug, "Don't know. Can't remember."

He lets out a disapproving hum, "Still operating on misguided principles." I tell him I don't know what he's talking about, and he says, "I hear you're moving back."

I nod.

"Is that why he hit you?"

I shrug. "No one hit me. I fell."

"Sure, let's go with that."

He turns away from me and looks over at his wife standing in a group of women beside the fire pit. She smiles at him, and he gives her a nod and then turns back to me. "You see your mom lately?" I shake my head, "No, not since I left here." He says, "I've seen her. She looks a lot better than she used to."

I say, "Well that's good." and he says, "I assume it's over the girl."

I shrug, and act like I don't know what he's talking about. He makes a show of looking around, nodding and giving a quick wave to some of the others.

I notice the way people are watching us. Obviously making inaccurate assumptions about why the chief of police has sidled up next to me.

I want to pull away, just walk off and act like I don't care. The way I used to.

Don says, "Look Camden, I've always known you were good kid in a bad situation, but the rest of these people don't know you like I do. They all think you're trouble, and you are and will be if you keep acting like that." My brow furrows and he says, "You can't let them get to you."

I nod because how many times is someone that has no idea what it's like to live on the outside going to tell me how I could have and should have done better.

Just not let it get to me.

Ignore and remain completely unaffected by the opinions of others because they don't matter. Right? We all come into this world on our own and we all leave on our own, but the part in the middle. The part everyone wants to act like doesn't matter, is heavily populated with people and their opinions, and as much as I used to act like it doesn't matter.

It does.

We are not all dealt the same hand. Some of us are born into disrepute and if there is one thing I know for sure. It's that if *they*, the right people, say you're ruined.

You are.

I wish I lived in a world where we all got what we actually deserved, because then maybe people would think twice before they used their power to hold another down.

Maybe people would do the right thing because it was the right thing to do, not because it was popular or accepted, or even expected of them. Perhaps if we were measured by our own deeds and choices, I wouldn't have had to leave, because I messed up, but I didn't mean to. I wasn't ruined by her. I wasn't her at all, but that's not what they thought.

Bad seed, bad plant.

I grew up guilty until proven innocent, and I turned out exactly how they said I would. Don lifts his drink to his lips and says, "I know what you're thinking. I can see the looks they give you just as good as you can, and yeah, I know. We can't choose where we came from, but we can choose where we go."

^^^^^^

Emma

Tatumn and Ethan walk in through the French doors at the back of the house. Everyone lifts their glass in the air and the DJ plays *Le Vie En Rose* as they walk out on to the dance floor and wrap their arms around each other.

Agatha is with me, she says that our dresses match so we have to stay together all night, and I see him there. Standing, *alone*, outside next to the railing. Lights twinkling all around his head. I want to go to him. Wrap my arms around him and sway together to the music, but I can't, because this day isn't about me.

It's about Tatumn. And Ethan. And Agatha.

^^^^^^

Camden

I know where I want to go.

^^^^^^

Emma

I'm dancing with Agatha. Her tiny hands are clasped in mine, and she has the biggest smile on her face. He walks up and she says, "Hi, Camden." like it's no big deal.

Like it doesn't matter at all that he's standing so close and everyone in the room has turned our way. They are all watching us, obviously wondering if I'll send him away, ignore him, treat him like the outsider they all think he is. I look back down at Agatha's bright innocent smile.

He says, "If this is too much I can go back outside."

I look up at him, "No, I want you to stay."

Acknowledgments

^^^^^^

I am fully convinced that nothing truly great ever happens all on your own. There are always people that come before you and support you in a way that makes your dreams possible.

First, I have to thank my husband, Brad. He is the prototype for my perfect man and the reason I am able to write about love with such honest fervor and passion. I literally could not have done this without you. Thank you for supporting me, listening to me ramble about my characters, being the voice of reason when I am freaking out, and constantly telling me that I can do this. You were the first person that ever believed in me, and I love you more than words can say.

So much gratitude to my children. Audrey you are a truly remarkable young woman. Thank you for keeping me on my toes, being brave enough to snap back when I need it, and showing me what it really means to love the life you live. Elliot you are one of a kind. Your honesty and support mean the world to me. Thank you for keeping me calm, and for your sometimes brutal opinions. They make me stronger. Better than I could ever be on my own.

Jo, this book wouldn't exist without you. Thank you for reading and re-reading my chapters, giving me feedback, and encouraging me to continue. Thank you for taking me to Montana, sitting on the porch with me, doing yoga and drinking wine. You are an incredible person, and I am so thankful to get to call you my friend.

Acknowledgments

Sam, thank you for supporting me, reading the book and telling me to continue. You are so full of life. Thank you for being the life of the party, brightening up every room, and keeping us laughing.

So much thanks to all the authors that have come before me. My journey as a writer began in the pages of your books. Thank you to S. E. Hinton and Suzanne Collins whose stories captivated me and are referenced in this book.

Unending thanks to my readers. As a reader myself I know how valuable your time is and I feel so much gratitude that you chose to spend some of it with me, lost in the pages of this book.

Author Bio

Tiffany Renée is an avid reader and author of *On the Outside of Everything*. She spends most of her time thinking about people that don't exist and trying to help them solve the problems she has single-handedly created for them. She enjoys long walks in the sunshine, yoga, and inappropriate jokes.

tiffanyrenee.author